Selected Short Stories
Of Thailand

Selected
Short Stories
Of Thailand

William Peskett

Edited by Robert Johnstone

A Cycad Books Production
Pattaya, Thailand

EX LIBRIS 3412091313

www.williampeskett.com

ISBN-13: 978-1515089704
ISBN-10: 1515089703

Contents

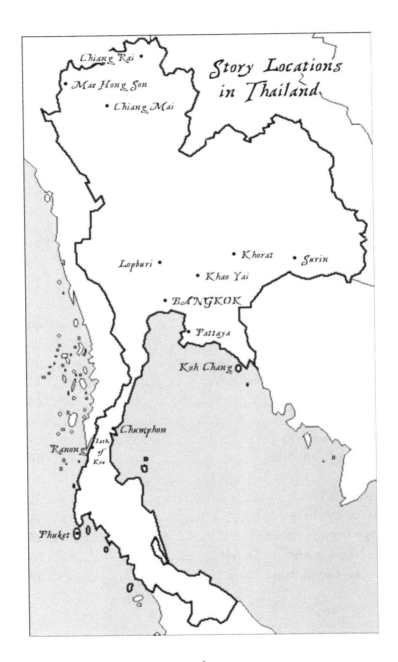

Story Locations in Thailand

- Chiang Rai
- Mae Hong Son
- Chiang Mai
- Lopburi
- Khorat
- Surin
- Khao Yai
- BANGKOK
- Pattaya
- Koh Chang
- Chumphon
- Ranong
- Isth. of Kra
- Phuket

Foreword

We must have been about twelve years old when William Peskett and I first met. We were in the same year at the Royal Belfast Academical Institution, as our school was formally called, back in the 1960s. I couldn't have predicted then that fifty years later he would have written a body of short stories that took the lid off the encounter between Thailand and the West, or that he would invite me, from his home way over there, to edit them.

Come to think of it, my predictions of our futures would have been much more unlikely. I might have envisaged myself, in my acceptance speech for the 2020 Nobel Prize for Literature, congratulating my old pal Sir William Peskett, head of the Royal Society, on receiving his Nobel Prize for his pioneering work on newts.

But Will really did go on quite soon to prove that the unlikely was possible. Before he had left school he had bagged a contract with a major London publisher for his first book of poems. I suspect I wasn't as impressed at the time as I should have been (since for us then all things were possible), but I knew it was the sort of thing that legendary figures like Arthur Rimbaud and Dylan Thomas might have got up to.

After studying natural sciences at Cambridge (where he caused consternation when he declined to participate in what he regarded as an unnecessary dissection) he lived and worked mostly in London, and had a successful career with a multinational firm. He published two collections of poetry but then (like Dylan Thomas) moved on to other genres, including two novels and a radio play.

Many years later I happened to meet the distinguished poet and critic Anthony Thwaite. Remembering that he had written about Will in the past, I mentioned our connection. At the time the 'Martian School' of poets had just passed through its moment in the sun as the most fashionable trend in British verse. I suggested that Will, whose poems often had sparky, original imagery, could be thought of as a sort of precursor of the Martians. Thwaite shook his head: 'He's much better than that.'

Maybe he's not really like the Martians. Maybe he doesn't have that much in common with Dylan Thomas. But there is one further little thing before we abandon this comparison. Like Rimbaud, Will moved to a far-off country. Admittedly, he didn't, like the French *poète maudit*, take up gun-running. He took early retirement, remarried, and set up home in Thailand's 'most extreme city', Pattaya. There he took up writing articles for a local English-language newspaper, and short stories.

He has published four story collections so far. I suggested that, rather than make a selection from his broad range of settings and styles (science fiction, tales set in England, fables, parodies of hard-boiled detective yarns), we should gather together some of the stories which give a fascinating insight into Thailand and its relations with the West.

Even those of us who have never been there are likely to have a vivid idea of Thailand, cobbled together from our relish for Thai food, reports of gap-year student trips, lurid tales about louche bars, newspaper exposés of sex tourism, images of beautiful dancers in fantastic costumes... On daytime television in Britain we are able to watch reality shows about Bangkok airport and ladyboys, and we might even catch a screening (denied by the censors to residents of the country itself) of *The King And I*. So our picture may well be sensationalised or romanticised, and certainly simplified. After all, it is easier to have strong opinions when we don't know all the facts.

To a Westerner like myself, Thailand seems vibrant and distinctive but also very open, both economically and culturally. It has a relatively strong economy, with low unemployment. It is the third biggest rice exporter in the world, and it is fully engaged with global trade. On a personal level it also seems open: short-term visitors do not require visas (the UK does not reciprocate), and retirees over 50 years of age can apply for special residential visas.

Then there is the phenomenon of Thais marrying foreigners. There are numerous English-language websites promising introductions to Thai women who seek partners. Is this simply an aspect of neo-colonialist exploitation? Since some of these stories deal with this situation (though in this book the Western men generally live in Thailand), I did a little research and found that often Thai women seek foreign husbands not so much out of financial desperation but more as a sort of protest against the particular form of gender stereotyping in their society. Western men are expected to be more faithful to their wives and treat them more considerately than local husbands.

Other subjects in this selection include the different ways in which people look at how the world works, for example in the clash between a scientific approach and a traditionalist Buddhist mode of thought. And some deal with the impossible yearnings that can motivate or destroy a person. Sometimes these may be shallow — a lust for drink, for money or for sex — and the characters absurdly comic, self-destructive or psychopathic. Sometimes the yearning may be for a better life that is thwarted by others. Sometimes the outcome may be tragic. And sometimes the yearning can be lyrical and full of beauty, however unfulfilled. In a way, these stories examine many different aspects (not just that of intermarriage) of the various forms of love affair that spring up between Thailand, its people, its culture and its environment, and those who have come to know it.

After reading Will's stories, which are written with intimate, first-hand knowledge and an undeceived eye as well as warmth and humour, I felt I understood much more about what really goes on behind the shock headlines and the easy clichés. There are more than sixty million real people — few of them reality television stars — living in Thailand, and all the people in these stories, whether Western or Eastern, good or bad, ordinary, corrupt, foolish or insane (or, in one case, simian), are real too, with human motives and foibles, and are portrayed with understanding. Once one starts to look at individual cases stock situations become humanised and we can begin to see that there are comprehensible reasons for the decisions that individuals make.

Will's father was the Principal of our school, and his family was English. Those two factors might have made life awkward in the insular and intolerant Northern Ireland of the time. But he (and his dad) seemed to sail through it all, as far as I could see, without a false step. One might think that as a Westerner living in Thailand he is again living a life slightly detached from the life around him, in a more extreme form. But that may be another simplification.

Will has always been interested in the natural world, but these stories show he takes the same intense pleasure in observing the people around him and in understanding their behaviour as thoroughly as any natural scientist would study his subject. Which is not to say that he looks through a microscope at specimens: there is no dissection taking place here. The author is describing a world of which he is very much a part, as one or two of the stories make explicit, and it is a world he is committed to, and finds amusing and delightful, quirky and strange, but also familiar. This strange new world, with its idiosyncrasies, is inhabited by recognisable, fallible human beings who are portrayed affectionately and with tolerance.

The author's qualities of open-mindedness, delight and amusement make his stories particularly refreshing. There is always some neat, new idea to pique one's interest. I would also say Will is a fearless writer, both in his subject matter and in the ways he chooses to present it. Some of the stories are simply funny, while some tackle quite 'difficult' themes. They are written from the inside by someone who speaks a little Thai and knows whereof he speaks. I find them all fascinating, each in its own way, and show that real life, and real human beings, are a lot more complicated and a lot more interesting when looked at carefully without preconceived ideas.

And did I mention that they are a lot of fun?

Robert Johnstone
London

Market Day

The counterfeit music stall is kept by Apem, a sallow young man in a droopy black vest and three-quarter-length blue denims. He has fine, wispy sideburns suggesting that he doesn't need to shave his cheeks though he's old enough to have two young babies at home. Attached to the concrete post is a battered black loudspeaker with horns that point two ways. On the plywood trestle table is a control box that Apem built himself. It has a sliding volume control which he adjusts fractionally every few minutes to get the level just right for each track. The song he's playing to this end of the market is a current favourite, *Love Me Tender* — Elvis Presley 1956.

Chompu wanders over from the stall across the dusty aisle and inspects a few of his CDs. Apem knows she's not going to buy one because she never does, but then he has no intention of buying one of Chompu's dresses either. It's an accepted rule among stall-holders that one trader doesn't push unwanted goods on to another. Suddenly Chompu notices that she has a potential customer at her stall. She returns the CD to the rack and hurries back.

Apem was born in Bangkok to second-generation Chinese immigrants. Though he has no interest in family history his parents maintain some of the customs learned from the previous generation. On special occasions and in company his father still drinks multiple tots of powerful baijiu from a decorated china flask and each year his mother buys mooncakes for the autumn festival. Apem himself doesn't speak a word of Chinese, not even enough to say Happy New Year.

Nong, short and muscular and happily married to a boring but dependable council clerk, has a young son who's doing well at school. She walks briskly by from left to right carrying a small blue rucksack embroidered with a fake North Face logo. She herself comes from the north, but is oblivious to the connection. Lest potential customers dismiss her as merely another market visitor carrying things around in a rucksack — rather than a trader with a rucksack to sell — she shows the bag off by waving it above her head quite gaily. After a while she comes around again, still walking purposefully from left to right and this time carrying a much larger black rucksack with a different logo. In the course of the market day Nong aims to cater to every reasonable hiker's luggage requirements.

Mut, dark-skinned and stooped, walks by pushing a small hand-made cart. On top of a battered cardboard Chang beer box are balanced a couple of whisky bottles refilled with clear honey and an arrangement of broken-off twigs on which jungle bees have built honeycombs of various colours, shapes and sizes, some as small as a matchbox. Mut comes from Chiang Rai, in the far north of Thailand. She has lost contact with her family up there, though the honey she sells is still harvested from high in the hardwood trees quite near where they live.

As Mut hobbles by, Jampah is passing the other way. Her cart is professionally constructed from an alloy frame and white laminate panels on which are printed the name of an ice-cream company and pictures of cones of three flavours. Attached to the rail that she uses to push the cart along is a bicycle bell which she occasionally rings and the stem of a wide, flat parasol that keeps her skin pale and prolongs the life of her frozen merchandise. At the end of the day, when Jampah leans over to scour out the cold tubs, the aroma of artificial vanilla which once made her crave a loaded spoonful of her own ice-cream now leaves her feeling quite nauseous.

As the two carts turn at opposite corners of the market they disappear from view. They are replaced by Noi who seems to block out the light as she approaches, dressed in black, and takes up residence on the bar steps. She is twice the weight that doctors would recommend for a woman of her height. She has big thighs and ankles and, head-on, jowls like a bloodhound. She wears a rough cloth cap, patterned a faded tartan, with flaps at the sides and back to keep off the sun. There's little she can do to stop herself looking like a fat Imperial Japanese soldier.

Noi is trying to sell carved black ornaments, African in style, perhaps because it hasn't crossed her mind that such incongruous items might not appeal to tourists in Thailand, though surely someone must buy them. The limbs of the nimble female forms, squatting and on all-fours, make a sad tangle in her big fleshy hand. Noi is cross that no-one is buying her statuettes today, or she may be more generally unhappy with her life. She comes from Rayong and shares a one-room flat with a much smaller girl who she's known since school. Noi has had quite a few boyfriends over the years, but never one that wanted to settle down with Noi.

To show her wares to customers in the bar, Noi has to lean over Heinz, a long-time Pattaya resident originally from Frankfurt where he drove a maroon Mercedes taxi, mostly on the airport run. Heinz is sitting on the top step with a mobile phone pressed hard against his ear because of the noise. He is talking loudly in pidgin English to Imm, his girlfriend of two years. Heinz learned English from his passengers who would tell him the name of a hotel and then say nothing until they arrived. With such inadequate tutoring he is ill-equipped to respond to an angry Thai woman whose English was improved by the eight years she lived here in Pattaya with a faithful but unhealthy and ultimately short-lived oil engineer from Stavanger. Imm has taken enough of Heinz's womanising and, having only last week spied him being sweet to a younger woman on Beach Road, has moved out of their furnished condo in Jomtien. His tone softens as he begs her to return. It's the sort of voice that people use when they're making a significant promise but Heinz is 59 years old and he is living a life in Pattaya without responsibility so means little of what he says.

Vladimir and Marina amble by with their daughter Alexa. Vladimir is wearing brief red running shorts cut away at the sides, a grey singlet with a number 6 on the back and flip-flops. Marina has not aged well and could easily pass for his mother. She's wearing a tired, sleeveless polyester dress with an indistinct floral pattern. Her big upper arm is pitted with the scars of inoculations which have helped her resist many of the microbial kingdom's most determined assaults. Alexa is thirteen and an only child. She wears a Union Jack on her T-shirt because she thinks it's a pretty design. Her pink velour shorts are even briefer than her father's and her blonde hair is in plaits pinned up in the shape of an arrow. When Marina and Alexa stop at Chompu's clothes stall, Vladimir goes to browse the CDs across the aisle. Apem has put on *Losing My Religion*—R.E.M. from 1991—and Vladimir nods his head rhythmically to show he's familiar with the song.

Marina riffles roughly through the clothes and before long she is trying on a pair of black leggings. For modesty, the manoeuvre is performed inside a full-length sarong with a large elasticated waist that Chompu provides for the purpose.

Miao, an elderly lady with a dark, round face appears as if from nowhere, dancing about the broken road like a woodland sprite. She has a small square of gold leaf stuck to the middle of her deeply-lined forehead. She's wearing jeans and a checked cotton shirt and holds a yellow tennis ball which she repeatedly throws up and quickly snatches back from the air, showing amazement at her own skill. She could be performing for money or be lost in some other happy world; it's hard to say.

Miao sits down on one of the lower chairs and beckons to Som-Oh who operates a dessert trolley on market days. Som-Oh brings her trolley nearer, takes a large clear block of ice from a cold box and dashes it vigorously and repeatedly against the blade of what looks like an upturned plane. She holds a plastic bowl underneath to catch the cascade of shaved ice. After consulting with Miao she ladles on to the bowl a selection of chopped preserved fruit and coloured syrup from large glass jars. Miao hands her two five-baht coins and settles down to eat her dessert with a red plastic spoon, the yellow tennis ball quiescent on her lap.

A skinny man drifts by holding a hinged wooden case filled with lottery tickets. He has laid them out neatly in numerical order and flagged with yellow stickers the ones that have particularly auspicious numbers. This is Satra, who came to Pattaya a year ago and has been sleeping on the cement floor of a partially-built house near the stadium, courtesy of his cousin who left their village in the North-East a year before he did and is working as a roofer on local projects.

Satra has been selling lottery tickets for six weeks now and makes enough for noodle soup twice a day and whisky at the building site in the evenings. He approaches Amir who is muscling through the market with his men friends Ekani and Kamal, visitors from Hyderabad on a budget. Satra talks up the providential power of his tickets, using facial expressions that involve a lot of work with both eyebrows. Kamal looks interested and rubs his fingers together to ask the price. Satra indicates the notes required but, after a show of considering the odds, the three Indian men pass on, pretending they can find a better return elsewhere.

Miao smiles at Lam forlornly as he pushes past her and struggles up the steps of the bar. Lam is a former chicken farmer from the North-East and has the desperate look of a man not wanting to fail at two businesses in a row. He has male-pattern baldness and is wearing a beige windcheater despite the heat. He approaches each table with his laminated wall-maps of Thailand and bunch of wooden back-scratchers, demonstrating the function of the latter on some of the bar customers' backs. Each annoyed refusal makes Lam more desperate and he leaves the bar in a rush, determined to be able to look back on the day as a commercial success.

Vladimir seems excited by the music on offer at Apem's stall and has carefully selected four counterfeit CDs which he wants to take home to play in his flat in Omsk where he works as a factory caretaker. Apem is slipping the four discs into a small plastic carrier while Vladimir holds up three banknotes. The words between them are not spoken. Vladimir knows the going rate for a fake CD is 100 baht but he's trying to negotiate what he considers a reasonable discount for quantity. Apem holds on to the plastic bag. He's not in the mood for discounts. He's thinking of the evening hours he spends copying the originals and printing genuine-looking labels on to the copies while his babies cry from the other room. Vladimir proffers another bill, this time a fifty, nostalgically confident that they'd go for it in the market in Omsk.

Marina holds the sarong up under her chin and looks at her legs in the mirror. She sees herself younger than she really is, before she met Vladimir even, when with her slim legs she had the pick of several young men in the canteen kitchen where she dispensed pork and cabbage to junior bank employees on their lunch break. Chompu tells her she looks beautiful but Alexa giggles. Marina drops the hem of the sarong from her chin and removes the leggings, handing the bunched garment back to Chompu with a grunt. As they walk past the music stall, Vladimir turns to join them with a determined shake of his head. He carefully returns the banknotes to his slim wallet and Apem replaces the CDs in the gaps they left in the rack.

Next to the clothes stall Gan is putting a frilly cotton dress on a baby rabbit. The hamsters lie around their cages on their backs like sun-bathers exhausted by the heat. Siamese fighting fish are segregated in Singha soda-water bottles. Five terrapins the size of ten-baht coins are looking for a way out of a white plastic bowl. Gan used to keep a dog at home but two years ago it was run over by a careless woman in a silver Nissan pick-up and she was too sad about her loss to replace him. She looks up when Apem plays that track: *Only miss the sun when it starts to snow*. She likes the tune but has no idea who is singing or what snow is. Nok, who keeps the towel cart, asks Gan to watch her stock while she goes to the toilet. Gan nods.

At a table in the next bar Mike from Birmingham is sitting with his younger wife Ngor and her family—her mother Nahm, brother Keow and two sisters Mapran and Porn. There are six dishes on the table—fried pork, fish cakes, two curries and two noodle dishes—as well as Leo beers for the men, rum for the mother-in-law and Cokes for the young women. The Thai conversation is animated. Mike drinks his beer in silence, nodding occasionally as Ngor translates a snippet here and there. Keow orders another beer and Pimm, who has waited on tables in this bar on market days for more than five years, quietly adds another slip to the pot that constitutes Mike's bill.

My place in the bar is raised a few steps above the road. All the cane chairs face one way, towards the market. On the glass-topped table in front of me there is a bottle of San Miguel Light with a slice of lime in the neck. My sunglasses have prescription lenses for distance vision. Nobody knows my name.

Coming from Latvia

He is strolling along Beach Road one evening alone. It is around six o'clock, the sky is darkening but the sand stays eerily illuminated. The deckchairs are all folded and stacked against the palm trees and the jet-ski boys are zooming around like fighter pilots pretending that they're putting their vehicles away for the night at Bali Hai pier, though anyone can see they're taking the long way around. After a day of trying to impress the girls on Pattaya beach, they're saying it's time for a bit of fun.

There are lots of places to sit along the walkway, and these are mostly occupied by elderly *farang* men— Westerners—some of whom are accompanied by younger ladies. A lot of the old guys look recently showered for the evening, in clean shirts but perhaps the same khaki shorts they've been wearing all day. A few are holding cans of Singha or Chang beer. Ken seems to fit the demographic, so he claims a vacant space to sit awhile and appreciate the reddening sun as it lowers itself like a cautious bather into the sea somewhere the other side of Koh Larn, the largest island visible from the shore.

There are a number of unattached women hanging around the walkway, as if placed into the tableau by someone skilled in flower arranging. Ken knows how to identify working girls: they hold eye contact that little bit longer. When it first happened to him, it came as a momentary shock as he is generally accustomed to look away from the eyes of strangers. He's still uncomfortable for the first split-second. Maybe she is, maybe she isn't. Is she a shameless sexual predator or merely unabashed? If she holds longer than the first blink, he can be sure. With growing confidence, Ken now considers that continued eye contact with a girl on Beach Road can be a thing to be savoured, to wonder where it will lead.

A woman sitting on the same wall as Ken stands up without fuss, moves a little closer to him and resettles. Ken will talk to anyone, and frequently does, much to the occasional annoyance of Mrs Boxer, now ex. When they were together he would sometimes find her tugging at his sleeve when she thought he was staying too long in a shop, perhaps to discuss the salesperson's favourite fly for salmon, or the power of the storm coming in from over the Atlantic like black poster paint in water.

Soon he is in conversation with Nook, or it may be Ning; she doesn't give her name. Not only is she a skilled conversationalist, but as her story unfolds it reveals an interesting coincidence.

*

Ken is a big man and has upper arms like thighs. He could lift Mrs Boxer above his head, back in the days when Mrs Boxer was willing to participate in such demonstrations of his strength. He has a ruddy complexion with a large, bulbous nose that an unkind observer might describe as the nose of a drinker. His hair is grey, curly and unattended. Although newly showered, he is wearing a crumpled green vest, possibly of military origin, and this reveals on his shoulder a tattoo of the noble profile of a Red Indian chief.

The Red Indian chief has been with Ken for a long time and has survived many changes in their relationship. When the ink was first applied, Ken was proud of the adornment, despite the pain and the expense; then came a period of regret. These days, Ken is more relaxed. He's getting on in years and can't really see the tattoo without a mirror, so now he doesn't think it matters either way.

Sometimes when Ken talks to strangers he likes to adopt a persona. This is a clever-sounding way of saying that he pretends to be someone he is not. He doesn't do this in the sort of places in which he might discuss salmon fishing or the weather, such as the shops he used to visit with the then Mrs Boxer. Those shop people knew pretty well who Ken was. No, his subterfuge is reserved for situations of certain anonymity, such as he finds himself in now on Beach Road, Pattaya.

He doesn't feel guilty about this deception. Should he ever be rebuked for it, he is ready with the philosophical challenge: 'Who am I anyway? I am many people and which one I choose to present to strangers in the street is my own business.' To which one could so easily argue: 'Yes, but who is the person doing the choosing, Ken? That's you. That's the real Ken Boxer.'

There's no-one around this evening who seems likely to rebuke or to argue, and Ken isn't overly concerned whether he's real or not. He is just sitting here on Beach Road watching the sunset when the woman, who could so easily be called Nook, slowly leans over, her hands pressed into the lap of her denim shorts, and asks him quietly, 'Excuse me, mister. Where do you come from?'

The woman is good-looking, small, perhaps in her early forties, yet with long loose hair through which large gold loop earrings grin. She's wearing a pink T-shirt with a strip of white lace around the neck. Her face is made up with precision. He can detect perfume vaporising into the diminished space between them. Mentally leafing through his portfolio of personae, Ken answers quickly but, affected by the closeness of the woman and the beauty of the setting sun, quite wistfully, thus: 'Latvia.'

Latvia is not where Ken actually comes from. Ken comes from Nova Scotia, a piece of land that hangs off the east side of Canada as if they were trying to get rid of it. Ken comes from Nova Scotia like Christmas trees come from Nova Scotia, like Donald Sutherland, lobster and the Trailer Park Boys come from Nova Scotia. Cut Ken Boxer's weather-beaten, leathery skin and he bleeds Alexander Keith's Red Amber Ale, that's how much he doesn't come from Latvia.

Since Nova Scotia is a big piece of land, Ken might narrow things down a little by revealing that he comes more particularly and most recently from Halifax, the provincial capital of Nova Scotia, though he was born not far away from there in Shubenacadie, a small accumulation of dwellings and businesses of which he is confident that his present companion is both unaware and unconcerned.

What he is doing in Pattaya can easily be explained. Pattaya, Thailand has something in abundance that is in short supply in Halifax, Nova Scotia, at least outdoors in winter, and that's heat. It can be distressing to consider the injustice of heat's distribution around the world. While the temperature range in Pattaya is said to go from around 21 to 34 degrees Celsius, in Halifax they're lucky if they can manage -9 to 23.

In Walking Street, Pattaya, they have a vodka bar — the Icebar — where the ambient temperature is air-conned down to -5°C. That's *minus* five. It's meant as a novelty, a place for temperate tourists enervated by the taxing tropical climate to have a laugh. You rush in, shiver in your sweat-damp T-shirt, down your icy shot and scoot. You're not meant to spend all day in the -5° Icebar, yet that's effectively what they do in Halifax on a warm day in winter.

Ken has a friend from Vancouver who keeps a house in Pattaya. He says, 'That which is solid in Nova Scotia is a vapour in Pattaya.'

Ken is mesmerised by the magic of his friend's words. 'Is it some kind of riddle?' he asks.

'I'm talking about water, Ken.'

Of course. The water in Nova Scotia is something you can depend on. You can stand on the water in Nova Scotia and drive your 4x4 on it with chains. In Pattaya, it's hard to get a grip on the humidity. It goes in through your lungs and comes out of your skin, dribbling down your chest like the footsteps of flies.

Ken considers the similar properties of water and blood. He imagines the frozen heart of Mrs Boxer, now ex, and sees enclosed within it the massed spicules of ice, like the fingers of frost around a window frame.

It is the expectation, encouraged by his friend from Vancouver, that in Pattaya the spaces of the heart are hot and humid that brings Ken so far from Halifax, Nova Scotia to discover these things for himself.

*

Ken has never been to Latvia; in fact he'd never been out of Canada until he was 22. However, he is determined not to let an untravelled youth limit his imagination. If he says he comes from Latvia then, for the purposes of his current conversation with the attractive lady on his wall, Latvia is whence he surely comes. As he considers the magnificence of the sunset that unfolds before him, he is quite proud of his quick invention, but apprehensive as to where the conversation might now lead. What's the capital of Latvia? Speak to me in Latvian. What's the most popular brand of beer in Latvia and how big are the salmon? His complete ignorance of such basic issues concerning the place he claims is his home country could easily expose him as a fraud.

But for the moment he is saved. Nook shows a miraculous sign of recognition and says, 'Oh that is interesting. My daughter is going to study to be a nurse in Lat... What is the name of your country again?'

'Latvia.'

'That is where my daughter is going.'

'Well, that certainly is a coincidence.'

'Yes, she will study in the hospital there. And work a little, but only in the mornings.'

'My country has need of many fine nurses,' opines Ken, considering himself on reasonably safe ground. He prays he is not over-doing it when he adds: 'I hope she will be happy nursing in Latvia, my beloved homeland.'

The edge of the sun has dipped into the sea as far as you'd be advised to dunk a biscuit in a cup of tea. Its light dances off the waves like a roman candle.

'My daughter is worried that she will have no friends in Latvia,' continues Nook.

'I'm sure the hospital will take good care of your daughter and help her to make many new friends.'

Nook looks worried. 'But my daughter knows nothing about your country—its people or its... You have a good heart. I would like you to meet her. She can learn from you. Can she find green papaya salad in Latvia? Are the beauty salons expensive? Where are the best chicken's feet stalls? Where is the nearest temple where she can make merit?'

The disc has begun to melt into the hot ocean. Its light is fiery orange.

Ken wants to give Nook and her daughter the benefit of his wisdom of which, concerning Latvia, he has painfully little. So, keeping the conversation as general as he can, he provides these consoling words: 'These are simple questions which the hospital will be able to answer in your daughter's first few days. There will be an orientation session for new students I am sure. It's natural to be concerned about travelling to a strange land but after a week or so your daughter will feel quite at home and wonder why she ever worried about anything.'

'But my daughter would be happier if she could hear this from you, a man who comes from Latvia itself. Do you say Latvian? What is your hotel and room number, please? She's gonna call at your hotel room tonight at 7.30. She is 19 years old. She is a very happy girl, very clean.'

The sun is nearly submerged, out of its depth, sinking. Its face is red.

'Don't worry about reception,' Nook continues assuringly. 'My daughter knows how to deal with hotel receptions.'

*

The thought crosses Ken's mind that he is being presented with an opportunity by Nook which, at first, he did not see. What if this young woman, her daughter, is attractive? What if they meet and she is drawn to him for his wind-battered, characterful face and powerful arms? If he could just keep up the pretence for long enough, soon, as he runs out of advice about nursing in Latvia, he might find her eyes drifting to his. Perhaps she would stand before him, take his big lion's head in her little hands and look directly into his ice-grey eyes for longer than a blink, enough to make him wonder. Their lips would touch, or they might. It has been a long time since he kissed a woman, a long time before the divorce even.

But Nook looks so innocent and helpless. He can't take advantage of her by seducing her daughter. What if they fell in love, Nook's daughter and Ken? His new lover would be cruelly snatched away so soon after their meeting. He would be left alone to imagine his new darling as she endured the long hours of study, the unpleasant chores—emptying bedpans, blanket baths, enemas—and fending off the advances of horny young Latvian doctors. It doesn't bear thinking about.

Further along the wall, an old man drops his empty beer can on to the pavement. It sounds like the tolling of a broken bell.

Ken comes to his senses, ashamed of this flight of lustful imagination. He considers Nook's predicament. She clearly loves her daughter who will shortly embark on a long journey to a strange land. Since the land is strange not only to Nook's daughter, but also to Ken, he can hardly imagine the difficulties she will encounter on arrival. Finding her way around Latvia could be a nightmare; it could be a piece of cake. It's the awful *unknowing* that gnaws so at the imagination.

Ken is a kindly man and wishes to help Nook's daughter with her charitable mission to care for the needy in her Latvian hospital. However, he feels he has imparted just about all the advice that he can muster. If only he had told

Nook that he came from Halifax, Nova Scotia. He would be able to expound for a good hour about the best places to eat in town, the best laundromat, a reliable all-night pharmacy, the maritime museum and Alexander Keith's brewery, which is open to visitors.

For a moment he considers saying, 'Actually, I'm from Halifax, Nova Scotia. Wouldn't your daughter prefer to go nursing in Canada? We need good quality medical personnel in our province. The prospects there are good, even if it looks as if the rest of Canada is trying to kick us into the Atlantic.' But it is too late. A person can't be from Latvia one minute and Nova Scotia the next. It's not honest.

'I think it would be better if she came here to meet me on Beach Road,' is all Ken can usefully add. 'Here we can watch the sun go down together and I can tell her all I know about Latvia. It won't take long.'

He knows he's pushing his luck. What if she accepts his offer? It will be embarrassing to sit here on Beach Road with an innocent young nursing novice, making up stuff about Latvia. 'Right around the corner from the hospital, down the road a-ways and on the left, you'll find a great place to buy snow-boots,' he would advise. Do they even need snow-boots in Latvia? He doesn't know. Latvia could be as balmy as British Columbia for all Ken knows. It's hopeless. He goofed royally by even choosing an alternate persona in the first place.

Nook has lost patience. She is beginning to regret investing time in this dishevelled old Latvian codger who seems to want nothing but to sit on a wall on his own and watch the sunset. In future she will choose younger and more virile subjects with whom to share her daughter's thirst for knowledge. And she will avoid Latvians at all costs.

'That is not so good,' she says quite sternly, giving it one last chance. 'Which hotel are you staying at please? Tell me your room number.'

*

Just as Ken will talk to anyone, so he finds it difficult to stop talking to anyone, but Nook's change of tone makes him suspect now that she is not quite as she first seemed. Folks back in Nova Scotia are more down to earth than this fiery woman. What you see in Shubenacadie is what you get. A Nova Scotian's word is his bond, solid as ice.

In the short time he has been staying at the house of his friend from Vancouver, Ken has noticed that things around here are not like that, not necessarily what they seem. Here in Pattaya, an understanding you thought you had can disappear as easily as steam from a bowl of noodle soup.

Is Nook for real, or is she spinning him a line? Does she want money? If so, is she offering to sell him something or trying to rip him off pure and simple? If he had a hotel room and he agreed to her request, what would happen when he found himself alone with Nook's daughter? Would her boyfriend burst in and accuse him of molesting her, would she stab him and steal his wallet, or would she suggest they have sex together in return for a suitable sum? Although he doesn't understand the scam, if a scam it is, he suspects it is a scam. Nook is pretending to be someone she's not, which makes his heart heavy.

We're both pretending, he realises. If we'd been honest with each other, we could have had a good long talk. She probably knows nothing and cares little about salmon fishing, but the weather could have been a start. Suddenly, he needs to go home.

As he pushes down on his knees and rises to leave, the sun has slipped below the horizon. It crosses his mind that it'll probably be up again tomorrow.

Reincarnation

As the lights came on, Angela awoke, though without the satisfaction of a full night's rest. To her right, Adam held the little pillow over his eyes. He was clearly feeling the same. The blinds were up; the bright light was unarguable; it was daytime. She wondered if she should brush her teeth and run some cold water over her face, but decided it wouldn't be worth the effort. Besides, the rather brusque hostess had just pinned her in her seat with a breakfast tray. She knew that under the foil lid there would be an omelette with a half-sized frankfurter, half a boiled tomato and a mushroom. There usually was.

Adam looked at his watch.

'How long till we land?' asked Angela.

'About 40 minutes.'

'Did you get any sleep?'

'I'm not really sure. I suppose I must have, but it can't have been much.'

They were on the British Airways flight from London Heathrow to Bangkok, the first time for Angela, though Adam had visited Thailand twice before. On this trip he was in transit to Laos and Vietnam. He planned to spend two days in Bangkok to help Angela acclimatise, then take a flight to Vientiane.

'So,' Adam began as he chased his single mushroom around the tray with a plastic fork, 'now I've got you trapped, what's the story with you and Bryn? Do you think you'll get back together again?'

'Second question first: no, I won't even try. Six years was long enough for a thorough assessment, to find out that he's not the man for me. He's a good bloke, I still love him, but he's not the one I'm going to grow old with. I need a completely new start, a new life. When you called the other week it had just happened and I guess I just wanted to run away and hide for a while. When you said you were going to Asia, and I had the summer holidays coming up, it felt like an opportunity to tag along with you, at least for the outward trip. It was a perfect chance to be out of touch for a bit, and I'd never have done it alone. So thank you.'

'Was that bit your answer to the first question?'

'Not really. You mean what made us break up? It was me that walked out. It was his lack of commitment. It was a feeling that grew over a number of years and I know women say it a lot, but it's important. I could never get him to commit to anything in the future. I like a plan. I like to know where we're heading. I felt we were just treading water, waiting for something to happen that would force us – force him – into action.'

'We're talking about babies really, aren't we?'

'And being accepted by his family as a permanent fixture, and getting a proper house, and marriage. Yes, I'm taking about babies. So what? I'm at the nesting age. The final straw was when he agreed to help a couple of our friends – lesbians, actually – by donating sperm. Don't get me wrong, it was a great thing to do and I was proud of him, but... sorry, Adam, I'm going to sound like a grade-A bitch... he never offered to donate any sperm to me.'

Adam nodded and went back to his breakfast.

Angela watched the aeroplane's descent through the window. Rows of strange buildings, canals and rectangles of water, clear sky, a shimmer of heat, and everywhere palm trees. Ah, Asia, she thought—huge, vibrant, different, unknown. The excitement caused a little pain to nag in the backs of her hands. Until this moment, she had never stepped foot outside Europe, and Western Europe at that. This new continent was already having a physical effect on her.

*

They took a taxi to their hotel near the Asok junction on the Sukhumvit Road and checked into rooms on the second and fourth floors. After freshening up, they met in the lobby and walked to Cabbages and Condoms for dinner.

'Isn't the heat amazing?' exclaimed Angela. 'It's like walking into a bonfire. And this place is just magic, the lights in the trees and everything. What's with the condoms?'

'It's run by a charity,' explained Adam. 'They do anti-Aids projects.'

'They do good food, too. That fish was amazing. I don't feel like going to bed, what about you? My body clock tells me it's three o'clock in the afternoon. What shall we do after dinner?'

'I'm going to take you to Soi Cowboy, if you're up for it.'

'I'm up for anything, but what's Soi Cowboy?'

'It's a party street. It's not far. I think you'll enjoy it.'

They split the bill, left a small tip and walked up to the main road, dashing over Sukhumvit just before the intersection. Then they crossed the busy Soi 21 on a long zebra crossing that the cars seemed to ignore, and turned from the relative quiet of the major traffic artery into the pedestrianised bedlam of Soi Cowboy.

Nothing had prepared Angela for this. Not Piccadilly Circus, not Pigalle Place on acid — the Paris district, not Angela. This was the brashest, brightest, loudest street she had ever been in. It was a narrow street, and relatively short, but into that small area were packed what must have been dozens of bars — or were they clubs? — each with coloured flashing lights, neon logos and crude names. Kiss, Spice Girls, Dollhouse, Long Gun and Suzie Wong — the nature of their business was in little doubt. The message flashing at Angela was commercial sex with a party twist. The bars were pumping out music at ear-throbbing decibels. In front of the bars, gaggles of women in their underwear held up signs advertising happy hours and discount draft beer, while loudly urging groups of ambling tourists to come inside. Welcome, handsome man: the unignorable greeting that speaks straight to the heart of any male with blood in his veins. Or his vains.

'Which one shall we try first?' asked Adam.

'Go inside? No, I don't think so, Adam. Unless I'm wrong, I don't think I'm going to be very welcome in any of these places. They're all men here. Well, mostly.'

'You'll be fine.'

'No, really, Adam. I'm no prude, but these are strip joints, aren't they?'

'Not really.'

'What then?'

'They're go-go bars. Come on inside and I'll show you.'

'Are you sure?'

Adam chose a bar on the right and dragged Angela by the hand past the girls around the door and through a black cloth curtain into the gaudy interior. A waiter rushed them to a bench seat. Before them was a small shelf which served as a table. The man took their drinks order. Angela sipped her gin and tonic and took stock of her surroundings.

No more than two metres in front of her was a stage on which about a dozen women were dancing dreamily to the loud rock music. They seemed to be dressed, if dressed was the word—in uniform—a pelmet-like gauze micro skirt with pink waist-band and a strip of similar material performing the function of a bra. Their boots were more varied in design, though platform soles were popular. About half the women were topless; and they were all effectively bottomless since it was quite easy to see through the wispy material that they were naked under their little skirts. They wore numbered discs on their wrists.

Closest to the dancers, customers sat on stools with their drinks before them on the stage. On the near side, they had their backs to Angela, but it was clear from the angles of their heads that their position afforded a good view up the dancers' skirts. A throng of people milled around the stage. Boys in white shirts directed newcomers to empty tables. There were girls in pretend school uniforms and platform boots who seemed to be delivering drinks. There were dancing girls who had left the stage or were waiting their turn to go on. A number of these women were naked but for their shoes. Some sat with customers. Some sat on customers. Raised slightly above the proceedings and to one side in an illuminated alcove was a man wearing a headset. He appeared to be the DJ. The music was his fault.

'Do you need me to explain what's going on?' Adam asked.

'I think I've probably worked out the various job descriptions,' Angela replied, raising her voice above the thumping bass, 'except her. Who's the woman in black?'

'That's the mamasan.'

'Oh, right, mamasan. What's that? Sounds Japanese.'

'She takes care of the girls. She makes sure they behave themselves, and that they earn good money for the bar.'

'What, she tells them how to dance?'

'Dancing is just the shop window activity. It's the girls' chance to show off to customers. They get paid to dance, but only a little.'

'How do they survive then?'

Adam put down his beer, smiled at Angela. 'This is a brothel,' he said abruptly. 'The girls get paid by customers who take them back to their hotels, and the bar charges the customer a fine for the loss of the girl's dancing services. Prostitution is illegal in Thailand, so the bars aren't officially involved in it. They're dancing establishments; the sex is a matter for the girls. The bar provides them with a marketing opportunity. Officially, that is.'

'Right, so I hadn't worked out the job descriptions. It all seems like a pretty fine line.'

'This is Thailand. Fine lines are what they do best. Here's another fine line: the girls are not on the game; they're just looking for boyfriends, no matter for how long.'

'But the men are all so old.'

'Yes, a lot of them.'

'And the girls are so young.'

'And?'

'Nothing. I suppose it's what I would have expected. But if this is a brothel for men to pick up hookers, why don't they mind me being here?'

'As I said, it's not officially a brothel as that would be illegal. It's wholesome family entertainment. You're drinking their drink, so you're welcome. You'd be even more welcome if you bought one of the girls a lady drink, even more so if you took one of them back to the hotel.'

'They do that?'

'Some might. You sometimes see couples bar-fining a lady for a threesome. This is Asia. You have to park your old-world ideas and catch the vibe. They don't look like you, they don't think like you, they don't act the way you do. That's why you're here and not in Malaga or Gran Canaria. You're experiencing another culture. Drink up. We'll try the next bar.'

Adam and Angela sampled five or six go-go bars as they progressed along Soi Cowboy. As the night wore on, the street outside filled up with bar ladies and their customers; many were paired off and heading for taxis at the ends of the street. Some of the men looked uncomfortable, others triumphant. Many were red-faced and the worse for drink. They held hands with young girls. Some looked as if they'd never held hands with a girl before; others appeared more suave. For the girls, now in a version of street clothes for the taxi ride back to their new boyfriend's hotel, it appeared to be a little more routine.

Angela was struck by the inequality of the relationships she'd seen forged on Soi Cowboy, no matter how temporary they had been. White with brown, old with young, rich with poor, educated with uneducated, seller with buyer. Whatever bonds were being made here, they were asymmetrical.

*

The next day, Adam led Angela on the tourist trail around some of the major Bangkok sights. He told her to wear a long skirt for their visit to the Grand Palace. They marvelled at the tiny Emerald Buddha in Wat Phra Kaeo. They sweated in the heat of the dusty National Museum. They lunched on noodle soup near the river and rode in a boat south from Tha Chang to Tha Oriental, where Adam insisted on treating Angela to afternoon tea at the hotel there. They took a taxi back to Asok, swam in their hotel's roof-top pool and read their paperbacks. In the evening they went to China Town to see the Golden Buddha, explore the alleyways around Sampeng and have an expensive dinner in a gaudy red-and-gold Chinese eatery.

It was Adam's last night in Bangkok. 'Back to the airport again tomorrow, I'm afraid. Then you're on your own. What's the plan?'

'Oh I'm just going to hang around town for a couple of days, then maybe take a trip to Kanchanaburi,' said Angela, taking the name a syllable at a time. 'I've heard you can stay on a raft on the River Kwai, ride an elephant, that sort of thing. And I'd like to go up to Chiang Mai and then back down to the islands. I've got three weeks, so I'm going to take it easy.'

'And you won't be lonely?'

'I don't know. I haven't been away alone since I've been with Bryn. We always went everywhere together. But this is my new life. This is something different. I'm actually looking forward to providing my own company. And anyway, if I go on trips, I'm bound to meet other people. They'll be couples and I'll be the gooseberry, but so what?'

'"What can you do?" as they say in Thailand.'

'Is that what they say?'

'You hear it quite a lot. It's an acknowledgment that so much is beyond our control. It's the Buddhist resignation.'

'I like it. That's going to be my motto.'

'Good luck with your trip, anyway. I won't see you in the morning because I've got an early flight to Vientiane. Keep up on Facebook. See you in Blighty.'

*

On her first day alone, Angela decided to follow her guide book's advice and hire a long-tail boat on the Chao Phraya River. The book said you could share with others, but she was in more of a mood to treat herself than she was to spend the morning with strangers, so she took the whole boat, large though it was.

Although she knew which sights she wanted to see, the boatman had his own idea of what would be a suitable itinerary. From his quick introduction, delivered in what sounded like phonetic English, there seemed to be a fair amount of overlap, so she was happy to lie back on the uncomfortable seat and allow herself to be guided.

He took her across the river and steered the boat up and down numerous narrow *klongs* on the Thonburi side where Siam's capital used to be; he moored at a riverside museum where royal ceremonial barges were on display; and he dropped her off at Wat Arun, the temple of dawn. Here, he signalled that she had 30 minutes to look around.

Actually, she didn't need quite that long. Wat Arun was a very pretty building but there was a limit to how many photos of it she needed to take home. Besides, the classic views of the temple were from the water itself or from the city side of the river.

In the grounds, there was some stone furniture for the use of visitors. Angela sat at one of the tables and read up about the temple in her guide book. Within a few minutes she became aware of someone standing close to her. She looked up and found a boy — a young man — who seemed about to speak to her. He was leaning slightly forward and was holding out a large, well-thumbed paperback book.

'Excuse me,' the boy asked. 'Do you speak English?'

'Yes, I do.'

'Please, I wonder if you can help me with my studies. I am teaching myself with this book, but it's better if I can talk to an English-speaking person. Where are you from?'

'I'm from England.'

'Perfect. Do English people speak the best English?'

Angela had to think about that one. 'Probably not,' she replied slowly. 'The Irish are probably better. Anyway, there are lots of ways of speaking English. Even in England we speak in many different ways.'

'But it's all English, yes?'

'Yes.'

'Can you help me with my studies?'

'Well, OK,' Angela said hesitantly, 'I can help you a little, but I have to go back to my boat in a few minutes.'

'Better than nothing,' the boy said, proud of his use of the expression.

He sat down at Angela's table and spread his book in front of her. The passage he had been studying was headed 'Tea'. Most of the section was in Thai, but a few phrases in Roman type within the text stuck out for her: 'Traditional British tea', 'Savoy Hotel', 'A selection of fresh finger sandwiches', and 'Delicious home-made French pastries and tea cakes'. Angela was surprised to find that such topics were taught to Thais as typical, presumably, of the British way of life. Personally, she had never been to the Savoy Hotel. And she preferred coffee.

'In Thailand, tea is a drink. In England also?'

'No. Well, yes. Yes, tea is a drink in England, though of course we don't grow it there. England is quite a cold country, so we don't grow tea. It comes from India and China.' She realised that her reply had become hopelessly tangled.

At home, Angela was a teacher. That was her job. She was trained as a teacher and had more than ten years' secondary school experience. She was trained to make complex topics accessible to her pupils. She could hold a class of 14-year-olds in thrall with her explanation of photosynthesis or the way a kidney worked. Explaining an afternoon snack to a young Thai man shouldn't be this difficult.

'Why is there a page about tea in my book if you have no tea in England? This is my problem with this book. There are so many parts I don't understand.'

Angela gathered her thoughts. 'Well, although tea doesn't grow in England, it is very popular. Over the years, tea has come to mean not only the drink, but also the food that people eat when they drink tea. It's similar to your expression in Thai, "*gin khao*". You say "eat rice", even though the phrase also covers eating the things that go with rice.' That practically exhausted the knowledge of Thai that Angela had gleaned from the dictionary section of her guide book.

'I understand, so people eat the sandwiches and cakes when they drink tea?'

'Yes, you got it.'

'The drink is called tea and the food is called tea.'

'The whole meal is called tea. Like breakfast and lunch.'

'You explain these things very well. But what is a "fresh finger"?'

'Ah, that seems to be referring to a fresh finger sandwich. You know what a sandwich is?'

'Yes.'

'Well, "fresh" means it has just been made, and "finger" describes its shape. It's long and thin, like a finger; that's what that means. There are no fingers inside.'

'Thank you. And now this page…'

'Actually, I'm sorry, but I have to go back to my boat. It has been nice to meet you.'

'What is your name?'

'Angela. It was nice to meet you. But now…'

'My name is Som. How old are you?'

'Oh, I don't think… OK, I'm 34.'

'I am 21. If you have a boat, I wonder if you could take me across the river. I will help you 50 baht.'

Angela hesitated, then relented. She decided there was no harm in giving Som a lift to the eastern bank in her huge boat, but refused his offered contribution to the cost. As they were leaving the temple compound, Som stopped to talk to two little girls who were sitting behind a stack of small, battered wooden cages. He seemed to be buying one of them. With an apologetic nod to Angela, he stepped aside and opened the cage to release what looked like a pair of finches. He prayed and looked solemn for a moment, then returned the empty cage to one of the girls. Angela and Som continued to the waiting long-tail.

'This is the best view of Wat Arun, from here,' Angela suggested when they were about mid-water.

'It is a very beautiful temple.'

'What were you doing with the birds? Why did you let them go?'

'That was to make merit. If I release a bird that's kept in a cage, then I make merit.'

'And that decides your karma,' Angela asked, remembering the idea from what she'd read.

'Exactly, the more merit I make, then the higher I will be when I come back.'

'After you die.'

'Yes.'

'You believe that you will come back as something else when you die?'

'Yes. All Buddhists believe that.'

'Will I come back after I die?'

'Of course. Everybody does.'

'But I make no merit, so does that mean I'll come back as something low—a worm or a toad? Or maybe I won't come back at all?'

'You are a good woman, so you make merit in your own way. In the next life you will be something very high. This happens to Christians as well as Buddhists.'

'But I'm not a Christian.'

'Then what is your religion?'

'I have no religion.'

Som pondered these words calmly. He was prepared for all eventualities. 'I don't think that makes any difference. But Buddhists like to be sure.'

'How do you know there's another life?'

'All Buddhists know that life goes on forever.'

'Yes, but how? Who told you?'

'I have known it since I was a small boy. I have learnt it from monks. I cannot doubt it.'

'You see, that's where I have a problem with your belief. I am a scientist and, to make it simple, I can't accept something as true unless there is evidence to support it. I'm not going to believe anything unless I can at least see a reason for it to be true. Now, if we're all going to be reborn as something different, it follows that, before, we were also something else. So how many people remember having a previous life? How many people remember being a dog or a finch?'

'Oh, there are many people who can tell you about that.'

Angela should have guessed this. Just as there is a certain percentage of the population in the West who consider themselves to be Jesus Christ, Napoleon or Elvis, there is bound to be a similar number of Thai Buddhists who remember being a prawn.

'Have you met these people?'

'No, I haven't, but the monks have told me about them many times.'

'And you believe them?'

'Yes.'

'So how do animals come back as people? How can a toad make merit? It's got a long way to go. It can hardly pay to release birds from a cage.'

'I don't know.'

'Let's say in your next life you're an elephant. Will you be able to remember being human?'

'I hope so.'

Angela wanted to continue, but could see she had no hope of winning her argument. She was going to ask what point there would be in filling an elephant's head with human experiences when it would surely be more advantageous to the elephant if it used its brain power to deal only with elephant-related issues. But she realised that she was thinking like an evolutionary biologist, while he…well, he wasn't thinking at all. He was regurgitating doctrines that he had heard from people in authority and had accepted without question.

Adam's words from the previous evening came back to her. She had to remember that this was a different culture. They don't think like us. She was beginning to understand what he meant.

Som was a polite, correct, friendly young man whose faith had survived Angela's preliminary battering. To challenge him further would overstep the little social credit she had earned by giving him a lift across the Chao Phraya River in her hired long-tail. His face was turned to the wat, his eyes half closed, a slight breeze ruffling his hair.

Reincarnation was a ridiculous concept, Angela was certain, but made for stimulating argument. It got to the very heart of what it is that we are. If it were true, which was preposterous, what exactly would it be that would 'live on'. If it was 'I', who, actually, was I?

If someone describes me, Angela thought, first it would be in terms of my body: 'She's a blonde woman, mid-thirties, quite tall, slim, blue eyes.' But according to Buddhist teaching, none of those characteristics would come with me to my next life — not if I came back as a lizard — so they can't constitute 'me'. What would make that lizard Angela? Would it remember having been a biology schoolteacher? Would it remember its relationship with Bryn? Would it recall its holiday in Thailand? Would it be called Angela? Of course not, otherwise surely I would remember all my previous lives. I would remember being a jellyfish or a geranium, neither of which experiences ring any bells at all.

So if the reincarnated self bears no physical resemblance to its predecessor, and shares no mental connection, in what sense is it reincarnation at all?

We're all made of atoms, some of which may well have previously been part of the constructions of other living things. Is that what this is all about? Is it all an allegory of perfectly rational biology? If so, the Buddha must have been a pretty cool guy, because surely no-one else was thinking like that 2,500 or more years ago. But that didn't explain the idea of advancing up some kind of hierarchy, boosted by merit-making. Doing good could hardly direct your atoms into some higher form. Making merit to achieve favour at the point of reincarnation was at best a wild extrapolation of what may have been an amazing insight and, at worst, part of a commercial enterprise that involved disrupting the lives of innocent songbirds.

Or, as Angela had always previously argued, it was a way of making the peasants behave themselves in a socially sustainable way and stop complaining about their miserable lives, hoping for better luck next time.

*

The long-tail docked and Som helped Angela up on to the pier.

'It's lunch time,' he said. 'Would you like to eat?'

'No, I don't think so.'

'It's OK,' he said. 'You can pay. You won't feel guilty.'

Angela looked at him, considering his challenge. She smiled. 'Alright then, just something light.'

Som found a barbeque stall that served papaya salad and ordered chicken and *som tum Thai*. 'I asked for very little chilli in your salad,' he assured her. '*Nit noi phet.*'

They sat on plastic stools on the pavement and ate grilled chicken, sticky rice and papaya salad from plastic plates.

'So when you come back,' Angela ventured, 'what exactly is it that comes back? It can't be your body or your mind, so in what sense do you return?'

'The part that lives on is your... Excuse me.' Som took out a small dictionary and spent some time flicking the pages to and fro. After a while, he held the book up to Angela with his thumb nail underlining a Thai word.

Angela read off the English translation: 'Soul.'

'What passes to another animal is your soul?' she asked.

'Yes.'

'So what is your soul?'

'It is you.'

'Yes, but which part of me?'

'The part that remains when all other parts are taken away. The part that goes on.'

'Sorry, I don't understand.'

'Look at it this way. You are always changing. The Angela that sits here now is not the same Angela I met at Wat Arun half an hour ago. Your body has changed and your mind has changed — for example, you are hungry now and you have new memories. Just as 'you' are continuous, even though your mind and body have changed, so your soul is continuous, even though your body is gone and your mind dies. It's your soul that is taken up in another living thing.'

'Som,' said Angela, 'that's a lovely speech, in very good English, by the way. The words are lovely and the ideas are beautiful, but there's not the least bit of evidence to suggest that they're true. You can't expect me to accept an explanation like that just because it sounds so pleasing. It has to be supported by evidence. Can you prove what you say?'

Som considered this for a moment and said: 'You're a scientist. Let me explain this in a way that will have meaning for you. What I am suggesting is a hypothesis. It's a way of explaining the facts as we currently see them. If, by experiment, we can add evidence to support the idea, then eventually the hypothesis will become accepted as a theory or a law. Until then, it's one of a number of ways of explaining what we know.'

'OK,' Angela said, tentatively.

'Will you accept my ideas on that basis?'

'I suppose so,' replied Angela, 'as long as you open your mind to alternative hypotheses. And as long as you accept that we have no evidence yet.'

Som was all smiles. 'It is exactly that which made me approach you in Wat Arun. I cannot find such stimulating challenges among Thai people.'

'Well, I'm glad to have been of service.'

'Thank you for your conversation. Now, I would like to continue our talking and I would like you to help me more with my English,' said Som.

'OK, fire away.'

'Excuse me?'

'What help do you need?'

'No, not here, I wonder if I could come to your hotel.'

Angela's mouth was burning from the salad, which Som had assured her had been prepared with her Western sensitivity in mind. She had come to Thailand looking for some kind of adventure. Som was attractive, there was no doubt, and he was clearly attracted to her which, in itself, was an attractive characteristic. Was this the adventure, a young man not much older than her A-level students? A man whose unshakeable beliefs had no basis in her philosophy, despite his ruse of weaving his doctrine into scientific method?

An image crossed her mind of the queue of older Western men steering young Thai women out of Soi Cowboy. Was she now part of that queue? Was this an asymmetrical relationship in the making? Did this have any possible future?

She had been hurt by the break-up with Bryn. She came away from England to think things over and find a way of starting afresh, of beginning again — OK, of being born again, if you wanted to carry on being allegorical. Here was a man who was convinced that reincarnation was a certainty. But it was that very conviction, that belief without evidence — that faith — that troubled her. She didn't think it was going to be that easy.

It was a life-defining moment, but she had to decide.

'No, Som, sorry,' she said firmly. 'I've enjoyed your company, but I'm going back now, alone. I'm happy as I am.'

Paddy Fields Forever

Paddy Fields had been in Thailand for no more than four days. He spent the first night on a camp bed in the living room of his friend Dermott O'Callaghan, who lived with his wife Oh in a one-storey dwelling in an Eakmongkol housing estate in south Pattaya. The O'Callaghans' living room was not air-conditioned, but it did have a fan and there was a thermometer on the wall, the mercury in which did not drop below 30°C the whole first night. Paddy was recovering from jet-lag and slept fitfully in the heat. Oh complained that his snoring was audible through the bedroom wall.

The next day, Paddy slept late, ate the lunch of burger, egg and chips that Oh prepared, unpacked his suitcase into the living room cupboard and walked around the block. He came back covered in sweat. In the evening, Paddy showered and went with Dermott on two motorbike taxis to the Sexy Lady bar beer in Soi 7, where Dermott knew most of the regulars. They played three games of pool, all of which Paddy won, watched snatches of a golf competition on the TV, talked about people they knew back in Ireland, and wisecracked.

The bar ladies in the Sexy Lady bar beer took good care of their customers and ensured that their empty bottles were swiftly replenished. Paddy ordered so much Heineken — each small bottle accompanied by a Jameson chaser — that, after four or five hours of uninterrupted drinking, he was no longer able to stand. Without warning Paddy sank from the view of his companions, struck his leg on the corner of the bar and collapsed on to a cardboard box of empty Heineken bottles that the wholesaler's boy was supposed to have collected that afternoon. As Paddy crashed to the floor, the bottle in the corner of the box met his left ocular orbit with some force, knocking him unconscious.

Dermott and his friends noticed Paddy's disappearance only some seconds after it had occurred, such was the discreet nature of his collapse. Alerted by Dao, the wife of the owner of the Sexy Lady bar beer, they crowded around his apparently lifeless form, asked him if he was OK, shouted obscenities at him and slapped his cheeks. When these ministrations produced no more response than could be expected from a large horsehair mattress, Dermott decided to switch on his mobile phone and contact a local hospital for assistance.

While they waited for the ambulance, Paddy regained a modicum of consciousness, but not enough strength to enable him to sit up, so he lay with his feet under the pool table until help arrived. The ambulance took Paddy to the Memorial Hospital on Pattaya Klang, where he spent the next three nights in an air-conditioned ward. In the hospital he received caring and efficient treatment for a split lip, severe contusion to his left eye socket, and alcohol poisoning. He also had a sore knee, but this was not thought by the professionals to need medical attention. He looked as if he'd been three rounds with Mike Tyson but, as he became aware of his condition, he had to admit that his injuries were all self-inflicted.

In his underpants, Paddy Fields weighed 148kg, exactly three times as much as Dr Kasamsun, the physician who attended him in the Pattaya Memorial Hospital, in equivalent underwear. Dr Kasamsun was curious to know how someone of Paddy's obvious maturity — he was in his sixth decade on Earth — should contrive to consume such a large quantity of alcohol on only his first night in Thailand that his liver required three days to metabolise it from his system. Perhaps he just wasn't used to it.

'You don't have alcohol in Ireland, is that it, Mr Patrick?'

'Oh we do,' Paddy replied, 'but I'm on my holidays. At home in Ireland I have to work, so there's less scope.'

'Oh, I see. And what kind of work do you do?'

'I'm in the police,' said Paddy, though the way he said it the doctor was led to believe that Paddy was a policeman, which wasn't strictly the case. In fact, Paddy Fields was more of a caretaker and cleaner in the Shannonbridge garda station than a regular officer of the law; though he was expected to report to work sober each morning, just as the policemen themselves were, so that part was true enough.

Dr Kasamsun explained to Paddy that, ordinarily, she would offer a patient who was suffering from his condition — though she hadn't ever encountered a case as extreme as his — a course of alcoholism counselling. However, considering that he would be in Thailand for such a short time, she recommended instead that he should report to Alcoholics Anonymous as soon as he returned home to Ireland. Paddy promised that he would, wondering at the same time what in hell he'd want to go and do a thing like that for.

Paddy Fields was discharged from the Memorial Hospital at noon on the fourth day, but only after a considerable number of euros had been extracted from his credit card account. Paddy was quite philosophical about the cost, considering it to be an acceptable holiday expense, and possibly one he had already budgeted for; he couldn't remember.

Later that same evening, Paddy Fields was sitting in the Shillelagh Irish pub on Road Two with Dermott and Oh O'Callaghan and their friend Clive O'Dowd. Clive O'Dowd's wife Ping was also present. Under the gauze pad that a smiling nurse had caringly taped to Paddy's face, there was what was known as a black eye, though the colours blue and yellow were also evident. Still, Paddy found 'black eye' useful shorthand when describing to those of Dermott's friends who hadn't been in the Sexy Lady bar beer in Soi 7 three nights before what sort of injury he had sustained. 'You should see the other fellow,' he would add.

Paddy's swollen lower lip was held together by two black stitches, each with a prominent knot. The arrangement reminded Dermott O'Callaghan of the bindings his mother would apply to a pork joint before roasting. The string knots would still be there when the meat was withdrawn from the oven and the time came for his father to carefully divide the crackling among the seven family members.

Playing on the wall-mounted TV in the Shillelagh Irish pub was the Six Nations rugby tournament, coverage of which was not available on the cable package to which Dermott subscribed at home. The Shillelagh had a couple of TV screens which showed every game of the championship live, no matter how late at night it might come on. In the same part of the bar was a loudspeaker which, disconcertingly, relayed the commentary from a football match that was being screened in an adjoining room. It was strange to watch a rugby match while listening to a football commentary. Occasionally, the pundits' descriptions of the action on the soccer pitch made sense to someone watching the rugby, but these moments of insight were quickly replaced by long periods of meaninglessness.

The fat manager of the Shillelagh Irish pub came in to see if his customers were happy.

'Everything all right, lads?'

'Could you not turn off the football?' asked Dermott.

'Unfortunately, the speaker has no switch, otherwise I would,' replied the manager.

'I'll bring my fucking scissors next time and get up there and cut the wire.'

The manager laughed. 'So who are you boys rooting for this evening?' he asked, ignoring Dermott's threat. Since the first game that evening was between Italy and Wales, it was not immediately obvious which team Dermott and his Irish friends would be favouring with their support.

'I fancy Wales,' said Clive. 'And yourself?'

'I support Australia, and whoever's playing against England,' said the adipose manager, apparently unaware that Australia was not included among the countries that contested the Six Nations title, and strangely biased against one of the participating teams. The manager was unapologetically Australian.

'That's not very sporting of you,' retorted Clive. 'It's the game that counts, not the inferiority complex nor the colonial baggage. You should support whoever plays the better rugby. That's the spirit of the game. That's what we do, right, boys? Unless of course it's Ireland playing.'

'That would be different,' agreed Dermott.

Ping was gazing at the screen with her mouth slightly open. She had seen games of rugby on television before, but had never bothered to ask Clive for an explanation of the rules. In her opinion, it was a very dangerous game, played by men considerably larger than her own male family members, though possibly matched for weight by some of the *farang* tourists she observed around town — like Paddy Fields, for example.

Behind her, the chef who served at the carvery counter had stepped out from behind his row of roast joints, carving knife and fork in hand, to get a better view of the televised action. To him, a game of rugby looked like 30 men simultaneously kick-boxing. It seemed violent and unstructured, with no obvious resolution to the vicious brawls.

*

Back in Ireland, it was mid-afternoon on general election day. The ballot had been called quickly, in part to resolve the debate that was brewing about whether the terms of a European Union loan which the country needed to survive an economic crisis should be accepted or renegotiated. Although none of the men sitting in the Shillelagh Irish pub in Pattaya had been able to vote on account of being abroad, they naturally took a keen interest in the election result, which early exit polls indicated would involve a trouncing for Fianna Fail, the party that had dominated Irish politics for 80 years and that the electorate appeared to have blamed for the current crisis.

Despite widespread disenchantment with the old order, Paddy expressed his continuing support for Fianna Fail.

After all, voting for the party was a family tradition that had been maintained by the Fieldses for generations.

'I'd have voted for them, sure,' he confirmed.

'You're a fucking eejit,' Dermott told him 'You're an arsewipe and a cunt. Who do you think got us into this mess if it wasn't Fianna Fail?'

'It was the immigrants, like I always told you,' said Paddy Fields.

'Immigrants? You fucking eejit.'

'You're a fucking eejit.'

'You're both a pair of fucking eejits,' broke in Clive. 'What's the good of blaming the immigrants, for God's sake? Sure, aren't we the biggest collection of immigrants ourselves in practically any country you can name? Do the Americans blame us for their crisis even though New York and Boston are packed with Irishmen? Do even the English blame us for theirs, when Kilburn is practically an Irish colony? For all I know, there's a bit of downtown Athens chock-a-block with Paddies, but you didn't hear the Greeks complain about us when they went tits-up. And look at everybody here in this bar, this Irish bar in Thailand. Micks to a man apart from that fat Aussie bastard. What are we to blame for here?'

'Drinking the place dry,' quipped Dermott, cocking his thumb at Paddy.

'And, really, how can you blame the government either?' continued Clive. 'They've hardly changed for 80 years and things only went pear-shaped this last year or so. And it's been the same everywhere anyway. I'll tell you whose fault it was; it was our own stupid fault. Our own. We were having too good a time for too long. And it was all on tick. We were drinking at the bar for all those years, putting all the drinks on the slate, so to speak. Sooner or later it was inevitable that we'd have to pick up the tab. A gentleman pays his bills. Pay up and shut up, that's what we have to do now.'

Having delivered this oration, Clive stood up and strode off to the toilet.

Dermott and Paddy were silenced by the impressive logic of Clive's argument. Ping was showing Oh her new handbag that Clive had bought in the Royal Garden mall for her birthday. The designer logo on it was genuine, not a copy.

Dermott ordered another round of drinks. When the waitress returned with their order, she slipped another bill into each of the wooden pots on the table in front of the men.

Clive came back from the gents and took a slug from his Guinness.

And so the night wore on. Rugby was played; an election was held; handbags were compared; drink was drunk. Results were recorded, curses were exchanged, but nothing of much significance was settled.

*

While Paddy Fields was in hospital, Oh's sister Lek had visited from Khorat, taking advantage of Paddy's absence by sleeping on the camp bed in the O'Callaghan's living room. Dermott and Oh drove to meet Lek at the bus station in Pattaya Nua. When she got off the coach, she was carrying a cardboard box in the sides of which a number of holes had been cut. When they got home, Lek presented her sister with the box; it contained a small black-and-white kitten, somewhat dazed by the daylight. Oh was delighted with her new pet.

*

Paddy Fields had come to Thailand for two weeks to play golf. His hospitalisation, so soon after his arrival, had unfortunately prevented him from attending the fairways of Pattaya Country Club for the first few days but, now that he was better, he had great hopes for an early start to his sporting vacation. However, when he got up from his camp bed the next morning, he found that it was raining, which extended his misery for another day.

Rather than wait with the men for the rain to stop, Oh told Dermott and Paddy that she was going to drive to the veterinary surgery on Road Three.

'That's alright, Oh O'Callaghan,' Dermott confirmed. It amused him to address his wife using her full name. In the early days of their marriage, he'd often call out, 'Hey, Oh O'Callaghan, licensed to kill,' though after eight years the joke had worn a little thin.

While the rain pelted down outside, Dermott and Paddy passed the time drinking beer in the kitchen. When it stopped, and they'd emptied half a case, they ambled outside into the cool, fresh air and looked studiously at the sky to assess the possibility of fitting in a round of golf before it got dark. Before they could come to a decision, Dermott noticed something on the roof.

'Jesus,' said Dermott, still looking up, 'that cat of Oh's is up on the bloody roof. Come on quickly and help me get it down before Oh gets back.'

The cat had evidently climbed the jackfruit tree that grew close to the O'Callaghans' house. It had probably ventured out on to a branch, jumped down on to the gently sloping tiled roof, and found that it was unable to retrace its steps to freedom. Now the animal was crouched about half-way up, its front paws outstretched, and it was miaoing peevishly.

'Come on down,' said Paddy to the cat.

'Here, kitty, kitty,' tried Dermott, making a wet sucking noise with his lips.

'Get the fuck down here, you little bastard,' yelled Paddy.

Such entreaties seemed to have little impact on the cat, which continued to look frightened, and went on crying.

'Couldn't we just leave it?' asked Paddy, taking a swig of Leo from his fourth large bottle.

'God, no,' replied Dermott. 'Oh will go mental.'

'I'll chuck a stick at it. That'll get it down.'

'No you will not chuck a stick at it. I'm not going to have to explain to Oh how her new cat got its head dented with a log. We'll have to get the ladder.'

The two men put down their beers and collected a long bamboo ladder and a wooden plank from the car-port. They leaned the ladder against the edge of the roof, where the guttering would be if Thai houses had guttering.

'There, up you go,' said Dermott.

'Why me? You fucking go up,' countered Paddy. 'It's your bloody cat.'

'I can't,' pleaded Dermott. 'I'm afraid of heights.'

'So am I afraid of heights.'

'Yes, but I really am afraid of heights. I've got arachnophobia,' said Dermott pathetically.

'That's spiders, you bloody moron. Heights is vertigo. Either way, they're both just doctors' names for a fucking poof.'

'Oh, go on. Would you? Please?'

Paddy Fields looked at his friend. He looked up at the ladder and sighed. 'I suppose Paddy Fields will have to save the day,' he said, 'but you're still a bloody homo.'

Paddy grabbed the bamboo ladder and climbed up until he was level with the edge of the roof. Dermott passed him the plank, which Paddy laid across the tiles as a crawling board. At the sight of this, the cat became even more agitated and retreated further up the roof.

'Jesus,' said Paddy to the cat. 'Would you bloody well stop your bawling and come the fuck down? Shite and abortion, come here, you little fucker.'

The cat went on miaoing. Paddy heaved his weight on to the plank and began to advance upwards on all-fours. When he reached the end of the plank, he tried to grab the cat, but it was still beyond range. That fourth bottle of Leo was beginning to make him feel dizzy. Nevertheless, Paddy decided he'd have to stand up to make any further progress up the roof. Gingerly, he placed one foot on a tile and slowly got to his feet. He swayed a little.

As he put more weight on his foot, there was an ugly cracking sound from the roof beneath. He straightened and turned to see if his friend had noticed. At the same time, Paddy planted his other foot drunkenly on the roof, causing another, louder crack.

On the ground below, Dermott watched Paddy with increasing alarm. 'What was that noise?' he yelled sharply.

'A bit of settlement, is all,' replied Paddy. 'Everything's going according to plan.'

'I wasn't aware we had a plan. Fucking be careful anyway.'

Paddy was a big man with wild red hair and an unruly beard of more or less the same colour. From where Dermott was standing, Paddy towered like some wild giant over the whole of the Eakmongkol housing estate. At school, Paddy's notable hair colouring had earned him the nickname

Strawberry Fields, an epithet used to this day by those who had known him the longest. This huge hairy man was now standing on Dermott's roof, waving his arms wildly above his head for balance, his cavernous mouth emitting a string of blasphemies against Dermott and his wife's cat. He looked the image of Finn MacCool.

That was the moment that the tiled roof of Dermott O'Callaghan's house became unequal to the task of supporting the weight of Paddy Fields. With an almighty moan and the doleful sound of crashing masonry, Paddy disappeared from view.

Paddy landed in the O'Callaghans' living room, his left arm striking the top of Dermott's flat screen television and his right arm contacting the edge of one of Dermott's black-ash-effect chipboard loudspeaker cabinets which, with its twin on the other side of the room, was an integral part of his home entertainment system. The TV broke off its plastic stand and crashed to the floor. Dermott's home cinema and his large collection of DVDs was now buried under a pile of broken roof tiles, joists and mangled plasterboard, among which Paddy Fields also lay, dazed and concussed. A pall of dust hung in the air.

Dermott O'Callaghan rushed from the garden into the house and looked up at the hole in his living-room ceiling.

'Bloody termites,' he exclaimed.

'I'm down here, you fucking eejit,' moaned Paddy indignantly from his position on the floor.

'Are you all right?'

'No, I'm not fucking all right. I just fell through your bloody roof for fuck's sake. Jesus, my arm. I think I've broken my fucking arm. And the other one. I've broken both of my fucking arms. And my arse. I landed on my arse. I've broken my arse, you cunt.'

'Right. Oh keeps a first aid kit somewhere,' said Dermott, beginning to panic as he tried to think where he'd seen the white plastic box with the red cross on it.

'I don't want a fucking first aid kit. I need an arse transplant.'

'OK, I know you're joking, but…'

'Get me to the hospital, you bloody eejit. Jesus Christ! And be quick about it.'

'Well, Oh has the car, so I can't drive you. I'll have to call an ambulance. What did you have to go and fall through my roof for? You're a fucking eejit so you are.'

'You're the fucking eejit for making me go up on your roof for a pissing cat. Call the fucking ambulance. Hurry up, you cunt.'

Dermott phoned the Pattaya Memorial Hospital and an ambulance arrived within 20 minutes. The paramedics examined Paddy and confirmed the diagnosis he himself had made of his left arm. It was broken. The rest of him would have to wait until it could be x-rayed.

'Are you coming with me?' asked Paddy pathetically.

'Christ, no. When Oh gets back she'll go bloody ballistic. I'll need to calm her down. We'll follow on to the hospital later to see how you're coming along.'

With further expletives, Paddy Fields was loaded head-first into the Toyota ambulance by the two paramedics, Dermott's help being required to lift his friend's considerable bulk. Finally, Paddy Fields was driven away.

Dermott went back inside and tried feebly to recover some of his electronic equipment from under the pile of rubble. He carried a few pieces of tile into the front garden, where he met Eric from next door.

*

Eric Ericsson was originally from Uppsala, in Sweden. He had come to Thailand about four years previously in an attempt to begin a new life after the break-up of his marriage. Eric's first wife had come from a very good family in Stockholm, Eric explained to Dermott at their second or third meeting over a couple of beers in the Ericssons' front room, but she didn't share Eric's dream of having a large family, so the union had sadly ended in divorce.

Eric was now married to the much younger Sap, who he claimed was an ex-fashion model and came from a very good family in Bangkok, even though Dermott was pretty sure he remembered her working in a blow-job bar in Soi 6 a year or so before Eric met and married her. No matter how sure he was that it had been Sap in the bar, Dermott didn't feel he should challenge Eric on the point, not least because it might elicit an enquiry from Eric about what Dermott was doing in a blow-job bar in Soi 6 in the first place, which would have upset Oh, should she have got to hear about it. Eric was a Lutheran, and concerned that his wives should come from very good families, preferably in capital cities.

Eric said that he came over because he heard an almighty crash coming from Dermott's side of the fence. He further said that he could now see the cause of the commotion and pointed unhelpfully towards the roof.

'Was anyone hurt?' asked Eric, showing neighbourly, but innocent, concern.

'Only a friend I had staying from Ireland. It looks like a broken arm. He's gone to hospital. He was only discharged from the same bloody place yesterday.'

'How did it happen?'

'Termites,' explained Dermott, not wishing to engage in a full post-mortem.

'I think my roof is maybe the same age as yours, and the same wooden construction. I'm going to have to check mine out.' Eric was good at English, but you always knew he'd learnt it late in life, after he'd finished with nappies.

'You should do that. Look out for fucking termites anyway.'

'Our cat was stuck up on your roof earlier today,' observed Eric, 'so that's one good thing: at least the noise seems to have scared him down. He's OK now; he's in our kitchen with a bowl of cat food, in case you were worried.'

'Your cat was on my roof?' Dermott prevented himself from adding, 'and why would I give a toss about the health or safety of your cat, the one that shits in our garden?'

'Yes, I could see him. I can see the top of your roof from our side of the fence.'

'Then where the fuck is Oh's cat? Oh will incinerate me when she gets back. Jesus, if her cat went through the roof with Paddy, it'll be under that pile of rubble somewhere. Shite and abortion.'

Dermott quickly terminated his conversation with Eric and rushed back into the house.

'Hey, kitty, kitty,' he called with increasing desperation at the heap of tiles. He scrabbled at the larger pieces of plaster that were piled on the remains of his home cinema system. He peered nervously into spaces within the heap as he'd seen earthquake rescue teams do in footage from countries more prone than Ireland to movement in the Earth's crust.

*

Dermott was on all-fours at the epicentre of his own cataclysm when Oh returned from the vet's. She got out of the car, lifted the cardboard box from the back seat and walked with it into the house. The ladder was still leaning against the roof. She had an uneasy feeling that something was wrong.

Dermott heard his wife approach and met her at the front door, trying to block the strong smell of plaster dust in the living room from reaching her before he'd had a chance to explain.

Then, before he'd had a chance to explain, Dermott noticed that Oh was carrying Lek's cardboard box, the one with the holes cut in it. Oh opened the lid and lifted the kitten out.

'You took the fucking cat to the vet's?' Dermott cried, incensed by this sudden realisation.

'Of course. How is she going to have her injections if I don't take her?'

'Fucking Jesus. Paddy'll fucking brain me when he hears this. I thought you'd just gone to get worm pills or something.'

'Worm pills? I can get worm pills from the pet shop. No, I went to get the injections. It's quite cheap.'

'Mary, Jesus and shite, was that strictly necessary? I mean, couldn't you have left the cat here with us?' Dermott said feebly, imagining that there were alternative versions of the afternoon's events which could be activated by simply imagining things differently. 'At least the fucking eejit would have half-killed himself for some purpose.'

'Don't be silly. It was better to get the injections.'

'That Strawberry Fields,' said Dermott. 'I'll pull his fucking tubes out. When's visiting time?'

Planter's Punch

He was working in his study when they arrived.

'Please Kuhn Fraser, your visitors are here,' Fon called through the half-open door.

'What?'

'The journalists. There are three of them in a green car.'

'Oh Lord, bloody nuisance.'

Fraser was working on the plantation accounts, adjusting the profit to a figure more suitable for the tax office. He completed an early calculation before pushing back on his leather chair and rising wearily from his cluttered old desk.

The entrance hall and sitting room, though large, were all one in Fraser's bungalow. Two visitors were standing among the worn rattan furniture, viewing the brass and wooden ornaments on his library shelves—elegant Buddhas, Ganeshes, monkeys and elephants predominantly—and the faded sepia photos and small dusty oils that filled most of the gaps on the walls. The dog, thrilled by the new presence in the house, pawed at the visitors, snuffling and grinning excitedly.

He was struck immediately by the way they were dressed—khaki bush shirts with pockets pleated and flapped; the same colour for their shorts, with as many heavy duty patch pockets—exactly as he was. It struck him momentarily that he was being mocked, that they had come to show him something about himself, something which, despite their straight faces, they found comical or ridiculous. But he remembered the lengthy email correspondence with Beth, he thought her name was. She had been polite and deferential to a fault. He had never doubted her motives in requesting the interview or suggesting the 'feature' as she insisted on calling it, and managed to shake off the doubts he'd briefly felt.

'Come away, Zara. Leave our guests alone. That's it,' said Fraser in an attempt to calm his dog. 'She seldom meets new people. I hope you don't mind.'

'No, I love dogs,' said the woman. 'I'm Beth by the way and you must be Fraser. Finally.'

'How was your journey?'

'Long,' she replied, looking at her companion. 'This is Simon, the photographer.'

Fraser shook their hands and, glancing at Fon, said: 'Did I hear there were three of you?'

'Three? Oh, you must mean our driver. I forget his name. He's outside.'

'Somchai, I think,' said Simon as he tried to avoid the attentions of the large Dalmatian, her muzzle level with his thigh.

'That's it. Somchai drove us up from Chiang Mai—very pretty country; fantastic jungle all the way.'

'You haven't been to Mae Hong Son before? I said come away, Zara. Sorry.'

'No, never, not to Thailand even.'

'I've been to Bangkok,' said Simon, but not "up-country". I had no idea how beautiful it was in the north.'

'Do you want to invite him in?'

'No, I'm sure he'll be alright in the car for a while. I think he wanted to smoke.'

'Why don't we sit down? You must tell me what it is you need. Oh, this is Fon, my housekeeper. Fon, a cup of tea for our guests?'

'Your own, I hope,' Beth said smiling.

'What? Oh yes, our own of course.'

Beth extracted a notebook and pen from her canvas bag and, sitting forward on the cushion of a rattan chair, curled a straight blonde lock behind her hair. She was younger than Fraser had imagined, barely out of childhood by his estimation, twenty-one or twenty-two. She had soft, pale features with sky blue eyes, full lips and that floppy blonde hair which seemed to need constant attention. Her figure was concealed in the regulation up-country clothing, but she was tall and seemed slim enough. She was direct, too, and he liked that: she held his gaze more surely than most of the kids he remembered in England and her hand-shake was confident. The correspondence they'd conducted had been brief and to the point and her spelling and grammar were better than most. Her pen was now poised over a clean page of her notebook.

'Shall I kick off?' she began.

Beth thanked their host again for agreeing to be interviewed for the colour magazine that her newspaper put out on Saturdays. She asked: 'I wonder if you'd mind awfully if I recorded the interview?'

'What's wrong with shorthand?'

'I know it sounds awfully lazy but it's better, believe me. It means I'll get exactly what you say, and I'll be able to concentrate on you better, rather than all that fiddling around. Also, I have to confess that they don't teach us shorthand anymore, not for ages I believe. It's all a bit high-tech these days I'm afraid.'

'How long will it take?'

'We have a flight booked from Chiang Mai at 9.30 tomorrow evening so I hope we'll have most of tomorrow.'

'A whole day? I don't know about a whole day. I have work to do; it's our year-end so I have the accounts to finish.'

'I quite understand, Fraser. Of course we can fit around you. We'll try to make the most efficient use of your time. Simon can take the photos as we're talking, then there's your beautiful house and the grounds to shoot. If you tell him where to go I'm sure our driver could take him around the plantation for the big outdoor shots, don't you think, Simon?'

'Sure.'

'Tell you what,' Fraser commanded, 'if we get cracking now; we can surely break the back of it over dinner, then you can take your snaps tomorrow.'

'I'd like some time for a portrait—perhaps half an hour, forty-five minutes.'

'I've never photographed well, I have to warn you of that, but we'll see. Look, the sun's going to set in half an hour and you must be tired. You came from London today?'

'I think we set out yesterday.'

'Yes. Why don't you spend a moment freshening up and getting yourselves orientated and we'll start the interview over dinner? How does that sound? I'm thinking about it as more of a conversation than an interview — that sounds much too formal. Would that suit you?'

'Well, yes.'

'Fon, would you show our guests to their rooms and the ablutions? Now where's your driver chap going to sleep? Fon, would you see if Billy's wife might put him up for the night? Billy's my foreman, lives half a mile away. If you could advance his wife a few hundred baht she'd be tickled pink and your driver would get dinner and a proper Thai breakfast; they can't be doing with toast and marmalade, and they won't drink tea. Give the money to Fon; she'll pass it on. There'll be a sundowner waiting for you out there on the veranda at six.'

*

When Beth emerged from her room, Fraser was already settled on the faded cushions of a reclining metal deck-chair which was showing signs of rust.

'Ah, come and sit down. Enjoy the show.' He waved his tumbler at the horizon where a thin strip of yellow light split the sky between two masses of swirling leaden sky. 'We had rain again last night; could be more tonight.'

The house was set on a slight rise. A drive curved up from the main track below, lined with palms. Opposite, the land rose again, the gentle swell covered in low tea bushes.

She was handing him two plastic bags from the duty-free at Heathrow when Simon appeared.

'Good, good, please make yourselves comfortable. Oh, I say, gin, whisky. For me? How kind. What would you like yourselves? Give Fon your order. You will not find her ungenerous with the measures. Sorry we have no tonic; our local woman doesn't run to that. Plenty of soda usually. Whisky's my tipple. Join me, why don't you?'

'I must say this is a beautiful house. How long have you lived here?'

'Is this being recorded?'

'Of course.' Beth took a small device from her bag, fiddled with the controls for a moment and set it on the low rattan table between them.

'Did you build it yourself?'

'Yes, yes, I built it myself, partly with my own hands but mostly using a local chap. It's all teak you know; a skilled job. It was in 1979 that I first came here. Bought the estate off the peg; I'd never set foot in Thailand before that, but you have to take risks in business. I knew the agent though; in fact I was at school with his brother, so I had a comeback of sorts if it'd been a lemon.'

'What made you buy a tea plantation up here?' asked Simon.

The host regarded him blankly, not appreciating the question. While Beth had her sex and charm to soften Fraser's natural hostility to visitors, Simon had neither. He was older than his colleague, late thirties at least, with a weather-beaten face and long brown hair swept back in a ponytail. He wore jewellery; nothing precious but what Fraser would call ethnic — a mass of leather thongs and beads on his wrists and various Hindu charms around his neck. His tight black T-shirt bore a slogan which Fraser observed with distaste.

'Tea because that business was fed me with my mother's milk; up here simply because it was for sale. I asked the agent to look for anything in Asia; I would have gone anywhere too — Formosa, India, back to Ceylon, though Ceylon was difficult in the 70s; Sri Lanka it was called by then.'

'You were brought up there, in Ceylon as it was,' Beth prompted, recalling the emails. 'Were you born there?'

'No, actually I was born in Zanzibar.'

Simon: 'Like Freddie Mercury.' Silence from the others.

'My parents were returning to England for my birth, but a combination of leaving it too late and my foetal eagerness to be born meant that I was delivered in Zanzibar. They'd stopped for a week to visit friends. After leave and recuperation in England, they took me back to Ceylon when I was about six months old. My father had to get back to his plantation — one of the biggest tea estates in Dimbula in fact.'

'By the way, would you mind if I checked spellings of place names before we go to print? We can do it on email.'

'Of course. Dimbula's spelt the way it sounds. It's in Central Province; one of the first places to grow tea after the coffee industry packed up. We're talking nineteenth century now, 1870s or thereabouts. I grew up in the 30s and 40s on the estate, playing with the servants and the estate managers' children. It was a perfect childhood; I was free to play where I wished and go where I wanted. I should have some old photos somewhere; I'll show you tomorrow if you're interested. There was a nanny who fussed about, and later a tutor who came in to teach me the basics, but being at large on the estate taught me most — about getting on with people in particular.'

'Were there brothers and sisters?'

'No, no, they stopped at me.'

'And school, was that in Ceylon?'

'Good Lord no. Like everyone else I was sent off to boarding school in England. It was just after the war and I was nine. You wouldn't send a nine-year-old half way across the world these days, would you? Not on their own. They'd have packed me off earlier if it hadn't been for the war.

'You need a top-up. Fon, give these people another drink, would you? Is dinner nearly ready?'

'Dinner's ready anytime.'

'Good girl. I'd be lost without dear Fon as you'll have gathered.'

*

Fraser took the head of the table and arranged his guests on either side as Fon served rice and brought four or five different dishes to the table — curries, a large fried fish, salad and a plate of small spare ribs, glazed with sauce.

'This looks delicious, Fraser.'

'I hope you like Thai food. Tuck in. And let's have some more drinks. Fon?'

After charging her plate Beth asked, 'I know you won't mind if I switch this thing on again.'

'No, please.'

'So you finished school in England.'

'I finished school in England and returned to Ceylon. I was to learn the ropes on the plantation and gradually take over. It happened more quickly than planned. My father was in poor health, but it was my mother who succumbed first. She was brave; she didn't want to make a fuss, but that stoical planter spirit was her undoing. It was months before she would agree to go to a specialist in Colombo and by then it was too late. Breast cancer. She was 48.'

'That's no age,' said Simon.

'No, as you say, it's no age,' Fraser replied, giving Simon a rare smile. 'And it was the beginning of the end for my father. He was already a private man. I don't remember him ever having friends. My parents would rarely entertain, apart from small dinner parties for duty — local officials, agents, the rector, visitors from home foisted on them by people far away who didn't understand the set-up. After mother died he became a recluse. He stayed in the house and finally took to his bed with a pernicious wasting disease. I was left growing the tea.'

'You were still young,' observed Beth.

'Not so young when father finally died — I was 32 by then. The business was booming. Ceylon had become the world's biggest exporter of tea and we couldn't produce enough of the stuff. But although I was making a good living, the sense in being there had gone.'

'The sense in being there?'

'Yes, the point of it. There was I stuck halfway up a hill surrounded by tea bushes and all alone. I craved company; connection, you'd probably call it, Simon. My school friends had all become schoolmasters, MPs, bankers and lawyers. They had wives and fast cars — and somewhere to drive them. It was 1968. London was the centre of the world.'

'The Swinging Sixties,' said Simon.

'As you so rightly say, Simon, the Swinging Sixties, but they were swinging somewhere else. The closest I got to swinging was a ten-day-old copy of the *Daily Express*.

'Can I help you to some fish?' asked Beth. 'We don't want to let Simon eat the whole thing.'

'No, indeed we don't. I'll have a little, thanks. And more drinks. Fon, could you do the honours?' Fraser toyed with the piece of fish for a moment, looking thoughtful. 'And then there was a girl, a woman, Irene. She was the daughter of the district commissioner. I was invited to some ghastly dinner to celebrate his retirement. In the course of that dinner, from Windsor soup to trifle, amazingly, we fell in love. Can you believe it? We were starved of love you see, she and I. A fortnight later she was gone, whisked back to England with her parents. I wrote every week; received one reply. It was friendly but non-committal, not what I wanted at all.

'Then there was the political situation. They were letting the Russians and Chinese in. The place was turning commie; nationalisation of the plantations was in the air. Life on a tea estate on a Ceylonese hill had lost its appeal. I sold up to a local to avoid the government taking it and went back to England. It was January 1968. I had no suitable clothes. I rented a damp basement flat in Battersea. An uncle took me into his estate agency. I showed people around houses. I discovered what it was like to live at the centre of the world.'

'Was it swinging?'

'If it was, it was swinging on a different frequency from me. I found it hard to adjust. I had no friends except the ones I went to school with, but that was 14 years before. If I met one it was a school reunion, not a meeting of minds. And there was no space. The flat was small and the streets were confining, claustrophobic; there was no horizon, no serpent eagle soaring out of the jungle.'

'No, I suppose not. And Irene?' asked Beth.

'By the time I got to England Irene was married; some worthy chap. She was elegant, beautiful; I should have known she'd be snapped up as soon as she set foot in London. Maybe I did; maybe that's what made me chase after her like that. Not quick enough, though; beaten to the tape. She died two or three years ago, actually. I read her obit in the paper. Dame Irene, she became; got in with the Lib Dems; big on committees.

'I was love sick for a while, then just sick; I wasn't resistant to the germs you have over there. I went down with one bout of flu after another. I stuck it out for eleven years before I realised it was England I was sick of.'

'What was it about England?'

'England had lost its moral elastin; it had begun to droop. The men on our estate in Dimbula, you know, many of them volunteered in the war. They set off from their villages in their sarongs and sandals to fight and die for that country in Burma, in North Africa, all over the place. They'd be horrified if they could see what they'd saved, what it had become. The seventies was a time of 'anything goes'. It was not like it was, not the way I'd remembered it.'

'What time was your ideal? When were you comparing it with?' asked Beth.

'It's a process, Beth, a history of continuous decline. It's a hell of a lot worse now; don't think it's stopped, not by a long chalk. Look at the clowns that run the place now. Politicians and big business, that's who's in charge now, big business — old boys, back-scratchers and thieves. The fifties; I was at school in England in the fifties. Then, a man was expected to resign when he'd been caught in bed with the wrong tart; or choirboy. I'm talking about politicians here. Now, he just has to lie low for a few months, become a do-gooder, and he can come back as a minister.

'Business is even worse. In the old days at least we knew they were crooks, but now they pretend to act responsibly — you've heard them, I'm sure, claiming the moral high ground. Just as their snouts are sunk deep in the trough their lies gurgle up through the slop. There's a level they reach, these company men, beyond which they're free to cock a snook at the rest of us. It's like passing through the clouds. Up there the laws cease to apply, the laws of morality, economics or of the land. They become gods.' He called through to the kitchen and when Fon appeared, said, 'More drinks, please, my dear, and this time leave the bottle.'

Beth paused before attempting to resume the conversation: 'So this takes us up to the purchase of this plantation in Thailand.'

'Yes.'

'Your return to the colonial life,' Simon observed.

'No, not at all. That's not it at all, young man. Thailand is not a colony and, unlike all of its neighbours, was never colonised by Europeans. If Thais are proud of anything, they're proud of that.'

'Not in name, perhaps, but the lifestyle has got to be the same or similar...'

'Simon, please,' said Beth.

'Colonialism isn't a lifestyle, Simon,' Fraser insisted, 'it's a relationship between two sets of people. I have no vote here and no influence. I am a guest in a sovereign nation; they call me an alien. How is that like British rule in Ceylon?'

'My guess is, in practical terms, not that different.'

'Go back to school, young man. Learn the basics of your country's history.'

'Alright I will, but for starters where do you stand on the Empire, Fraser? Was it a good thing?'

Beth quickly intervened: 'Simon, please, I'm trying to conduct an interview here. You'll have your moment tomorrow when you take your snaps. Fraser, I'm sorry about this, I don't want to get side-tracked.'

'No, I think Mr Simon here should learn some manners. The British Empire wasn't designed to be *a good thing*, young fellow, it was designed to make money — it was a business — and in that it occasionally succeeded and occasionally failed. My tea estate in Dimbula, though a very small part of the Empire if a part of it at all, I think we can judge a success. It was right for the time. Incidentally, I believe it belongs now to a Sri Lankan educated at Cambridge. So I'll thank you to remember that you are a guest in my house and check your facts before expressing yourself.'

'Sorry, Fraser, but I find that a bit trite.'

'Simon,' chided Beth, 'we've come a long way for this. Let's get back to the job in hand.'

'OK, you're the boss, but surely the job in hand is to present our readers with a profile of Fraser here, a true representation of the man, an accurate account of his life, warts and all? Tomorrow I'll do my best. I'll get shots of the estate, hopefully of the people that pick and process the tea; I'll get a portrait of the man and shots of his bungalow. Readers will judge him from his face, his wrinkles, the look in his eye, his clothes, his background. They won't deceive.'

'OK, that's fine. That's how it should be. But that doesn't make it acceptable to insult the man in his own house.' Beth turned to their host: 'Fraser, I'm sorry. Simon didn't mean to challenge you. This isn't what I wanted. To my editor — to me — your life is remarkable. It's... well, there aren't many of your kind left anymore. He — my editor — thinks your story will play well, and I agree: you're a lovely man with an interesting life and a fascinating story to tell. My job is to record that, to represent it accurately. It will make a great feature. Please don't take any notice of Simon, he's...'

'He's accused me of being trite, that's what I recall.'

Simon drained his glass, helped himself to a refill and said: 'You don't mind? Thanks. Look, I'm just the photographer, but my pictures will take up more pages than Beth's editorial, so I think that gives me a right to contribute to this *recording* of your life. Yes? Look, I live in England — in London, actually, Bethnal Green — and I've seen a bit of the world. I've travelled in Africa, South America and Asia on assignments and you, Fraser, you're telling me about *moral collagen* or whatever. So, you decided you were sick of England — that was the word he used — because of its corruption and greed and you escaped to... where? You came here, to Thailand where corruption is a way of life. This is where you found peace of mind, lodgings that are not damp, neighbours who have somehow retained their *moral elastin* — sorry, it wasn't collagen — and, I'll be willing to bet, a decent income based on cheap labour.'

Fraser took a slug of his drink to settle himself and compose a reply. Beth put her hand gently on his arm in an attempt to head off a response but it was in vain.

'I grow tea here because it won't grow in England. You people in the West are prepared to pay a certain price for their cuppa and I'm part of the industry that meets that demand. I know how to run a tea estate, that's what I contribute, plus the capital to own and develop it.'

'I don't see that as sufficient justification to exploit local people as slaves. Sorry, Fraser, but I've seen the conditions described on the internet.'

Fraser, red in the face now, raised his voice and spat angrily: 'I don't exploit anybody in any way, let alone as slaves. What repository of internet lies did you get that from, you ignoramus? I need people to run this place, of course I do — women to pick the leaves — others to operate the machinery. I pay them the going rate. If I paid less, I'd get useless staff or no staff at all. If I paid more, I'd create such problems with the other planters — and other employers — that the whole local economy would come crashing down.'

'I'm sorry but I still see it as imperialism, Fraser. That's why the magazine is doing this piece, don't you realise? You're a throw-back, a museum piece. They're setting you up to be gawped at, disapproved of by most readers, ridiculed by others.'

Fraser's anger had reached a critical state. He spluttered a few words but could hardly form a coherent response. He felt indignant, unfairly condemned and cheated by people he had brought into his house as honoured guests. Simon's face was close, looking serious, challenging for a response. Fraser did all he could to control his frustration, but it was too much; his oppressor had to be silenced. He set his jaw and, staring the younger man fully in the eye, curled his liver-spotted old hand into a fist, reached back and punched him squarely on the nose.

*

He was working in his study the next morning when Fon called through the half-open door, 'Please Khun Fraser, breakfast is ready.'

He put down his pen and went to the veranda where the housekeeper had laid out toast in a rack, marmalade and tea.

'Sit with me, Fon. I want to apologise for last night.'

'Oh dear, such a row.'

'Did you see our guests leave?'

'Yes, they asked me to phone Billy at seven to recall their driver. They wouldn't eat breakfast, not even a cup of tea. They said they were going to take photos of the estate.'

'They're not coming back?'

'No, they said they wanted to look around Chiang Mai before their flight. The lady asked me to apologise to you. She said she'd email when she got home.'

'I'm sorry about what happened. It must have been embarrassing for you to listen to.'

'Not embarrassing, but I'll have to soak the table-cloth to get the blood out.'

'Do your best, Fon.'

'He had two black eyes.'

'Oh dear, like Zara.'

'I thought he was a very rude man.'

'So did I, Fon; he was ill-mannered. He called me a colonial, can you believe that?'

'I don't know what a colonial is, Khun Fraser.'

'No, of course you don't, and now they're gone, there's no point in explaining it.'

Confectionery

*From the private diary and correspondence of Arlo Aresti,
chief financial officer.*

14 July, Phnom Penh

Get in from Seoul at 10.40pm, take a taxi to the Raffles Hotel
and it's now way past midnight. The business in Korea is
doing well. Market share is up 1.5%, despite the price hikes in
January. They're affected by cocoa prices like everybody, but
profits for the year are still 9.6% higher. David will be
pleased; I know he was worried about Korea and Japan, but
they've both delivered above expectations in trying
circumstances.

I spend time on the plane preparing for tomorrow's
witch-hunt. At least first class provides room to work.
There's going to be blood on the walls, the only question
being: how much?

Not hungry, very tired. Shower and bed.

15 July, Phnom Penh

An excellent breakfast—one of the reasons I always stay
here—it sets me up for the day. I think it must be the coffee
they use. A driver comes at 8.30am and I get to the office by

nine, straight into a meeting with Samnang, known as James, our operating company MD. Why James? James Bond, possibly, though there's no obvious resemblance. I've never seen him order a martini, so I'm left guessing.

The point of spending three days here, rather than my usual one or two, is to get the unpleasantness out of the way before reviewing the year-end accounts. I've got only one day for the review, but I'll also be seeing the books today, and together that should be enough.

We've known about it in outline since early June—that persons known and possibly unknown have been colluding with tax officials to forge invoices, falsify the accounts and cream off a large sum of money from the company that was supposed to go to the government in tax. We're sure our financial controller was leading the scam from our end; he has already gone. What I need to do today is discover which of his people were also involved so that they can be removed. I also need to satisfy myself that James isn't implicated. It was he who alerted David to the scam, and that's a point in his favour, as long as he wasn't acting from necessity—for example, because he thought the plot was going to be uncovered by someone else anyway. Really, I'm David's rottweiler on this mission. He's livid and wants to see heads roll.

I outline my objectives to James, leaving out my scrutiny of his role, and he seems ready to co-operate. I spend the morning going through the paperwork with him and confirming the total loss. It looks like $1.1 million over two years, so not disastrous from our point of view, but we'll still clearly have to pay this sum in back tax, plus a fine probably. It's a huge amount to the guys who stole it, on the salaries they earn, so I can understand the motivation.

Lunch in the office.

*

In the afternoon they set up one-on-one interviews for me with all the finance people. Being the hatchet man from London head office is not my favourite role, but we don't have anyone locally who could do this. James himself is out of the question until he's cleared personally.

They come in at 15-minute intervals. I reduce about half of them to tears, men and women alike. There is a box of tissues on the table between us, of which extensive use is made. A couple of the men confess and name names, both on our side and in the tax office. I'll have to check the spellings later with James. There is broad agreement between the confessors and confirmation that the financial controller is the most culpable, but then he's easy to blame since he has gone.

I ask them specifically, and confidentially, if James was involved and I'm satisfied that he was not aware of what was going on. I reason that the guys on their way out are unlikely to stay loyal enough to lie for him to the bitter end so, on balance, I'm inclined to believe them. His not knowing about the plot is in itself a serious shortcoming in an MD, of course, and I'll have to consult with David as to whether it's bad enough for him to go. I expect to have to plead James's case.

Apart from the dosh we've lost, the much more serious issue is that the commerce minister has threatened to withdraw our trading licence, for an unspecified period, for not controlling the business properly. It's controlled a bloody sight better than any local outfit, but that's not an argument we can use. If we got barred for as long as a year, we'd be seriously stuffed, with idle production and office staff with nothing to do. The competition would be laughing like drains and scrapping for market share. I have a meeting with the minister tomorrow to try to avert disaster and be told our fate.

Around 6.30pm I take James to dinner at the Foreign Correspondents' Club or, as it's known locally, the FCC, or even the F. I love the faded colonial atmosphere; I don't ask whether James feels the same. The place has only been going for 20 years or so, so it isn't truly colonial, more like my college junior common room. I think you'd call the menu 'fusion' — Khmer and Mediterranean, perhaps; certainly some Italian influence is noticeable.

It's time for a frank talk with James. We agree the list of people who have to go — only three of them in the end. It's James's job to wield the axe, and he'll do that tomorrow. No notice; instant dismissal. I tell him how seriously we view the whole affair and the dim view we take of his failure to manage risk in the business effectively, though I call it 'our business' to remind him who's in charge. I say that, personally, I would like him to stay on because not only has he produced good numbers in the six years he's been with us, but also I consider he has the local and company knowledge to put in place the structures we need to avoid any more unpleasantness in the future.

Although that would be my recommendation to David, there are two further obstacles facing James. First, David may not agree with me. He's a stickler for doing the right thing and he may take the view that James has ballsed-up once and could easily balls-up again. Second, the minister may ask for James's scalp as a condition of our keeping our licence. I tell him if it comes to that, we'll choose the licence over him. I feel ruthless, but this is business. James gulps heavily on a piece of chicken before nodding his acceptance. I know he has four kids in education.

I decide that this is a good time to leave James to think things over, so wind up the dinner, getting James's driver to drop me off at the Raffles. I get back by 10.00pm, leave my jacket and tie in my room and go down to the Elephant Bar for a couple of drinks.

*

I count two or possibly three hookers in the bar and find myself sweating a little, despite the air conditioning, wondering if any will qualify. The third is carrying a bag that could be an attaché case, which means she is probably a guest; I don't want to put my foot in it there (shades of Manila last year!). I make eye contact with the taller of the two obvious candidates and, after about ten minutes, she comes over. I take in the tight red mini-dress and fantastic legs, long and slender.

I buy her a couple of drinks, putting her under close observation as she speaks. She says her name is Josie and she's Vietnamese. She's very elegant, gentle and sophisticated. She claims to have an accountancy degree, which I find hard to believe to look at her, but I determine not to be chauvinistic. Her English is better than the usual, so she may be telling the truth. We talk mostly complete drivel, skirting around the main business with chatter about where I come from, my job and so on. I say I'm into candy, which she takes as some kind of erotic code, though I can't work out the double entendre, beyond the obvious.

Moving our chairs closer, she touches my arm and, occasionally, my leg. She has large hands with slender fingers, which I take as a good sign. Her throat is slim and smooth, with only the slightest movement when she swallows. Double-X or chondroplasty? I'm getting quite feverish with anticipation. When she stands up to go to the ladies, there's that delicious gangliness about the way she unfolds her limbs from the wicker chair which has me frantically guessing, but her rear view leaves me in no doubt: those slim hips!

I have to have her.

As soon as she returns, I ask her to wait for me in the lobby, sign the tab and take her up to my floor. She doesn't know that I know. In the lift, she leans over and says, 'I have a surprise for you.'

Bingo!

I tumesce.

*

Five seconds into the room, I pull down her strapless dress and scoop into her bra. Perfect breasts that feel utterly real. I take her over to the desk-light to look for scars. She's a fine piece of work.

Most of all, Josie is fun. She's always laughing and joking. A little black G-string doesn't take much to remove. The moment of truth and double bingo! She's had the works, the full enchilada, as if she'd been born a girl.

The rest of the evening is a blur of pleasure. I spend it fervently worshiping Josie's spectacular body which, incidentally, she tells me was 'made in Bangkok', and enjoying myself in all her possible places. She seems to love watching me having such a lascivious time with her body.

She wants to be paid extra for no condom, which I don't see as a problem. Then I take her in the backside. I must be mad; could it get more dangerous? I'm on a high. And I'm supposed to be the king—the emperor—of risk management.

Unbelievable!

She offers to stay overnight and I am seriously tempted, but I need to get some sleep before the minister tomorrow, and I suddenly have the sense to realise that I can't really face the red mini-dress at breakfast, so I chuck her out around 2.00am. She tries to make a date for tomorrow; I say we'll see. She says she has left her number on the desk if I change my mind. She's such a minx.

Email to nan1975@hotmail.com

I'm now in Phnom Penh, Cambodia, and spent the day sorting out the corruption thing with James, the local MD. I think we've got to the bottom of the scam and fired the culprits, though I can't be sure. Asians are so damned inscrutable. I just hope we haven't missed a monster cover-up. It hasn't cost as much as we'd feared and we'll be watching more closely to make sure it doesn't happen again. James may survive, though he should have spotted the plot earlier. I just hope David doesn't get the idea that I should have seen it coming too. And the local auditors. Probably not terminal for me, but my bonus could take a kicking. Fingers crossed. Had dinner with James, but got back to the hotel early as I'm knackered.

Tomorrow I have to face the minister of commerce to plead with him to let us go on making chocolate bars in his country.

That doesn't sound good about your mother. Are they going to keep her in or can she go home? I know she's strong and she's a fighter, so don't worry.

Love to the kids. Tell Jason I got his iPad jelly case in Seoul, actually at the airport – purple silicone, just like he wanted. I'll get things for Mabel and Sam, so tell them not to be jealous.

Love you lots. I'll get Derek to meet me at Heathrow, so see you at home on Saturday. Sleep tight.

Arlo xxx

Text to +66 mobile number, saved in phone memory as 'Jack Anderson'

Tik, don't forget I arrive BKK 17 July. Plane lands 21.10. I will meet you in hotel lobby 22.30. Marriott like before. Call me if you have problem. Arlo xxxxx

16 July, Phnom Penh

Wake early, shower and shave. It's the black Armani, white shirt and the blue Bulgari tie that I think Nan gave me for Christmas. I take time for an inspection in the mirror. The general impression is good — tall, still quite slim (thanks, gym), tanned, all my own hair, grey at the temples. I'm confident that I look the successful, even imposing, Western businessman, not tranny-whoring pervert. I snarl like a werewolf at my working-day image and then laugh. If only David could see me now, I think. Since the knighthood, he won't even set foot in a go-go bar in case he's recognised. He fears the headline in the *Sun*: 'Knight On The Tiles' or some such garbage, brought out on the morning of the AGM probably, with some potty shareholder planted to ask him what his entertainment allowance is meant to cover. That would be one for the chairman to field, methinks. I try a few smiles and perfect a culpable-but-contrite expression for the minister. It melts my heart. Tie straight. All set for breakfast.

James and his driver pick me up in the lobby at 9.30am and we drive to the ministry. Traffic in Phnom Penh is frantic, bordering on the mental. The intersections are the hairiest, with uncontrolled streams of pickups, tuk-tuks and scooters coming from all directions. Worse than Naples! God, I do miss my Vespa 200 Rally.

The minister's invitation — or summons — was to me, but I've brought James along because he's in charge of the local business and because he's Cambodian, which I think may help. The risks are that they'll yammer on in Khmer, which of course I don't understand, and that James's future may be one of the topics of discussion. If it's the latter, he'll just have to leave the room, but I'm more comfortable having him with me.

We're made to wait for about 15 minutes, mostly in silence as James and I did our business yesterday evening. I don't want to ask him about his family in case we're just about to put them out on the streets. James confirms that the guilty three have been dismissed this morning. I'm wondering if I should seek out Josie tonight or take pot luck with someone new. I still can't believe my good fortune and I'm swelling slightly, here in the ministry of commerce reception area, just thinking about last night. Josie would be the safe option, but maybe also the boring one? Extraordinary how quickly I can tire of such an exciting woman. A bird in the hand is worth less than two in the bush if it's the hunt that turns you on, rather than the barbecued bird. A bit long for a proverb.

I park the decision as we are ushered into a large meeting room. They have five men lined up on their side of the table. I feel outgunned. James suddenly looks very small by my side.

The man in the middle explains that the minister is otherwise engaged and that he is to deputise. He introduces himself and his underlings, but I don't catch their names. I wouldn't know where to start, spelling them. I signal to James that he should write them down for me. The deputy minister is friendlier than I expected. He asks me what happened and I recount the story from the moment James discovered the fraud, through the dismissal of our financial controller and my investigation, to this morning's sackings.

One of the men on the deputy minister's left is small and effeminate. He looks down at his hands while playing with his pen, and then looks up at me with big doe eyes.

Concentrate, man!

I ask the deputy minister what measures have been taken at the tax department and he says 'appropriate steps will be taken' or some such waffle, by which I take him to mean that the people caught with their fingers in the till on that side will get off scot-free as the cash was seeping up through the ranks, to what level who knows? Still, what can I do?

The deputy minister's English is excellent. He wants to know where I'm from. When I say London, he says, 'No, originally.' I say Naples and he smiles broadly: 'Ah, Napoli!' I think for a moment that he's going to break into *O Sole Mio*, a surreal image indeed. He is very fond of our Greek temples at Paestum and has detailed memories of Pompeii and the Salerno coast. Throughout his travelogue, I maintain one of the smiles I practised this morning in the mirror.

'Then there's the matter of the licence,' he says suddenly, as if just remembering the point of the meeting. I try to read which way he's going on this and sense that it doesn't look too good for us, so I interrupt him as respectfully as possible to play my only trump card.

I explain that we plan to launch the Silk Ribbon chocolate range in the Asean region and we're currently looking for the best production site. It will mean a completely new line with perhaps 50 new jobs in total. It's a premium, high quality range of products, taking on imported European brands head-to-head. The production line will be state-of-the-art, requiring skilled technicians to install and run it. We will provide all the necessary training. We're currently looking at both our Asean sites — in Cambodia and Indonesia. James, sorry, Mr Samnang (at which point I realise I have no idea if this is his given or family name or which I should be using anyway) has assured me that he and his colleagues are strongly committed to taking on the new production here in Cambodia, training the additional sales force and increasing our exports in the region. Now, it just depends on the outcome of talks with the two governments.

I expand on the proposition a little, using the words 'skilled', 'jobs' and 'exports' liberally. I even mention 'import substitution' and throw in 'foreign exchange' and 'strong cash generation'. I stress the importance of Mr Samnang's experience in leading the development. The man to the deputy minister's left is smiling. I'm certain he's winking at me, though it could be a flutter. He has very long eye-lashes. He's wearing a business suit, and there's no sign of any breast development, but I'm thinking that that might be a little too much to expect of a civil servant at his level, even in Cambodia. Fantasising again. I conclude that he's a camp gay, so no earthly use to me. I keep my eyes locked on to the deputy minister, who sees nothing amiss.

The deputy minister says he understands my position and would like to consult with his colleagues. Since nobody moves, I take this as a sign that we are dismissed and so lead James back to the reception area. After nearly an hour, we're invited back in. We're told that the government is satisfied with the measures we've taken and our trading licence will not be revoked. No charges are to be brought against our ex-employees, dismissal being considered sufficient punishment. He tells us the operating company should consider itself on probation and hints that the heavens will fall in and dragons will breathe fire on our kinfolk if anything like this happens again. I nod that we've got the message. I made up the stuff about dragons, but he does seem quite adamant.

He goes on to explain that the government is highly gratified that we have chosen Cambodia as the best location for production of the range of Silk Ribbon confectionery and they look forward to discussing the details of this important investment with us. The government has prepared a brief joint press release to announce the investment in principle. A detailed briefing will follow when the full package has been agreed. David will go ballistic when he hears we've been finessed. I'm going to have to persuade him that we have no choice if we want to keep the factory running. I'm not looking forward to that phone call.

The deputy minister stands, followed by his staff. We all shake hands and the ministry guys leave the room. The poof is the last to go. I notice he doesn't glance back, so he must have got the message.

*

We take James's car back to the office and have a working lunch with his senior people. I brief them on the licence and make it clear that James will continue as MD. I tell them it has been a close call and stringent measures will need to be taken to ensure that discipline doesn't break down again. We're an international company, I remind them, and we must work to the strictest standards of probity. This time it was in finance, and the guilty people have gone, but it could just have easily been in purchasing, sales or production. I'm not pointing a finger at anyone, but I expect to find no loopholes when I conduct a thorough review of systems at Q1.

They all look a bit stunned, but they needed to be warned, even if it wasn't their departments this time. I tell them Silk Ribbon is definitely coming to Asean and it's still a toss-up with Indonesia, though we received very encouraging noises from the ministry today. That relieves the mood somewhat. I'll have to brief David before we tell the troops, but he's still in bed.

I review the accounts with James all afternoon. Car to the hotel by 6.30pm. Knackered, to tell the truth.

Shower and change. My current choice: something to eat, a trawl of the nightspots or a phone call to Josie? I decide on a beer. I take my complimentary copy of the *Phnom Penh Post* down to the Elephant Bar and order an Angkor. I've hardly read the headlines when I'm aware of someone standing close to me.

'Of all the gin joints in all the world…' the man says. It takes me a moment to recognise him and even then his name doesn't come to me.

'Arlo,' he says. 'You remember me? Kenneth Mann? You were president of Personal Care.'

'Of course,' I finally click. He was finance director in corporate when I was heading up my last firm's soap and deodorant division. 'God, what brings you to Cambodia?'

'Same as you, probably: an honest buck. You alone? Mind if I join you for a beer? Corner of a foreign field and all that; not forgetting you're Italian, of course, but an honorary Englishman for all that. How's Nan?'

'Nan's fine. Angkor OK?'

'As long as it's wet.'

And so we natter on about old times at HQ in Buckingham Palace Gate. I'm actually quite glad of the company. Kenneth was always a bit pompous, but I respec him for his judgement. Learning under him made me a CE so I'll always be grateful to him. He has left the old fir officially retired — and spends his time as a non-exec on boards, one of which requires his occasional presence in Asia, and of course only the Raffles will do for our Kenneth.

I can talk!

After a few beers, patrician Kenneth suggests we go to eat. (He never has been Ken, not to anyone, though it's hard to imagine his wife screaming 'Kenneth' at moments of climax. Oh dear, I need to erase that image from my mind!) He mentions a place called Frizz, which I don't know but I'm willing to try.

'Not really walking distance,' Kenneth says. 'Let's take a tuk-tuk.'

Dinner is fine. Good Khmer food in a friendly atmosphere. Conversation is surprisingly easy and enjoyable. We have lots of acquaintances in common. I don't mention the unpleasantness back at the OpCo in case one of his companies is a competitor. Well, you never know. So I'm here for the year-end review and that's going well.

A couple of bottles of wine have made Kenneth a bit impish and, after dinner, he suggests we inspect a few bars. I remember Kenneth. He's up for a good time if a good time is offered. On the other hand, what's in it for me? I'll have to watch him pawing a succession of young hostesses while I'm thinking that there's meatier prey out there just waiting to be snared. Basically, we're not in the same hunt, Kenneth and I.

I decline, citing tiredness, but tell him he mustn't call it a night. 'You'll have a better time on your own,' I assure him.

So I pay the bill, say I may see him at breakfast and hop leaving him on the pavement, looking this way ne opportunity might present itself.

I want the Classic, which he says he frequently changes names. I've been es, a 'cabaret show pub' they call it, covering off all the angles. The huge barn of a place is dominated by a laser-lit dance floor. There's a stage on which a number of drag acts perform to a thumping soundtrack. The exotically-dressed staff and performers alike are available to keep customers company and it's not long before I'm joined by Lola (which reminds me of a Kinks number about a transvestite) and a little later by Maly, which she tells me means flower. Maybe. Lola and Maly are sassy chicks with all the right characteristics. They've both had boob jobs and it takes me only a few rounds of drinks to discover that Maly is post-op, while Lola is still saving up. This talk of gender reassignment gets me quite excited. I decide to switch to mineral water in case I'm required to perform.

Although I'm very taken by my two companions, they are not in Josie's league at all. Josie was a class act; these two are a bit of rough, clearly boys with tits and thick make-up. I begin to think in terms of taking one of them back to the hotel. Lola suggests a threesome, which I resist at first, then realise that it's the asymmetry of their, er, surgical progress that has me so turned on. Two in the bush? Why not?

*

We bundle into a taxi and race back to the hotel. I'm aware that, as we pass the attendants on the door, I look like a sad old Western pervert with a couple of rather obvious ladyboys on my arms. But, hell, I'm rich. I brazen it out and manage to reach the lift. The doors are about to close when a hand reaches inside to stop them. It's Kenneth. Fuck!

The blood leaves my head. I am so embarrassed I could die. There is absolutely nothing I can do except deal with it man to man. I drop my arms from around the two ladies' waists and wait for Kenneth to speak. He smiles in friendly acknowledgement, but nothing stronger. He's very calm. I say, 'I couldn't sleep: jet-lag still, possibly. So I went for a walk and bumped into a couple of friends.'

The explanation isn't supposed to sound true, but it gives Kenneth the cue to speak. 'Oh, that's nice,' he says. 'I hope you have fun, catching up.' With that, the lift pings for his floor and he's gone. Kenneth knows everyone in the City. Now I'll never know who he's told, and who's laughing behind their hand. I'll have to invite him for a golf day when I get back to assess how discreet he plans to be. I have a few stories on him I may be able to hint at.

Email to nan1975@hotmail.com
The meeting at the ministry went better than expected; we're still in business. Back at the hotel, I bumped into Kenneth Mann, who I'm sure you'll remember. Wife Nicole, rather exotic, bright red hair. I had dinner with him in a local restaurant, now I'm ready for bed.

I'm really sorry to hear about your mother. Call me any time if there are developments. It must be awful for you, my darling.

Three big kisses for the kids and here are some for you.
Arlo xxx

Text to +66 mobile number, saved in phone memory as 'Jack Anderson'
I'm thinking about you, Tik, you beautiful woman. We'll have two whole days together. Arlo xxxxx

17 July, Phnom Penh
David won't allow first class tickets on flights under four hours so I'm in business, but the lounge is the same either way—Le Salon VIP lounge, which is where I am now, waiting for the 8.00pm flight to Suvarnabumi. I think the penny-pinching must be due to David's Calvinist upbringing.

I swear he wears a hair shirt under his business suit. The man's not human.

I didn't get the chance to write up last night. My two roguish companions proved lively company, though I was a little too tired to appreciate it fully.

I'm not gay. I'm not gay. I'm not gay.

But I do like a woman who has a cock and balls. That was Lola. I think of them as particularly swollen female genitals. There you go, I'm beginning to tumesce just tapping these words into my laptop. She tries to hang on to me, begging for my mobile number, email etc, clearly hoping to add me to her list of 'subscribers' to fund the op, but my heart is of stone. Tik is enough for the time being.

I eject Lola and Maly around 1.00am and phone David. I've worked with him for eight years now and I still can't predict his reactions accurately. This time it goes the right way and he is pretty relaxed about the Silk Ribbon deal, though he makes the point that he'd rather have taken the decision (maintain a degree of freedom, as he puts it) than be forced into it, even if it's the right way to go, which in this case we don't know because Indonesia didn't get a chance to bid. But we cocked up so we have to accept the repercussions.

I buy a gold necklace for Tik. It's supposed to be duty free, but comes out expensive at $320. Thai ladies love gold, considering it a convertible asset rather than mere personal adornment. My flight's boarding now.

17 July continued, Bangkok

There's a car waiting for me at Arrivals which gets me to the Marriott by around 10.30pm. Tik is waiting in reception, a small and demure figure dwarfed by the opulent surroundings. When she sees me, she jumps up and runs over, her steel high heels clattering on the marble floor. She throws her arms around my neck and says, 'I love you, Candyman.' Despite many attempts to teach her, Tik is never going to manage 'Arlo'. We've tried it as a word and we've tried it a letter at a time. She gets the hang of the 'r' and we move on to the 'l', by which time she has forgotten how to say the 'r', and so on.

'I love you too.' I have been seeing Tik twice a year for two-and-a-half years now and I regard our relationship as reasonably settled. When we first met, she was a man. It feels strange to type this now, but it's true. I have supported her throughout the change process, right up to her operation which took place in February.

I check in for two people and a porter carries my bag upstairs (Tik has no luggage), discreetly not even glancing at Tik. Employees of Bangkok hotels have seen it all before.

I give Tik the necklace. She seems grateful, curtsies and says thank you, but puts it straight into her handbag. Just as I said: it's loot, not a gift to treasure and use.

'Are you hungry?' I ask, knowing the answer will be yes.

'Room service,' she decides excitedly and buries herself in the menu.

This all delays my discovery of Tik's new body. I can see the tops of her enhanced breasts already, and can hardly wait to inspect what the surgeons have made of the rest. I paid for it, so I reckon I should be allowed to play with it.

When the meal is delivered and we've eaten it and placed the trays outside the door, I get to work. It's an amazing job. Her body was always slim and boyish; now it's fully feminine. She has lovely tits, with little sign of scars. Her new bits are fully functioning, as I soon discover.

We sit up in bed to watch TV.

'How long are you going to stay?' she asks.

'Two nights.'

She lets out a small wail. 'Only two nights? Not enough.' She snuggles closer. 'Tomorrow we go to the British embassy to make a visa, OK?'

'No,' I say. 'Not OK. How are you going to get a visa?'

'I can say I'm a student, or a tourist.'

'I don't think they're going to go for that, Tik, and anyway, where would you stay?'

'With you, *ting tong* Candyman.'

'You can't stay with me, Tik. I'm married.'

'Married!' she cries. 'Married? You didn't tell me you were married.'

'Yes I did. I told you I have three kids and I'm married.'

'But you have no ring. I thought you were joking.'

'Not all *farang* men wear wedding rings, Tik. I have no ring, but I do have a wife. I told you.'

'But we were joking. I told you I have a sister.'

'You do have a sister. I gave her 20,000 baht for her market stall at Mo Chit. Oh, you mean you really don't have a sister?'

'Just joking.'

'You do or you don't?'

'No, no sister.'

'Why did you lie to me? What did you do with the money?'

'I've got to live,' she shouts. 'How am I going to live without food?' This logic transcends the moral imperative to tell the truth to the man you love.

'How did you live before you met me?'

'Oh, I was OK. I have a German boyfriend and an American boyfriend.'

'You had before or you have now?'

'They send me money, but I don't see them.'

'You told me I was your only boyfriend.'

'You don't give me enough. I have to live.'

She sulks for a bit. I try to watch some old movie while considering how I've been shafted. After some time she says, 'You're not going to marry me, right? Right, Candyman? You just want candy, Mr Candyman, you don't want a wife. I'm your sweet candy girl, but I want to be your rice, I want to be your noodles. I want so you cannot live without me, but you can live without chocolate. You can live without me.'

She gets out of bed and starts getting dressed.

'I want to be your rice.'

'Come back to bed.'

'I cut off my dick for you,' she shouts.

'Tik, that's just not true. You've wanted to lose your dick since you were 15.'

'I wanted to lose it for a man who would love me. I thought that was you. I had surgery so I could be your wife.'

I protest, but she heads for the door.

'Call me if you can love me,' she says as she leaves.

Ten minutes later I call, but her phone is switched off.

Text to +66 mobile number, saved in phone memory as 'Jack Anderson'
Of course I love you, Tik. Come back. Candyman xxx

18 July, Bangkok
Sarawong's driver picks me up at 8.30am and I spend the day at the office. It's routine; the accounts are in good shape and

the business has done well, with turnover up more than 5% and profit 7.2% ahead. Sarawong has done well. He suggests lunch, but I tell him I'd prefer to make it a celebration after the review is finished tomorrow. He understands.

I call Tik many times during the day, but without success. Does she expect me to chase after her? I have only the vaguest idea where she lives — in an apartment block somewhere on Sukhumvit Soi 79, I think, but I have been there only once to drop her off from a taxi. I'm sure I couldn't find it again. She may even have moved.

At 5.00pm, the driver delivers me back to the hotel. I shower and change and wonder how I am going to spend the evening. I wander down to the street and order a Singha beer at a bar on Soi 5. It's time for reflection.

I realise that Tik is controlling me again. Ever since we met she has had this talent for making me do what she wants, at my expense. She has extracted large sums of money from me, not by direct cheating, but by putting me in a position where I want to give it to her. Lying about having a sister, though, was a 24-carat fraud.

Now, I have the prospect of an evening alone. I can't look for anyone else in case Tik decides to turn up. She has won again. It's infuriating.

I decide to have dinner in the restaurant on the corner of Soi 5 and then take a stroll to Nana Plaza, just to pass the time. I make for Obsession, on the ground floor at the back, and drink a couple of beers, feeling rather lonely and dejected. I buy drinks for a few of the girls, who are all pre-op in this bar, and allow one of them to play with me, but I don't come because my mobile starts to vibrate. It's Nan. I pay the bill and leave to find somewhere quiet to call back. That whole area is so raucous, I'm back in the hotel before I can make the call.

Nan's mother has died. The cancer was quick and I hope not painful. I tell Nan how sorry I am, that Bridget was a lovely lady, eccentric but strong. She has been brave to the end. I tell her I'll be home on Saturday and will be able to help with the funeral and other arrangements then.

I drink all the Scotch and all the beer in the mini-bar (four miniatures and four cans) in front of the TV. I fall asleep in my clothes.

Text to +66 mobile number, saved in phone memory as 'Jack Anderson'

I leave for London tomorrow. Your last chance, Tik. Candyman xxx

19 July, Bangkok

I wake at 5.00am, get undressed, clean my teeth and go back to sleep until 8.00am. Sarawong's driver has been waiting for 20 minutes by the time I get to the lobby.

I finish my business in the morning then take Sarawong and his senior people to lunch at the Banyan Tree as a special thank you for a great year. They're a good bunch and the natural flow of conversation takes my mind off my troubles with Tik and Nan for a couple of hours.

It's late afternoon before we finish lunch. I have all evening before my midnight flight back to London. I'll need to call in at the hotel to check out before taking a taxi to Suvarnabumi.

First, I hail a cab to Siam Square. I continue to call Tik from the car, but her mobile's still off. She will have a few dozen missed calls when she finally boots up, but I'll be gone by then, pushed that little bit too far. I put Tik down to experience; a good one by and large, but just an experience.

In Siam Square I get a digital camera for Mabel, a Play-Station for Sam and some binoculars for Jason, as the iPad cover didn't cost very much. They're good kids and I rarely spoil them, but I've been away a lot this month.

Guilt gifts, perhaps.

I go looking for jewellery for Nan; I know she likes to make an impression at formal occasions. I buy an emerald necklace for a little over 190,000 baht. They're not Thai emeralds, but the setting is from Thailand. I hope she thinks of it as something she can love herself then pass on to Mabel one day, and that it will remind my daughter of all her father's travels in Asia.

WILLIAM PESKETT

Snake Eyes

Coming up to fifty-five, he'd torn down all the straights and cornered most of the bends just like it said in the manual. Three children, the best he could have hoped for, were at university in England, or would be by next year. He'd made regional-level director in his company, which was more than he'd ever dared consider his goal. And he'd ditched only one wife along the way. It could have been more, he realised, as he had no illusions that he was an easy man to live with. Knowing the truth of that, after the split he'd dedicated himself to his work and to abstract painting, rather than to filling the emptiness he'd created in his own life.

The posting to South-East Asia had changed the dynamics. The old void his divorce had left was filled within a year by a simple country girl who knew how to please her man. She came with two kids of her own, now nearly grown up, so there seemed no need to make more babies.

That was eight years ago, and while his newish wife still knew how to cook a spectacular masaman curry, the intimacy that had driven him to her when they first met was now, while not non-existent, at best sporadic.

It seemed to suit them both. He had no desire to augment the physical love he shared with his wife by accepting any of the many commercial offers that living and working in Bangkok frequently presented to him. Nor was he attracted by any of the bustling women managers he encountered at work. He was reaching that age, he sometimes thought, when it became necessary to make use of the word 'libido'. The depressing thing he learnt was that it was a word you only needed to describe something that was in decline.

A year or so previously he had discovered — or rather rediscovered — the easy satisfaction of composing his own pleasure. It was ridiculous to think of it as a revelation, since the simple equipment and knowledge of its workings that now gave him such enjoyable sensations had been with him all his life. Rather, he thought of it as a re-evaluation of a pre-condition, a second chance to experience joy from a situation that was, basically, nothing new.

He first began on this new journey in bed. He would lie awake at night, unable to sleep perhaps because of a niggling worry that he'd left some piece of work undone, or because he was running through the possible kinetics of a meeting that he'd have to attend the next day. His wife would be lying next to him, quiet and still. If she was asleep or awake he couldn't tell; she didn't snore.

At first, it was merely something to hold on to, like a comforter. He would cradle it in his right hand and feel its relaxed, compliant bulk, like a long balloon of warm water, perhaps, a raw sausage or some item of uncooked pastry. What did a spring roll feel like before it was fried? He had no idea. But the difference between all these comparators and the real thing was that the real thing felt so good. It was not only good to hold (the sensations that came to him from his hand) but good to be held (the sensations that came directly from his penis).

On nights when it was clear that his wife didn't want to make love—and those were frequent—the pattern was repeated; he would clasp his penis softly until sleep came. This was all he needed; this was all his libido demanded. Every boy did a lot more, he was sure; his behaviour was nothing that caused him any anxiety or guilt.

But it became more serious. At work, he would sometimes find that, while walking along the corridor or passing between the desks of his subordinates with his hand casually pushed into his trouser pocket, he would make glancing contact with his new friend and enjoy a frisson of forbidden pleasure.

One weekend when his wife had gone to the market and left him sitting on the secluded balcony of their condominium with a pot of coffee and the *Bangkok Post*, on impulse he unzipped his fly and pulled his penis into view. He stared at it for some time before coming to a new realisation: it was beautiful. Until now, he hadn't appreciated what a handsome organ it was—structured yet amorphous, soft yet powerful. He longed to make it the subject of a painting and wondered how he could abstract its essence without alarming his wife. He would hang the finished picture in their drawing room and call it something obscure like *Insight 3*.

It looked back at him blankly, its vertical slot of a mouth seeming to express shock or surprise, but of a very familiar kind. This was part of him after all; they'd come through a lot together. He'd shot the DNA to make three kids through that mouth, he mused philosophically, plus a lot more that had gone nowhere in a genetic sense. And he hardly wanted to think about the tankers of beer.

He smiled at his penis and, with help, it smiled back, though the expression was awkward as its head was upside-down, like the smile of a limbo dancer. If he twisted the whole thing around, he found he could engage with it properly, face to face and the right way up. The little puffy cheeks below its mouth bulged like jowls; above was the high, noble forehead; and behind that brow rolled the comfortable ruff of prepuce, like the neck of a fisherman's favourite old sweater.

One negative he considered was that it was blind, and this insight suddenly made him think of his organ as a massive underground grub, pasty pink and etiolated because it had never been allowed access to the light. If only there were eyes in that wide flat head, he mused. If only their communication could be more than blind and he could express his gratitude for the pleasure it gave him. That would bring perfection to the joy of their blossoming relationship.

His new hobby was getting more serious. In bed now he would persist with his caresses until his penis was fully engorged. He found he could achieve this with the minimum of movement, and thus not risk waking his wife. He would maintain this state of tumescence for five minutes or so before replacing the foreskin and relaxing into sleep.

He took a pair of his weekend shorts and unpicked the stitching in one pocket. If his wife had noticed, she would have put the damage down to understandable wear and tear, but in reality, he used the aperture to reach through and hold his penis while in the most public places. Accompanying his wife to the supermarket, for example, was an ideal opportunity to bring it to life. Bored by the purchase of groceries, he would stroll among the displays of fruit and vegetables, his hand in his pocket, coaxing his penis to erection. He would jingle the keys in his other pocket to disguise any movement that might be required to create this exquisite pleasure.

He began to worry that his interest in his penis had become an obsession. But what if it had? Was it an obsession that was causing anyone harm? Was it an obsession that could escalate into evil behaviour? He thought not. Was he obtaining satisfaction from his own caresses that should have been provided by his wife? Was he supplanting her from this role? Possibly. This did cause him some pause for thought. But his wife and he did still make love, and the extent of this seemed to be all that his wife required, so his feelings of guilt were quickly assuaged. Without guilt, he became more honest about his own feelings; he had to admit it, he had fallen in love with his penis.

He quickly assured himself that this wasn't an exclusive love. He still loved his wife of course; he loved his three children naturally. This was a love that he could indulge in addition to these human relationships, despite its special nature. There was no denying the singular bond that existed between a man and his penis.

One Saturday, his wife suggested a trip to the zoo. It was somewhere they'd been before, but not often. It was a huge place, and included a pleasant park in which they could stroll while observing the animals. He'd been entertaining clients the night before and so considered that the walk and the fresh air would help clear the residue of unmetabolised alcohol still in his blood.

They drove to the zoo in her car. Together they walked and chatted and enjoyed the plants and animals until they reached the reptile house. Inside, down the steps, it was dark and hot. The smell of the scaly inhabitants was musty and close. He gripped the wall beside a glass window to clear his head and found himself staring at a python on a branch. The snake didn't move except for an occasional flick of its tongue. Its neck lay along the branch, long and thick. Its bulbous head extended beyond the end of the limb, held up by the stiffness of its neck.

The heat was becoming too much. He felt heady and weak. The eyes in the snake's smooth high forehead stared. In a flash it came to him that the lack of air in the reptile house was stifling him and before he could leave the building he realised he had something very important to do.

*

He told his personal assistant he'd be gone from the office for the afternoon and instructed his driver to take him to a large Bangkok hospital. It was one his wife and he used regularly for minor matters. In the back of the car he was pleased to note that a large hole had appeared in the right pocket of his office trousers. As the car jerked through the heavy Bangkok traffic, he took comfort from his own attention.

At the hospital he located the cosmetic surgery department and told the receptionist that he wanted to speak to a doctor about an elective procedure. After a short wait, he was ushered into a small consultation room; he was soon joined by a doctor.

'How can I help you?' she asked.

'I would like to have a small operation, nothing very serious.'

'I see. What operation would you like?' She had a notepad in front of her and twiddled a pen in her fingers.

'It's to do with my penis,' he said, quite calmly and without a hint of embarrassment.

'I see. Is it to increase the length? The girth? What exactly would you like us to do?' The woman was very attractive. He very much liked to hear her talking about him in that way.

'No, it's not the length, and it's not the girth. Both of those dimensions are quite satisfactory,' he smirked, then worried that he may have given it a little too much swagger. However, the doctor showed no reaction.

'Then what?' she asked.

'I would like you to insert...to give it some eyes,' he said quickly.

'Eyes? I see.' The doctor faltered momentarily, but swallowed and continued. 'May I ask why?'

'So it can see.'

'I see.'

'Yes.'

'Why do you want it to see?'

'I want our relationship—between my penis and myself, you understand—to be more equal. We are very much in love. We give each other physical pleasure of course, but I want to extend that to make our relationship more...'

'Sharing?'

'Yes, sharing's a good word.'

'And companionable?'

'Yes. Thank you for your understanding.'

'But that's my job! What you're asking for is a penile ocular transplant, what we surgeons call a POT. Actually, I will be honest with you: we don't get so much demand for this procedure. I shall have to consult with colleagues. Please excuse me for a moment.'

With that, the doctor left the room. He sat at the doctor's desk and waited. On the wall was a poster showing two women, one with small breasts, and the other with large breasts; when he finally looked at their faces he realised they were the same woman. On the desk was the doctor's notepad, still blank.

After some time, the doctor returned and said, 'Yes, we can do as you wish, we can perform a POT. But we do have a small problem.'

'What's the problem?' he asked.

'It's getting the right donor. People commonly donate their eyes for transplantation after their death, but this is normally restricted to facial use. Obtaining authorisation for penile transplantation is very rare. There could be a long wait. I'm sorry.'

'I don't want people's eyes,' he replied quickly. 'They would be much too big and very scary. It would be very weird thinking about who had owned them — and looked into them — before. No, I want something a lot smaller than that, something alert yet loving, like a snake.'

'Oh, I see. I'm sorry I misunderstood. Then it seems we do not have that problem. Finding a suitable snake donor is much easier than locating a human one for the simple reason that the snake has no choice. Ha ha,' the doctor laughed quickly. 'Please excuse me for a moment.'

After a short while, the doctor returned with some papers. 'You're all booked in for, well, immediate attention. The procedure will cost 430,000 baht. Please sign here and if I could have your credit card?'

He signed the document and handed over his card, which the doctor took out of the room. She returned again with the slip, which he signed.

'If you would now please undress and lie on the bed,' she directed, while snapping on some rubber gloves.

He lay naked on the small examination couch as the doctor approached with a hypodermic syringe.

'You have the snake?' he asked as she pierced his skin.

'Just leave the arrangements to us,' she replied, soothingly.

*

When he awoke, he was still in the same room. He lifted his head slowly and was surprised to find his wife sitting by the side of the bed. He was confused.

'Did it go alright?' he asked.

'Did what go alright?' his wife replied.

'The... thing. You know. My... no, sorry. Actually, why am I here?'

'You passed out.'

'I know, but... what? When did I pass out?'

'About two hours ago. You fainted at the zoo, in the lizard house. You hit your head on the step.'

He put his hand to his head and felt the bandage. Glancing down, he noticed he was still wearing his shorts. He put his hand in his pocket. It felt too normal. He couldn't find the sort of post-operative wrappings he'd expected.

'Come on, sit up,' his wife encouraged bracingly. 'How do you feel?'

'Kind of weak,' he replied.

He sat on the edge of the bed for some minutes and drank half a glass of water before deciding that he wanted to leave: 'Come on, let's go home.'

'If you feel better.'

'Yes, I'm fine.'

'I'll just go and pay.'

'I've already...'

'How could you have done?'

'No, right. You go and pay, sorry.'

He felt a little dizzy as he got up and walked slowly from the consultation room, a confusion that increased as he emerged through the front doors of the building and realised that he was leaving quite a different hospital from the one he'd entered.

'I've got my driver here,' he said weakly, wondering really if it was true.

'No you haven't, darling, it's Saturday. We're using my car.'

Sweet Song of the Siren

I am Henry Purt and this is my story. It isn't one of which I am proud. While the choices that I made appeared the right ones at the time, their effect was to lead me to disaster. The story I am about to relate will be cautionary to many readers and I hope to prevent much pain by candidly opening my heart to you. Although if I saw it written I would believe none of it, I can assure you of the truth of what I am about to confess.

*

I am a New Zealander, born the second of two sons to hard-working sheep farmers on the South Island some 100km west of Christchurch. Although I loved the child's life on the farm, it did not instil in me an ambition to become a stock-breeder. While my elder brother stayed at home to help manage the business, I moved to the city to make my way in the more mundane world of accountancy.

I qualified with one of the big international firms and began my career successfully as a tax specialist. My job allowed me to live comfortably in Christchurch; otherwise, although I devoted most of my waking hours to the firm, my professional life is not essential to my story. My engagement to Shelley, however, occupies centre stage.

Shelley was all I ever imagined I would need in a wife. We dated since our second year at Canterbury. She was bright, supportive and passionate. She felt strongly about social and environmental issues and wanted to dedicate her life to making a difference. Her friends joked that one day I'd be the prime minister's wife. It's wonderful to think now of those student days when every option was open and our lives took off like fireworks.

As Shelley struggled to make a name for herself in local politics, my career advanced and we rented a flat together in Christchurch. For nearly a year we lived the couple's life and talked about marriage and family. However, before the end of the year I discovered an inconsistency.

I am a trained auditor. Inconsistencies are what we look for—not normally at home, granted, but when they are presented to us we cannot ignore them. The details are as sordid as a corporate fraud review where some feckless loser with a speedboat he can't explain is found with his fingers in the petty cash.

We shared a car. I had it serviced. The odometer reading was recorded by the garage. Shelley told me she was meeting a girlfriend in town. The next day, the reading was up 220km.

When I pointed this out, Shelley became flustered and said the engineer must have made a mistake in the logbook. Flustered was the clue. I'm an auditor. The accounts are merely a shadow of the company's workings, as dusty fossil footprints in a museum drawer are of the blood and gore of a stone-age hunt. Flustered senior management is the clincher.

I began to observe Shelley's movements with more care. She had clocked up a couple of hundred kilometres on what she told me was a trip downtown. But perhaps she had been arranging a surprise for me—scouting out a romantic retreat up the coast, perhaps. If that was clutching at straws, I wanted to eliminate from my concerns the possibility that she was concealing something bad from me.

I loved Shelley so much that when I finally had proof of her deceit I thought my life had been liquidised. It was as if she'd taken our careers, our love and our future — a delicate three-dimensional structure — and chucked it in the blender.

It was actually someone at work who provided the compelling evidence. After a weekend when Shelley had been away in Auckland at a party conference, I found myself at the coffee machine with a colleague. Filling in the awkward moment that occurs while the machine grinds the beans, Jean mentioned casually that she'd seen Shelley in a tavern in Coalgate the previous Sunday. Coalgate is near where I was brought up, where my parents still live. It's here, on the South Island. Auckland isn't.

That evening, I confronted Shelley with the two pieces of information — the distance she'd racked up in the car and Jean's sighting of her on the wrong island. I'd heard her explanation for the car trip; how could she account for the other inconsistency?

For a moment, she seemed stunned. I hoped she'd tell me that Joan had been mistaken. I hoped she'd calmly produce the receipt from the Auckland hotel. But no. The line she took, like the All Blacks coming off a scrum on their own five-metre line, was one of determined attack. I spent too many hours at work. I had no time for mutual friends, only my own. I had changed since university. I was serious and domineering and she had no opportunity to express herself through her own interests.

'That's why you go to the country?'

'Yes.'

'Fine. It sounds great; so why lie to me? Why can't I come too? We could call in on my parents; you were pretty close.'

'Don't be ridiculous.'

'Why is it ridiculous?' I realised that a conversation like this would take us nowhere. I looked for the exits. 'Shelley, what's going on here? Something is very wrong.'

Shelley began to cry. She made a big production out of blowing her nose repeatedly, crumpling the tissues and disposing of them in the pedal-bin. This all took time, enough for her to compose her response. I wasn't expecting a confession.

'I've been seeing Carter,' she said in a voice as small as a sick child's.

'Seeing?' I recoiled from the word, my head feeling light. It was such an innocent word. What's the harm in seeing? But 'seeing Carter'? This seemed a much more loaded admission. How could she see Carter? He lived 100km away on a farm.

But she'd said it. The words were there to be understood; it just took me time. She'd shaken the sediment in my brain and I had to wait for it to settle. I said, 'You're seeing Carter? You're having an affair with my brother?'

*

We shouted at each other for a couple of hours. No plates were thrown, but in the course of our fight my confidence in Shelley, in myself, in the future, in my ability to make relationships, all of that became worthless. As in a stock-market run, what previously had value turned to junk. The currency in which I had so fervently dealt, the coins of our friendship, the banknotes of our love, were transformed into so much paper and brass.

I began thinking of the ramifications of what I'd learned. 'This will devastate Mum and Dad.'

There was a big pause. She had exhausted nose-blowing as a diversion and began walking around the flat instead. She directed her response at the bookcase: 'They already know.'

'They already know?'

The walls of the apartment and the rugged coasts of my beloved country suddenly began to squeeze me like an elastic band. In an instant, New Zealand felt too small to accommodate both me and my family lined up against me.

*

We tried to work it out but it didn't work out; Shelley moved out.

At work the next day I told my manager I was interested in an overseas assignment. He supported this and told me to keep my eye on the firm's intranet. I didn't really care where it was, as long as it was a number of time zones from Christchurch. First up was a year's secondment to our Bangkok office; I applied and was accepted.

Thailand. It wasn't in my plan.

In the following month, I saw Shelley move out, gave up the lease on the flat, paid my bills, emailed my parents a chilly farewell, sold the car, put my other belongings in a small shipping container and took a taxi to the airport.

If you ever go to live abroad, do it as the employee of a big, profitable multinational firm. Mine sent me to classes on living in another country, taught me some rudimentary Thai, arranged the move and found me a condo, a doctor, a dentist, a bank and an office buddy, a Chinese called Cheng who had lived in Thailand since he was a boy. Cheng showed me how to get the most out of the Bangkok bus system, how and when to *wai* (the Thai greeting) and how to ask for a milder version of the explosively spicy *tom yam* soup. He also showed me where I could find the sexiest bars and where I should scuba dive.

As in New Zealand, the day job in Thailand was enjoyable, interesting and fulfilling but, as I've said, my work is incidental to the main narrative I mean to relate. Scuba diving leads us closer to the heart of this story.

In early conversations with Cheng, possibly in one of the less noisy bars we visited, I discovered that he was a keen diver. I had done my fair share in New Zealand, the climax there being a trip to the Poor Knights off the Northland Region of the North Island. But that was before the business with Shelley and I was keen to take up the hobby again.

Cheng told me that I—or rather we—should set our sights on the Andaman Islands, a vast archipelago west of Thailand that belongs to India. We waited until I had earned some leave before making the arduous trip, and flew the dogleg via Kolkata to Port Blair. From there, it was a matter of taking a ferry to Havelock Island and joining smaller dive boats to the best, and sometimes most remote, spots.

The quality of the diving among the Andamans was spectacular. The colours of the pristine reefs and the extraordinary variety of life I witnessed on them were enough, had I not been breathing through a regulator, to make me gasp. Manta rays, barracuda, moray eels, puffer fish and lionfish were easy to spot around the coral while great shoals of mackerel and tuna cruised by. My favourite finds were the turtles. Impossibly massive and wonderfully serene, they wore their millions of years of existence on this planet — and quite possibly in these very waters — with obvious pride.

Perhaps because the archipelago is not that easy to reach, the dives we made on the first few days were not crowded and we were always guaranteed to see more fish than other divers—more groupers than groups, as the guides would say. Nevertheless, Cheng and I still agreed on an urge to get away from the others and one day we hired an old fishing boat with a couple of berths, loaded it up with food, beer and spare tanks, and went off in exploration of truly uncharted waters. To be honest, the underwater scenery was no better off the beaten track than it was in the popular dive areas (and with hindsight this was to be expected), but the sense of discovery was enough to keep us pressing on, every day further and further from our base.

We would cover the miles in the early morning, then complete two dives a day, stopping between for lunch and a couple of hours reading and relaxing. In the evenings, we'd bob about at anchor, fry up some fish in the galley and drink beer until the stars speckling the canopy of our enormous world had heard enough of our trite wisdom and commanded us to sleep.

When using air, we always dived together in the approved manner, but one afternoon while Cheng was busy writing his journal I decided to snorkel to a nearby islet alone. The rock had little coral within view, but it was host to other fauna—a garden of anemones, urchins and sensitive tube worms waved their arms in the nutritious current. I decided to swim around the rock. It was when I reached the far side that I caught my first glimpse.

Diving masks give a surprisingly restricted field of view so I wasn't sure what I'd seen. Thinking I might have been on the trail of a monster tuna or, more likely, a shoal of them, I turned and swam in the direction of the flash.

I could find no fish and soon gave up the hunt. However, diving down a metre or so along the face of the rock, I found a dark space in the wall, an underwater cave, perhaps, that momentarily caught my interest. Intrigued, I came up for a lungful of air and went down again. What I saw in the mouth of that cave was the most astonishing sight I have ever experienced. The shock of coming face to face with that apparition was enough to make me choke on the small amount of seawater in my snorkel, flounder violently for a few seconds and struggle back to the surface for air.

Treading water, I tried to collect my thoughts. Was it a composition of the light filtering through waves, was it merely an unusual coral formation, was it the fierce sun affecting my brain or had I just seen a human face — a living, female human face — at the entrance to the cave, and had she smiled at me, and had she raised a small white hand and beckoned me to follow her?

There's little time for rational contemplation when you're treading water and trying not to drown. I readied my mask and dived again back to the cave. The horrific thought came to me that what I had seen was indeed a woman, drowned while snorkelling like me, and that the movement I'd seen was her dead hand wafting in the ocean's ebb and flow. I prepared myself for confirmation of this awful possibility, but it didn't come. The woman's face had moved further from the darkness and was now clearly dappled by light from the surface. Her lips smiled playfully, her eyes flirted with me. This time, she beckoned with both of her hands, one after the other, cycling slowly in an unmistakable invitation to follow her into the cave.

While struggling against my buoyancy, I attempted some signs in reply — I raised my eyebrows, hunched my shoulders and held out my hands like some Jewish comedian in an exaggerated attempt at 'Who are you? What do you want? How come you're living underwater in an Indian cave?'

She didn't reply to any of these quite reasonable queries. Instead, on my next descent, she reached out and touched my wrist, pulling me gently towards her. Her expression had changed. She now seemed to be saying, 'Why not? What are you afraid of?' In my own urgent sign language I replied, 'I can't do more than a minute of this. I need air.' On the surface again, I remember thinking, why doesn't she?

When I dived again, she held me as before, this time pulling me further into her cave. I resisted at first because I was aware of the dangers of being caught underwater, snagged between rocks without enough puff to return to the atmosphere. But then I saw the unmistakable silver light of a water surface inside the cave. She drew me gently up towards it. The softness of her touch beguiled me and I flowed like a floating cloth into the cave and up into air. The woman broke the surface with me and we found ourselves face to face and out of water for the first time.

She said nothing, though her face was alive with soft expressions which seemed to say, 'Well, that wasn't so bad, was it? You're safe here. Welcome to my home.'

Mesmerised by the woman's beauty, I pushed back my mask and stared at her, probably for longer than was polite. I turned about to take in my surroundings. We were in a vertical shaft, some two metres across, which connected below water with the horizontal cave through which I'd swum. The surface of the rock around us was smooth and its shape quite regular as if worked by human hand. Above, there was a domed ceiling, three metres or more in height. One side of the shaft opened on to a wide platform. This also seemed to have been constructed as it was quite level, about ten centimetres above the water surface. The space was lit by half a dozen apertures high up in the ceiling, through which the sun's rays penetrated.

The woman seemed to float without effort, keeping her head and shoulders quite still above the water. Despite having so recently surfaced, her face was dry, the droplets of seawater being cast off by her skin more quickly than by mine. Her light brown hair, too, appeared unnaturally dry. It was thick and lustrous, falling to her shoulders. Something else that was odd: the irises of her eyes were gold, like tiny wedding rings.

I grabbed hold of the platform and rested one arm on the rock. This seemed to amuse the woman. She copied my action, raising herself up in the water and revealing her naked breasts. I can only guess what the expression on my face meant to her. In response, her smile seemed to say, 'I'm glad you approve.' After a moment, this clearly changed to something like, 'Well, what do we do next?'

The air was breathable in the cave and my escape route was clear and short. Reassured, I pulled up on the edge of the rock and leapt out of the water, sitting on the platform with my legs in the water. She let out a small giggle and did the same, slithering up on to the rock beside me.

I've seen theatrical double-takes in comedy shows but they are nothing compared with my reaction when I realised that, from the waist down, my companion was a fish. All my earlier fears returned that I was suffering a hallucination. In such situations, the custom is to pinch yourself to verify your vision with some physical sensation, but there was no need. The mermaid had reached over and placed both of her tiny white hands on my arm. She looked up at me, her eyes and lips moving minutely to suggest, 'I know this is a shock for you. Relax and everything will be fine.'

I wasn't sure that my face was as expressive as hers, so I tried some spoken English: 'Who are you?'

The mermaid giggled.

'What is your name?'

A quizzical look, like a sparrow locating a sound.

'My name is Henry.' I indicated that I was talking about me, and then pointed at her. 'What is your name?'

She giggled again and caught my hand, pressing it between her breasts. Her skin was warm.

I tried more conversational gambits, but without success. Then she spoke, softly and at length, murmuring lilting syllables with a rhythm that ran like the tides. All the while she gazed into my eyes and the beguiling music of her voice washed over me like cooling surf.

'I have to know who you are,' I insisted, but she silenced me with a tiny fingertip on my lips.

Suddenly, she slipped into the water, reached up and beckoned me to follow. She indicated that I should put on my mask, dived and led me down through the shaft and further into the cave, away from the mouth through which I'd first entered. After a few metres she drew me up to another circle of meniscus. We were in a second chamber, bigger than the first and this time furnished as a dwelling.

To one side there was a bed; on the other a low table with plates and bowls. The room was lit as before with small skylights. The mermaid slithered effortlessly up onto the rock floor and drew me into the room. I struggled up and found myself close to her, literally in her arms. She held my gaze for some moments before leaning down and pressing her lips to mine. The kiss was salty with the water of the ocean.

My head felt light. The Andamans, Cheng and the boat, my flat in Bangkok, my work as a tax accountant, Shelley and

Christchurch all seemed unreal to me now. My mind swam through coral seas, weaving through underwater caverns and opening to unseen, unimagined worlds beneath the waves. I had lost my fear of hallucination; this woman was real, was now the only reality. An hour ago all this would have been impossible, then as she drew me into her life it became merely wonderful. Now I was in her arms, the gaze of her golden eyes seemed all that mattered. I drew her head down to mine and savoured her kiss again. After some moments in this embrace, I fell back and lay in her arms. She began to stroke my hair and temples with gentle, rhythmic caresses. I felt quite at peace, the only sound the gentle lapping of the ocean's swell against the walls of the cave.

After a while she began to hum — a soft, melodic refrain that seemed to possess its own harmonies. As she sang, her voice changed, from a hum to a single voice and from there to a choir of voices, swelling and receding in volume, rising and falling in pitch. I closed my eyes and gave myself up to the stroking of my hair, back and forth, and the waves of her sweet song, swirling in my ears.

*

As love-struck as I was, I hadn't forgotten my buddy Cheng. I'd been gone from the boat more than two hours and he would soon begin to worry; he may already have set out to look for me.

I signalled to the mermaid that I had to go but promised I would be back. I was certain that she understood. As I recovered my mask and made to enter the water again, she clung to me gently, in a way that let me go but also meant she wanted me to stay.

I made my way back to the open sea. I swam quickly around the rocky islet, my arms pumping manically, my brain awash with the experiences of the last hours.

When I got back to the boat, Cheng was lazing with a book and a bottle of beer.

'What's with the alcohol?' I asked. 'Aren't we going to dive this afternoon?'

Cheng was annoyed: 'You were gone so long, I thought you'd decided to call it off, so I cracked a couple of beers.'

It suited me. We were approaching the end of the fishing boat charter anyway, so I suggested we head back to Havelock Island. On the way, I decided to confess everything to my friend. Cheng had been a good buddy to me since I arrived in Thailand, but by the time I'd uncovered the last detail of my adventure, he could hardly conceal his view that I'd lost my mind.

He was reminded of something: 'In Thailand we have the Ramakien, our national epic story. We all get taught it at school. It's the tale of Rama, prince of Ayutthaya, who defeats the evil Tosakan with the aid of an army of monkeys.'

'Thanks for the local colour, but what's the relevance?'

'One of the characters is Suphanna Matcha, the golden mermaid. She ends up falling in love with Hanuman, the monkey king.'

'So there are precedents for Thai mermaids?'

'The story originally comes from India.'

'Even better. We're in Indian waters now.'

'Henry, there are certainly precedents for Western men falling in love with exotic Eastern fantasies.'

'Yeah, well, I didn't expect anything different from you. Fantasy or not, I'm going back for her.'

'What, are you kidding? When?'

'Just as soon as I can deliver you back to Havelock Island. I can't involve you in this any further. You don't even believe she exists. You think of her in the same way as you think of a monkey king.'

'You're not coming back to Bangkok? What about your job? We're expected back in the office on Monday morning.'

I tried my best to persuade Cheng that my destiny lay here, but as we chugged across the calm blue ocean, surrounded by jungled islands, I slowly came to realise that he was right. I shouldn't throw away my career when a compromise was possible.

*

I worked hard for the next few months, until I had accumulated enough leave to return to the Andamans and the woman I had left behind. My idea was to re-establish contact with my mermaid and bring her back to share my life in Bangkok.

Although I could see many difficulties with this plan, when it came to putting it into action, everything worked well. I retraced the route I'd taken with Cheng only months before, found the islet and swam to the mermaid's lair. She wasn't there, but the place felt lived in, so I lay on her bed to await her return.

Before long, and without a splash, my love was in my arms and showering my mouth with kisses. It was just as it had been in the crazy daydreams I'd had every day since we'd parted.

We stayed together for a day in her secret home, establishing a means of communication, swimming and making love. Mermaids don't exactly have the same physical arrangements for this as land-based women do, but we didn't allow this flaw to compromise our devotion; we coupled spontaneously and passionately, as if every act of love should be like ours—a blend of opposites; a union between West and East, between land and sea.

We understood each other in bed, but things were less clear out of it. I still hadn't learnt her name, if indeed mermaids had names, so I decided to call her Kiri, after the celebrated New Zealand singer.

I explained to Kiri my plan to take her back with me and she seemed pleased. She would do anything, she seemed to say, if she could be with me. I took her as far as the mainland wrapped in a blanket, explaining to everyone who asked that she was sick. The airline even provided a wheelchair. In Kolkata, Kiri applied for a passport; I got her some shirts and a ticket to Bangkok and before long I was wheeling her from the airport with a long sarong concealing her tail.

We soon settled into a routine. I would spend the day at the office, Kiri would wheel herself around the flat, watch TV and cook our evening meal. She began to learn English from a set of DVDs. In the evenings, we would often go out. Bangkok's pavements are not designed for wheelchair users, and the difficulty of getting her into a taxi without exposing her tail ruled out that means of transport, so I bought a car with a wide back hatch and a chair-lift. The roof was high enough to accommodate Kiri in her wheelchair; it was a bit like the Popemobile. In this vehicle I would drive Kiri to one or other of the many shopping malls in the city. Kiri loved to look at the expensive stores and I bought her many gifts of tops, handbags and jewellery. We would occasionally dine out at seafood restaurants.

I began to sense that Kiri wasn't truly happy. After a couple of months in the condo, she told me what was wrong. The flat was too dry and her wheelchair-bound life too restrictive, she longed for the freedom of the ocean; she missed her family; and her scales were out of condition.

I cursed myself for my insensitivity. Of course it couldn't be right to keep a woman adapted to the sea on the seventh floor of a city tower. It hadn't occurred to me that Kiri would have a family of her own kind, but it was obvious, of course she must. And what she said about her lower half was easily apparent—the beautiful mirror-bright scales that had alerted me to her presence when we first met had turned dull, gunmetal grey. I bought sacks of salt in an attempt to create a seawater bath in the condo, but I can't have got the mix quite right; the shine would not return.

I could see only one way forward that would give Kiri the freedom she craved and maintain our relationship as a couple: we would return to her islands together. Within a week, I had resigned from my job. I sold the Popemobile at a huge loss and left most of my possessions with Cheng. With a couple of small suitcases, we flew back to the Andamans.

*

At Havelock Island, I bought a small dinghy which I thought would be useful, and chartered a boat to take us and the dinghy to our new home. The return to her islet was like a refreshing tonic for Kiri and she couldn't wait for our boat to chug the last few hundred metres to her home. When the captain's back was turned, she leapt from the wheelchair and over the side. Pausing to tear off her shirt, she dived like a dolphin and I watched as she streaked ahead of the boat. When we caught up, I loaded our luggage into the dinghy, paid off the captain and waved as the boat turned in a wide circle and motored away.

This was my new life. With that wave goodbye, I had left the world of my kind and come to live among the merfolk. I was apprehensive, but the strength of my love for Kiri made me supremely confident in the future.

We settled into Kiri's two-roomed cave. I tried hard to adapt to her customs, but still retained some of my human ways. I wore clothes, for example, read from the few books that I had managed to fit into my suitcase, and began to write this journal. As for food, Kiri caught fish and gathered a huge variety of other creatures — crabs, prawns, shellfish, urchins — as well as algae of different colours. Using these ingredients, she took great care in preparing our meals which she earnestly hoped I would find tasty. Occasionally I did, though I was slow to get used to eating everything raw.

In the course of our first few days together, Kiri was loving and attentive. The nights I lay in her arms after love-making confirmed that, despite the privations of living on raw fish in a damp cave, I had made the right decision.

The family that Kiri had missed so much in Bangkok soon made themselves known. The first to visit our cave, after a couple of days, was a young merman who Kiri introduced as her older brother. To my great surprise, he arrived on a seascooter, a small device not unlike a torpedo which pulls you through the water. When he had gone, I questioned Kiri about her brother's toy: 'Where did he get it?'

'He bought it from a trader.'

'You mean you have underwater shops?'

'Not underwater, the traders come on boats. They're fourlegs, so cannot come down from the air.'

'Fourlegs?'

'That's our name for your kind.'

'Your people do business with humans?'

'Of course, we buy whatever we need.' She indicated the plates, knives and other equipment in her kitchen.

'What does your brother do for a living? Where does he get the money?'

'He hunts as we all do. We can sell lobsters to the traders. My sister bought him the seascooter.'

'Does your sister have a job?'

'No, not a job, but she's married to a fourlegs.'

'Where do they live?'

'Quite close.'

*

The next day, Kiri announced that she was taking me to see her father and mother.

'Should we swim?' I asked, wondering if I should dress in my Sunday best for such an encounter.

'Of course, silly Henry,' she replied.

We swam to an adjacent rocky island and through a cave entrance not unlike the door to our own home. Inside we met an older mermaid, who I took to be Kiri's mother, and two young mermen, one of them the brother I'd met before.

Kiri's mother smiled and sang softly to me. I took this to be a welcome. When she spoke to Kiri, her daughter translated: 'Mother says you're very handsome. You must be a strong swimmer.' I thanked her.

We sat in a wide circle and smiled at each other. Kiri exchanged occasional chat with her mother and brothers, but there was little that she thought interesting enough to translate for me. After a while, a man's head appeared in the entrance. Kiri's father had white hair and a full white beard. He joined the group, but did little to acknowledge my presence. Instead he directed a number of urgent remarks to his wife, and to Kiri. He seemed to be giving instructions.

After a number of such exchanges, Kiri turned to me sadly: 'My father says it is not right for me to live on my own with a fourlegs. According to our custom, we must move into the family home or be married.

'Oh. Well, let's talk about this when we get home.'

On the short swim back I turned over in my mind the patriarch's decree. My first reaction was to refuse, but that would mean having to live with Kiri's parents, almost certainly restricting the intimacy I was now used to.

Was it sensible to commit myself to a woman I'd known for such a short while, and who wasn't technically a woman anyway? Then again, I was in love with Kiri and fully intended to be with her forever, so why not marry her? If that was the way things were done around here, I should go along with it.

When we got home, I proposed to Kiri. She went to get something from the back of the cave. It was a colourful and beautifully polished shell, like a clam, the size of her palm. She pulled the two halves of the shell apart. 'When these two shells join again,' she whispered, 'then shall my love be proved untrue.' And with that, she deftly threw one of the pair up, through the largest of the cave's skylights, and into the vast ocean beyond. The other she kissed and put away in a box I had given her to contain her precious jewels.

*

I confess I didn't look forward to our wedding, but the occasion was much less stressful than I had anticipated. Kiri took me to a distant island where there was a large cave filled with merfolk and, I was astonished to find, a number of humans, all of them men.

The guests sat in groups chattering in their melodic language. In the centre was a huge array of the food with which I had become familiar, and many bottles of Indian beer. There was no official ceremony that I could discern. Kiri and I were told to sit at one side, while the guests made their way over to us one by one for a greeting. Each guest presented us with a small gift, a shell or shark's tooth or, in one case, a carved cuttlefish bone. With my fellow humans I exchanged a few embarrassed words. I felt our common bond should make us friendly, but they seemed quite integrated into the merfolk community and were as uncommunicative as if they themselves had fishtails.

Everyone got merry on the beer and the party continued long after nightfall. Just as I was thinking it would be a good time to leave, we were approached by Kiri's father. Kiri translated as he said to me, 'Welcome to our family, fourlegs.'

'His name's Henry, father.'

'Oh well, welcome to our family anyway. You have enjoyed the wedding feast I think?'

'Oh yes, very much. The food was delicious, spectacular.'

'And you have taken our daughter as your wife.'

'I have. I promise always to love her.'

'That's good. For the party—food and drink and hire of the cave—and the bridal dowry, that'll be 800,000 rupees.'

Kiri translated these words without demur. She and her father waited for my reply. I was shocked. Nobody had mentioned a dowry. That was about 18,000 dollars New Zealand, a sizeable proportion of my savings.

'I didn't know about this. I'm not sure...'

'The party must be paid for, fourlegs. We cannot scoop beer from the ocean.'

'No, of course not. I'll pay for the party, but a dowry...'

'It's our custom, Henry,' explained Kiri softly. 'My family will lose respect in the community if their second daughter is valued as worthless by her husband.'

'But it's not my custom. We don't buy and sell women in New Zealand.'

'You're not in New Zealand, Henry.'

'Well, anyway, I don't have that much cash. I could hardly row the dinghy all the way back to Havelock Island.'

'That's no problem,' intoned the old man cheerfully, sensing he'd won the negotiation, 'we take credit cards.'

That night, Kiri was even more loving than usual. She assured me that she would never be unfaithful and that her family's demand for money was a one-off.

The next day, on leaving the cave, I was disappointed to find that my dinghy, which I had secured to a rock, was gone. I swam back to the cave to report this to Kiri and she told me in an offhand manner, 'Oh, my younger brother took it.'

'Oh did he? And when will he bring it back?'

'I didn't think you'd need it any longer, now we're married. Merfolk don't use boats. I told him he could sell it.'

With hindsight, I should have seen these two events as warnings. While the dowry was the largest amount of money I was asked to pay, it certainly wasn't the last. Over the next months I was presented with request after request. Many of these I declined, but when the pleading was done by a wife as beautiful and persuasive as mine, and the cause was one that appeared just, then some requests for money were impossible to refuse.

In human terms, the merfolk were poor. They lived in caves with the minimum of luxuries, they had no utilities, no source of food except what they could catch, and no comforts except those they could buy from human traders in their floating emporia. Kiri's technique — and I see it now as such — was to gently remind me of the disparity in the wealth of our two families. It was also to accept my refusals, though I found that each refusal was quickly followed by another, different request. When I said I wouldn't buy a seascooter for her younger brother, she seemed to understand, but a week later she told me she was worried about her mother's bed; it was giving her a bad back, she said. I paid for a new bed.

Over the months, Kiri went fishing less and less, pleading a wifely obligation to take care of me. Instead, she bought our food and provisions from the traders, turning to me for the money to pay them. The traders made shopping as convenient as possible; they had a machine to process credit cards and were always willing to give cash from a card withdrawal, on payment of a hefty commission.

With so many expenses at home and around my extended family, I soon lost track of my finances. Without bank statements and with no means of checking my account, I had to make do with keeping a running balance in my head. Before too long, the inevitable occurred — the traders told me a transaction had been refused and I owed them 9,000 rupees. This wasn't a huge amount of money, but nevertheless I didn't have it, nor did I have the means to earn it.

I explained the situation to Kiri, as casually as I could. I wondered if her father might lend me some money, after all he had her dowry. My wife flew into a rage. It would be quite out of the question to return any of the dowry, even as a loan. Her family would lose face and be a laughing-stock.

'I don't know what else I can do,' I said morosely.

'Are you telling me that you have no money?'

'Well, yes, I am.'

'But you are a fourlegs! You must be rich. How can you be penniless?'

'I was OK before, but living here is expensive.'

'Henry, you cannot stay here. The shame would be too great. You must go.'

'Go where?'

'Anywhere. Go and make some money. You have a wife.'

'And a wife's family,' I muttered bitterly.

It was meant as an aside, but she'd heard: 'Yes, my family. You want me to be ashamed of my family?'

The situation was beyond argument. I couldn't stay with my wife, the woman I loved, because I'd run out of funds. For nearly a year I had lodged in her heart but now I could no longer pay the rent.

I persuaded the traders that the best way to get their money back was to give me a lift to Havelock Island. There, I slept rough in a disued beach hut and got a job of sorts helping out at a dive school. My plan was to rebuild my finances and return to Kiri in solvent triumph.

It didn't work out quite like that; I earned very little money as a diving coach. More important, the longer I stayed away from Kiri, the less I wanted to return. What had I been thinking? I had married someone – something – who I now realised belonged to another species. Our lovemaking began to seem weird, then a gross perversion. Had I really coupled with a fish? It became like a dream to me now, a dream from which I would wake to find the horrific reality: Kiri's top half had been human only in my imagination, her breasts a fantasy, her arms and lips mere wishful thinking; I'd find myself in bed with an enormous tuna. I recoiled from the memory of my shameful acts and resolved to escape as soon as possible.

I saved enough for a flight to Kolkata. I had no idea where I would go from there, but it seemed like the first step towards home, wherever that was.

*

It proved to be the last step I would take for a while. As I write this journal, I am still in Kolkata. Still penniless, I live on the streets with hundreds of thousands of others. I'm taller than most and, under the grime, whiter, but otherwise I'm just like them. I receive rice and vegetables from a mission; I sleep under a trestle table in the market and scavenge for glass and plastic bottles which I can sell for a pittance by walking four clicks to a recycling dump.

I dream occasionally of heading home, of dragging my filthy body into the New Zealand consulate in Kolkata and saying, 'You're not going to believe this, but I'm a Kiwi.' Then reality returns: at best they'd contact my next of kin, my parents. Perhaps the call would go through on a Sunday. Mum would be preparing the salads for lunch; Dad would be outside, turning lamb chops on the barbeque. Carter would be slugging from a bottle of Cassel's with his arm around Shelley, his pregnant wife.

Mum would stop at the back door with the phone: 'It's a call from India, darling, something about Henry.'

I've moved from a condo to a cave and from a cave to the gutter, but there are some things I could never do.

Boxing Days

26 December 1975, Boston

This has really been the most trying Christmas ever. Granny Braid is losing her mind and Grandpa Braid has lost his hips. You'd think between the two of them they'd constitute one decent grandparent, but it doesn't seem to work like that. How much more jolly it would be with the Nelsons. But I suppose it's because they're so much more capable that they're spending Christmas in their own home.

We have been practically confined to the house since Granny and Grandpa arrived on the 23rd and, since then, the place has been like a sanatorium. Every downstairs room is strewn with half-drunk cups of tea and there are biscuit crumbs all over the furniture. I sit down to watch something on TV and the sofa is gritty with ginger-nut granules. Granny reacts to everything with a look of extreme surprise, as if to say: 'Gosh, I've put my dentures in upside down again. Oh look, there's bread sauce all down my front. I look like I'm in a porn movie!' If she hoists her eyebrows any higher I swear they'll disappear under her wig.

When Granny gets in a scrape, Grandpa gallantly goes to her assistance but, what with the two sticks, by the time he's made it across the room, the crisis has usually been averted.

Poor old boy. I don't know what's worse: to lose your pins or your marbles. Mum's being *faux* brave; Dad's just being Dad, like a marble statue of the Laughing Cavalier. Nothing seems to faze him.

Christmas has always been a magic time. You wake up on Christmas morning and it's nothing like waking up on any other day. Its specialness lasts all day. This year there was a fair amount of champagne at lunch so some of us — those who could stand unaided — went for a bracing walk around the village to sober up.

Going for a walk on Christmas day is special. It's not only that there are so few people about (or that you exchange festive pleasantries with the ones you do pass), it's the very idea of doing something as ordinary as going for a walk on a day reserved for revelry and celebration. The air seems to be Christmas air, the pavements Christmas pavements. I hope I never lose this feeling. I hope that, if I have kids, I can relay this feeling to them.

Mimi's boyfriend Stephen joined us in the evening for Christmas dinner, so I suppose it must be serious. Either that or he had nowhere else to go (and that's possible). So there were eight around the table: Mum and Dad, Dad's parents, Mimi and Stephen going all doe-eyed across the steaming turkey, Lucy, and me.

Stephen's OK, but I'd prefer it if he didn't consider his best chance of getting into my sister's knickers (where I'm pretty certain he has yet to venture) was to fawn shamelessly over everything Dad says. Even when Dad tells us the same story he related the day before, Stephen guffaws like a hyena as if Peter Ustinov himself had dropped in to impart a freshly-minted anecdote. Dad has probably been wearing a yellow waistcoat since they were fashionable sometime in the last century. Blow me down, but Stephen turns up yesterday wearing a yellow waistcoat. My Dad's is threadbare, but at least it looks as if it was once a class piece of schmutter, possibly even tailored; Stephen's has the M&S label hanging out the neck. Not really, but we get the idea.

The worst thing about Christmas this year is that I'm not spending it with Jo. I miss her a lot. I've called her every day since I got here a week ago, being careful to do so in the evenings, while the others are watching TV and so unable to hear me in the hall. Then I go out into the garden, look up at the stars and watch my breath disappearing into the cold air. Somehow it makes me feel closer to her, to think that she could see the same stars from Edinburgh and that, in some small way, we are breathing the same air.

I thought about the pheromones that moths exude to attract mates. The female squirts out some infinitesimally small amount of scent which, carried on the breeze, gets diluted so much that, downwind, the hapless male is left sniffing around for single molecules of the stuff to give him a clue as to where the talent lies. He flaps his way up the concentration gradient, the smell getting stronger and stronger, until he finds himself in the arms of his highly scented beloved (for which read, the wings of some strange female with whom he will shortly have his way). That's how I'd like it to be with Jo. She's up there in Edinburgh, taking the night air. She senses a beery molecule that has wafted up from Lincolnshire and gets all broody, images of chubby caterpillars in bonnets clouding her reason, and tipsily prepares for the imminent arrival of her moth-prince. She has only to wait until 17 January when, glory of glories, we'll be together again in Norwich.

We tried to spend some time together earlier this vacation, but with two sets of family obligations it just wouldn't work out. We could have gone up to Cromer for a couple of days, or even down to London. These were our fantasies. Family obligations were one thing, but money was another. Although we're both in our third year, neither of us has two new pence to rub together and we had to admit that splitting off back to our families for Christmas was really the only financially viable option. We're both having to deal with geriatric relatives but at least the central heating's free.

I had six family presents to buy, which is always a bit of a strain on a grant, and this year I had Jo to buy for too. That was something completely new. I had no idea what she would get for me. I didn't want to be mean and I didn't want to over-do it. Jewellery? Not really feasible, so I got her a sexy camisole top, *Ariel* by Sylvia Plath, Bob's *Blood on the Tracks* and some perfume. The perfume was the most difficult. There's a scent I sometimes catch in the street, when I pass well-dressed women, that makes me want to follow them and give them babies. I suppose it must be my pheromone trigger. I wanted to find that exact perfume for Jo, but nothing smelt quite so good in the cosmetics department of Jarrold's. I sniffed so many scents that the girl was getting annoyed, so I bought a bottle of Chloe which the girl said is new and which she described as 'romantic with an intensive floral aroma' in a broad Norfolk accent. I suppose it could have been a Norfolk Broads accent. I thought, doesn't that describe every perfume? But I bought it anyway, just to get out of the shop without further embarrassment.

Anyway, Jo's middle name is Chloe and I couldn't find a perfume called 'Jo', so I reckon I did as well as a boyfriend of one term could be expected to do. We exchanged gifts on our

146

last day together. Jo gave me a rucksack with the promise that we'd hitch around Greece together after our finals.

26 December 1980, Derby

A couple of months ago in a pile of old papers I found the one-day diary I wrote exactly five years ago. I've decided to turn what I probably intended as a one-off (anyway, it *was* a one-off until now) into a tradition: jot down snapshots of a single day that will aid my memory of the intervening events.

This is our first Christmas away from home. With the house sale only completed in October, it has taken us until now to get the place in some sort of order. It's small but it's very cosy and we love it so much we really didn't want to leave it over Christmas. There was a bit of pressure from Mum because Lucy and Mimi were both going to be at home, so I just had to brazen it out and promise Boxing Day instead. Jo's parents were fine about it. Her sister has a new baby (their first grandchild) which was probably enough to distract them.

We went completely crazy with the decorations. We had a real tree with flashing lights and glass balls which we decorated together last week. I spent at least three evenings making paper chains out of strips of gummed paper from Woolworth's. These go from corner to corner in the living room and I also strung them around the walls of the dining room. We hung Christmas cards on loops of tape around the picture rail in the hall. Jo made a holly wreath for the front door, but I don't think we've had a visitor since she put it up, apart from the postman, who we had to tip. We don't get milk delivered.

We wanted Jane and Garry to come over for Christmas dinner, but Jane's father is a widower and Jane herself is an only child, so they felt they had to go to his place in Birmingham, as they have for the last three years. I almost heard myself suggesting that they bring him along too, but I thought better of it. It would have been a charitable act of quite sickening proportions, but his presence would have completely changed the dynamics of the occasion. Also, I suddenly thought, what would I buy Jane's Dad (whom I've never met) for a present?' The faithful socks idea would have been a non-starter as the old boy has only got one leg, though I suppose he puts a sock on his plastic foot, just for symmetry, so maybe it would've all worked out OK.

As a consolation, we went out for a drink with them last Friday. Garry and I had been to the office Christmas party the night before so were feeling a bit fragile. Jo's was a sit-down lunch with six members of her department in an Italian restaurant. She hates them all, so was determined not to enjoy herself, but she still managed to drink so much Valpolicella that, when she was sick in the waste paper bin under her desk, it was red. She found her boss asleep in the boardroom and, the next evening, helped me fantasise about how she might use the information. Despite having a laugh, we decided it wasn't really very incriminating; in fact, his peers would probably admire him for connecting so effectively with his staff.

We decided to have our turkey at lunch time on Christmas Day. However, what with one thing and another, we didn't get up until late and it was only around 10.30am that Jo read the cooking instructions which were stuck to the bird. It was going to take four hours to cook and she hadn't stuffed it yet. We began thinking in terms of four o'clock for lunch, which meant we had to have a big breakfast to tide us over. We drank buck's fizz with our toast and yoghurt, got dressed and started on the red wine around midday, to go with the present opening. I'd bought six bottles of some rather pricey claret. I think that was when we thought there would be four of us.

I gave Jo a winter coat and a pair of shoes, both of which she knew about because she'd had to try them on, and actually chose them. I wasn't sure about records because *Slow Train Coming* was a bit of a shock last year, but I bought her *Saved* anyway. It's not my fault if Bob's got himself born again, though I'm a little confused about how a Jew can get reborn as a Christian. Even if it's bad, she still needs it to keep her collection complete. I also gave her Seamus Heaney's *Selected Poems* and, as a complete surprise, a gold and amethyst necklace which she really seemed to like. Jo gave me a shirt and a jumper and a circular saw, which I had dropped a couple of hints about. That's for redoing the floorboards in our bedroom. Also some silver cufflinks for work. Rolls-Royce likes the men to wear suits, and if I'm going to go along with that I might as well do it properly. Garry's always pretty well turned out, so we're going to have an escalating fashion war, which I will win.

Christmas lunch itself, served pretty close to dinner time, was fine, though the turkey was still a bit pink (isn't that supposed to be dangerous?), the potatoes didn't crisp like my Mum's and the sprouts were over-boiled. Still, it was our first attempt and I'm sure we'll get better at it over the years. We have our whole lives ahead of us! We'd drunk so much claret by the time the meal was ready that we both had difficulty staying awake to eat it. We forgot to pull the crackers and neither of us could manage any Christmas pudding, despite the effort Jo put into the brandy butter. It'll keep.

*

Today, we drove over to Mum and Dad's (as I now refer to the house in which I was born and which I used to call 'home') for lunch and to exchange gifts with the family. Grandpa Braid was there, newly mobile having had two new hips inserted over the last couple of years. He's walking with only one stick now. Also in attendance were Granny and Grandpa Nelson, popularly known as Sheila and Barry. They still seem to be reasonably with it and both now apparently play golf which was a new one on me and of course twice as bad as one of them playing golf. Today they wore matching polo shirts at lunch because they'd played nine holes in the morning. It must have been a very geriatric form of the game because Barry's nearly 80 and Sheila can't be far behind. Barry's quite robust for a man of his age, and still tells funny stories, though they're not quite as funny as I remembered. Sheila has taken to finishing his sentences for him, which he seems to regard as a useful service. Jo said afterwards that she'd throttle me if I ever did that to her.

Lucy is in her last year at Oxford and is thinking about doing a PhD. She has turned out to be the brainy one of the family. What did she want to do her PhD on? She was interested in family migrations in 18th and 19th Century Wales. I said that, fascinating though the peregrinations of antique Taffies undoubtedly was, I thought the whole point of being an anthropologist was that you got to spend three years living in a grass hut in Polynesia. She saw my point but explained *sotto voce* that that wouldn't work because of Peter who was a forestry consultant.

'A forestry consultant to whom?' I enquired.

'Mostly national parks,' Lucy said.

'National parks where?'

'Oh, places like Snowdonia and the Brecon Beacons.'

'So Peter is basically Wales-based then.'

'Yes.'

'And Peter is…?'

Peter is her significant other. It's very sweet to see Lucy so coy. She hasn't introduced this guy to Mum and Dad yet, and this conversation was conducted in conspiratorial whispers, though she didn't ask me not to tell anyone. Maybe I'm supposed to be her conduit for leaking the news.

Mimi was heavily pregnant. I knew about this, of course, but it was still a shock to see my sister with a bump. The next generation. My immediate thought was that she was going for a virgin birth, though Stephen had an unattractively smug look about him that I haven't seen on Joseph's face, not as represented by the figure in Mum's crib anyway, so he may have worked out how to do the dirty deed. It just goes to show how inept Joseph must have been.

At lunch I found myself sitting next to Stephen, so I felt I ought to converse. I knew he was something in local government, but asked for more detail. 'How local? Did he collect the bins or what?' He smiled long-sufferingly. I'm Mimi's younger brother so, now they're married, he feels he can treat me like a younger brother too. It's an unpleasant side-effect of the in-law thing. He's apparently a manager in the planning department of Lincolnshire County Council.

'That must be a busy job,' I commented sarcastically, thinking about the space centre and yacht marina not being built in Boston, and the high-rise financial district which hasn't been suggested for Spalding. Sarcasm can be a cruel weapon to use on a council official but, honestly, how much planning does a pea field really need?

26 December 1985, Lincoln

This is the third year we've been invited to Mimi's for Christmas. She's the one with the kids, and Christmas is a family occasion, so it does seem logical. The age range at lunch went from Grandpa Braid at 91 to Jack Halpin at just over one. I suppose Mum and Dad are looking to me to produce the next grandchild, but right now that doesn't look like happening any time soon.

I am aching with love for Miriam and could hardly bear to think of her yesterday, stuck in some awful loveless Christmas horror movie with the loathsome Ian. Actually, to be fair, having never met the bloke, I can't speak for him being so completely odious, but he hasn't been such a good husband to Miriam. The attention he pays her, he deserves to lose her.

I couldn't contact her yesterday as it would have created too much suspicion, but this morning I walked around the block and called her from a phone box when I knew Ian would be out with his football mates. She was a little tearful. She's ready to leave him and wanted to know what I would do. I said walking out on Jo was impossible but that I loved her deeply. Miriam's waiting for me to jump ship first.

We had 12 for Christmas lunch: Grandpa Braid, Sheila Nelson, Mum and Dad, Mimi and Stephen plus Herbie and Jack, Lucy and Peter, Jo and me. I was watching Jo and thinking how well she copes with my family, no matter how strange they might be. I still love her. I couldn't do anything to hurt her. Yet I'm so glad I met Miriam. I feel trapped, loving two women. Can that ever work?

Lucy seems happy. I love my lovely sister Lucy. She's so sweet and doesn't seem to mind Mimi's role as rising matriarch of the Braid clan. She's got a teaching job at Cardiff

University and is working for her PhD at the same time — something about people migrating between villages. I didn't catch the detail but then I never do understand PhD topics. Perhaps that's the whole point of them. Peter seems to be making her happy. He's a nice guy for a tree consultant. I always expect him to look like the Green Man and smell of resin. His vegetarianism is a little awkward at Christmas, but Mimi managed to palm him off with a quiche and he seemed pretty happy with that, at least for a tree consultant.

I couldn't get Jo anything too soppy this year as it would have felt like hypocrisy, and disloyal to Miriam, so I bought her a CD player with a few discs, including *Empire Burlesque*. I knew she'd hate the idea of having two formats, but vinyl can't go on forever. She may even have to start re-buying her whole collection on CD. She'll come round to the idea in the end. She gave me some clothes which were so exactly right that I nearly burst out crying on the spot. I've known her for ten years and we operate like one person. I feel like a bastard, but I'm not a completely free agent. Other people are involved.

26 December 1990, Bristol

Although we have lived here for nearly five years, yesterday was the first time that my parents had set foot in our home. The visitation was surely a sign that bygones have been examined and discovered indeed to be bygones, or it could have been a climax to the tension that was surely building, especially in my mother, from having not yet seen their latest set of grandchildren in person.

Photos of chubby proto-humans, no matter how strong the family likeness, are unlikely to satisfy a grandmother for long. The pressure built up behind the dam, the masonry creaked and the deluge arrived on Christmas morning. My mother kissed me lightly twice, Miriam once, and then submerged herself in the cheeks, chins and cheekiness of Oscar, now three, and Gwen, only 13 months.

My father was more interested in the shelves I had put up and the shed I'd had installed half-way down the garden. He was intrigued to see how I'd moled a little tunnel between the house and my new male hideaway to take an electric cable, a branch from the mains water and a phone line. As the railroad had civilised the West, so had I brought modernity to previously unconquered parts of the garden.

'You could get quite a brew-up going in here,' my father remarked.

'I was thinking more in terms of diluting my Scotch,' I said, showing him the niche I'd made to take two bottles.

He looked a little disappointed, as if he were a teetotaller, which he isn't. It's natural to have higher standards for your kids than the ones you observed yourself at a similar age; otherwise we'd be on a gradient of steady decline.

Oscar and Gwen are grandchildren numbers three and five, Lucy having produced Fiona somewhere between our two. I think my mother blames Miriam for the breakup of my marriage to Jo. She doesn't make eye contact easily with my wife and she is a little more explicit in her disagreements with Miriam on points of baby-care than I would expect from a guest in our house, even if it is my mama. I'm pretty sure it doesn't matter that much how you respond to a cry in the night, as long as it doesn't involve firearms.

My father probably has a better grasp of what actually happened. He sometimes gives me knowing looks which I think are meant to say that he's a man of the world and understands the motivations that guide those unfortunate enough to possess a Y-chromosome. But I believe his knowingness is a construct, designed to keep him and me on the same side. My mother was almost certainly his first lover. Though he may have had an eye for a girl or two in the brief period between reaching sexual maturity and marrying my mother, I really don't think it went any further than having an eye. So, when he looks at me in that way, it is as if to say that he has read about my predicament in books or seen screen lovers agonising in similar circumstances. I don't value his sympathy any less for that, in fact I find the effort that he makes to be my pal very touching.

I opened a bottle of champagne when my parents arrived and, after the excitement of becoming acquainted with the grandchildren had died down, we exchanged gifts. I bought Miriam a watch (quite expensive) and some diamond earrings (very expensive). When we first met, she defined Bob in terms of *Blowin' in the Wind*, but last year, after constantly replaying what I thought was a great album, I saw her mouthing some of the words from *Oh Mercy*, so this year I gave her the CD of *Under the Red Sky* and she seemed not unpleased. She has an easy way with smiles. She gave me a Canon lens and a pair of cowboy boots which she'd had to send away for to London. They're a perfect fit; I feel the part.

Miriam is a calm and competent cook and the feast we consumed on Christmas Day was prepared to perfection. I tried to keep the level of joviality high by introducing standard activities like pulling crackers and so on as if they were the greatest comedic innovations, but even so Christmas was a fairly sombre occasion, enjoyable but serious.

Today we went to a matinee of *Snow White* in town. Dad couldn't hear what was going on and Gwen grizzled through most of the second half. Pantomimes can be very long. We nearly agreed to leave before the curtain, but Oscar remained enthralled to the end, so we stayed for his sake.

Mum and Dad are leaving tomorrow. I hope this has broken the ice and that we'll be able to get over to Boston more often in the future.

26 December 1995, HMP Horfield, Bristol

After last year's turkey roll—for which read, all the bits of a turkey that weren't recognisable enough to go into a Drummer—yesterday I opted for the halal beef Italienne. I thought it would be a suitably surreal culinary accompaniment to another day of pointless tedium.

That was Christmas.

There is never much to do in this place. Even less so at this time of year when the non-essential staff are on holiday, so there are no classes, the workshop is closed and visits are not allowed. I have a stock of books and I was permitted to watch television until six o'clock this evening, at which point it was deemed to be bedtime. It was probably dark outside, so they may have had a point.

The men's skin is the first thing you notice; smooth, pale cheeks like waxworks, apparently blemish-free. It's the ultra-violet light, and perhaps the wind, that makes men on the outside so rugged. Keep us in the sheltered dark for a few years and, like mushrooms, we grow ghostly white with a flawless epidermis, suitable for boiling, stir-fry or serving raw. The black boys complain of the same thing; they say they're growing pale without the ripening power of the sun of the Caribbean, or of Lagos or Addis Ababa. They're going stir-crazy imagining they come from anywhere but St Paul's.

Whatever their original colour, there were a lot of long faces in here yesterday, and some tears too. Hard men were feeling sorry for themselves. Christmas reminds them that they have families who are growing up without them. The chaplain comes around more often at this time of year, looking pious, and the governor gives us sweets to show that the society he represents has sympathy for our plight, but only to the extent of a handful of toffees as weighed against five years of confinement. It is not my view that society should feel sorry for me. I am being punished for committing a crime. If they regret the sentence, let them show their repentance by knocking off some time, not with jelly-babies.

The chaplain would be better employed ministering to the victims of these bad men. In my case, that would be awkward as my misdemeanour was as close to a victimless crime as you can get. The shareholders of my erstwhile employer may have suffered to some extent, but probably unknowingly, and their loss would surely have been offset by insurance. The impact of my offence was therefore highly dissipated. I didn't so much shoot a fox as stamp on a nest of ants. Few people shed a tear for a squashed insect.

*

'Steal a little and they throw you in jail; steal a lot and they make you a king,' as the man said. Those words have rumbled around inside my head these last few days. Next it'll be some line from David Bowie or it could easily be Jethro Tull. There's no telling how these gems bubble to the surface. Bob Dylan doesn't often get it wrong, and he's probably spot-on this time too, for the *general case*. But what makes me so smug, and will get me through until the end of next year — my designated release date — is the knowledge that, although I was indeed thrown in jail, I had not stolen a little; and, while they did not see fit to bestow on me the crown of the realm and all its attendant privileges (it was, after all, already taken), they do seem to have given up looking for the spoils of my larceny to which I will have immediate access on my release.

I was allocated to this most unglamorous of clinks in response to a request from my brief that, if it please the court, I wished to be close to my young family. In exchange for pleading guilty, it was the least they could do. Thus accorded convenience, Miriam would bring the kids to visit me often, so maintaining the bonds of fatherhood which, in so many cases, moulder and slip away from lack of use. And so it was for the first couple of years. We had painful, emotional, tense meetings in the visitor centre, and occasional phone calls, me standing in my Perspex bubble with a jeering queue along the landing.

Now, Miriam's aim is to draw away from me as you might try to rid yourself of a drunk on the late-night bus. The shame of having a husband in choky is more than she can bear and I feel sure that, being a beautiful young woman, she continues to attract the kind of attention to which she will eventually succumb.

I have constructed my litter and I am required to recline thereon.

My children are a different matter. I haven't given up on them as I am prepared to do with Miriam. However, as they are now eight and six years old, they are capable of understanding that their daddy has done something bad. They are old enough too to realise that my current domicile is a loathsome billet. I would prefer it if they did not associate their father with his present circumstances. I am actually quite relieved that they no longer visit. I will be out soon. I will be rich. I will pick up with them at a point when the moonlight fell on us softly — before the rozzers came to call —

rather than the last time I hugged them in the blinding fluorescence of the linoleum hell they reserve here for family contact.

The fraud was so simple I could hardly believe my luck. Being in procurement I knew I was under a risk-management spotlight; I thought that each time it worked would be the last. I'd send off the documents expecting with that action to feel a mighty fist gripping my shoulder and hear some gruff agent address me in cod-Scotland Yard: 'You're nicked, Sunshine,' or similar.

It was this very expectation of imminent discovery that coaxed me to be prudent in processing the spoils. A more confident felon might have stuck it all in a Halifax Easy Access savings account. But I reasoned that, once they'd rumbled me, they'd be into such an instrument before nightfall; hence the numerous conferences that I reluctantly attended *sur le continent*. If I said to Miriam it was Belgium, it was Liechtenstein; if I said it was Holland, it was still bloody Liechtenstein. They don't ask many questions in Liechtenstein if you need help to lift your suitcase of cash on to the counter. I find a bank an invigorating place to do business when I have a copious supply of what they want (money) and clearly have no regard for what to them is anathema (scruples).

When I leave, and re-acquaint myself with my nest-egg, before I make contact with my children and come to an accommodation with their mother concerning our future relations, I plan to spend some weeks — no, months — lying on some expensive beach, all the while being fed *amuse-bouche* and sweetmeats by caramel-coloured maidens whose only wish is my contentment. I'm thinking of St Lucia, Thailand, Fiji, wherever is the most expensive.

26 December 2000, Marriott Hotel, Bristol

Having lost the freehold of the house in Clifton to Miriam, and having not been offered a bed for the night in the guest room, I am staying here for two days to take up my rights of visitation.

Not that I have many rights, Miriam having cited my criminal nature and my adultery with May as reasons that I should never see my children again. Hey, but it's Christmas and the ice-maiden has relented, at least to the extent of seven hours on Boxing Day.

I flew in on Christmas Eve, hired a car and drove with some trepidation straight to Mimi's house in Lincoln. The place was a riot of children and other young persons. Herbie's 19 now and Jack 16. Lucy's three girls, Fiona, Sophie and Kate, range from 13 down to about six. Good ages. All ages are good. Stephen was rushing around in an apron fixing drinks. Mum was a little unsure on her feet, but got up with the aid of a stick when I arrived.

I haven't seen any of my family since my incarceration and their smiles were grim, but they *were* smiles. I suppose the way they see it is: I didn't murder anyone; I brought shame on the family but I've been punished and it's all over. Mimi greeted me with a bracing kiss on the cheek, Lucy with a hug. I also got a hug from Mum, which is unusual for her, so a true sign of forgiveness. Herbie punched my knuckles in greeting, in recognition perhaps of the kudos he has acquired by having an old lag for an uncle.

Christmas Day was a simulation of Christmases past. All the requisite activities were there — the same tree, the same crib (really; Mum seems to have brought it with her), the same feast — but the personnel had changed. No grandparents anymore, not for a long time, and no-one sitting in the chair that Dad always liked, but these ghosts have been replaced by a hoard of lively youngsters who bring a different joy to the occasion.

I brought gifts for everyone from Bangkok, where I stopped off for two days *en route* from Koh Chang for Christmas shopping. I think my family looks on me as a little exotic. Stephen was keen to know about my circumstances in Thailand, by which I took him to mean where and how I lived. I told them about the beach hut and the house we're building behind it, now perhaps half complete. Who had designed it, he wanted to know. I did, I explained quite proudly, with the assistance of a local builder whom I trusted. And did I need planning permission? I explained that consent wasn't a problem. We bought the plot in May's name and could build what we wanted, as far as I knew.

'You'd love it,' I said to Peter as my confidence in their acceptance of me grew. 'We have coconut palms, sea almond and casuarinas along the beach and, higher up, yellow cassia, frangipani, coral trees and breadfruit. Those are just the ones I can name. We also have a large variety of palms. You must come out with Lucy and the girls and help me identify all the trees.'

'I'd have to read them up first,' he replied ponderously. 'I'm more at home with the temperate flora.'

'Who's Temperate Flora? I want to know why you're more at home with her than with me,' joked Lucy while being mauled by Sophie, standing on her mother's lap.

Mum plucked up the courage to ask about May. I explained that we'd met in Chiang Mai more than three years ago when I first went out there and had done some travelling around the country. She's 22 years old and we were married in her home village last year.

'But, Richard! How could you marry someone so young?' My mother risked bursting the wobbly bubble of our new accommodation.

'She's not *that* young, Mum. She's 22,' I replied, artfully.

'Young compared with you, I mean.'

'That's very common in Thailand,' I claimed, playing the *different culture* card. 'It means nothing to them and, if it means nothing to May, it means nothing to me.'

'But she'll want children.'

'She will. But that's all right. I'm actually only 46. That's not so old. Anyway, she's five months pregnant.'

That knocked the wind out of their sails. Mum and Mimi bristled; Lucy offered her congratulations.

The conversation drifted on like that for most of the day. It was OK with me. I had nothing to be ashamed of anymore and I reasoned that the more they got to know the new me, the better it would be for everyone.

*

I drove the four hours here to Bristol, starting early this morning, and picked up Oscar and Gwen at midday. We went for lunch at a pizza place, then packed in as much as possible into the time we had — ice skating, shopping and the planetarium. I brought them back to the hotel for supper from room service. I wanted them to remember me in some kind of home. Even though it's only a hotel, their memory of me will probably be in this room, at least until I can arrange for them to visit me in my natural habitat in Koh Chang.

My children thought it very grand to have food delivered to their bedroom by a man in a black waistcoat. After supper, they jumped on the bed until it was wrecked.

I sketched them a floor plan of the new house, with labels for 'Oscar's Room' and 'Gwendolyn's Room', showing that each had its own bathroom and toilet.

'You don't have to call it *Gwendolyn's*,' my daughter pointed out, deflecting for a moment from her excitement of having her own suite. '*Gwen's* will do.'

I delivered Oscar and Gwen back to Miriam at seven o'clock. She didn't invite me in. Still no room at the inn. I hadn't asked Oscar if Mummy had a boyfriend because I suspected she would grill him later to find out how jealous I was. I decided I didn't care. On the doorstep (of my old house) I told Miriam I would try to get back to England every couple of years and would be grateful if I could see my children on these occasions.

'It's OK if it is only every couple of years,' she said.

26 December 2005, Koh Chang, Thailand

By rights, this should be the last entry in my quinquennial journal. I'm 51 years old, I have two families that I love, I'm married to the most exciting woman on the island of Koh Chang, I've built my own house in paradise, and I have enough money in the bank to make our enjoyable little business merely a hobby.

By a trick of arithmetic, my diary year was not 2004. A year ago today was when the tsunami struck, killing a quarter of a million people, adding a word to the average Thai's vocabulary, providing newsreel pictures for the locals here to watch in silence for two or three weeks, but not really touching their hearts.

Mum was on the phone within 12 hours, imagining the bloated bodies of her son and his young family swilling around amid the sodden wreckage of their lives, as was the case for so many. For her it looked close. For Koh Changers, it had struck across the bay and the other side of the isthmus. If they had no family down there, it was just one of those things that happen. It takes more than a sub-sea earthquake to send a ripple across the Thai countenance.

For us, it nailed a question mark over the site we'd chosen for our home, not that we could do anything about it except sell up and leave. The house is no more than 50 metres from the beach, perhaps one or two metres above sea level at high tide. We would take the slap of a tsunami right in the face. We built our house stronger than the local standard, but not strong enough to stop it falling over on first impact.

If a tsunami is unlikely — and historically it is — we have rising sea levels due to climate change to be concerned about.

But do we worry? Of course not. If we get flooded out, it's just one of those things that happen.

On the beach in front of our house is where May and I first lived on Koh Chang, in a two-room bamboo hut that we rented from someone who clearly had no right to build it there. Later, when our house was complete, we bought the hut and demolished it as it obstructed the otherwise perfect view from our front rooms.

We used the bamboo poles and screens to build a bar-restaurant on the beach, a little off to the right. It's a ramshackle affair, not very waterproof when it rains, not very sand-proof when the wind blows; but it attracts a certain demographic from among Koh Chang's visitors. It provides a challenge for May and a social life for us both. During the monsoon, we take it down, put the materials and furniture into storage and take a three-month vacation.

The place is called May's Cookhouse. We have a cocktail bar and a restaurant area with ten tables and forty chairs. I don't think we have ever filled them all, so a reservation is not required. I choose the music. *Hotel California, Take Me Home, Country Road* and *Bad Moon Rising,* which are played in all other bars on the island, seemingly on tape loops, are banned. Bob, Van and Joni are the staples. It surprises customers to find they're listening to *Love and Theft* on a hick island beach in Thailand. They often come back because of it.

Yesterday, for the first time, we did a special Christmas menu. May saw it as extra work, but I persuaded her to make the change as a bit of fun. We roasted a turkey and a goose, both brought in at some expense from Australia, did roast potatoes, sprouts, parsnips and all the traditional stuffings, gravies and sauces. We charged 450 baht a head, a huge premium on our usual tariff, but managed to sell 28 covers. We shifted a lot more wine than usual too, so the total take was enormous, and we'd only done it for a laugh. I saw May smiling as she counted the money around three o'clock this morning. I didn't say, 'I told you so,' and she didn't acknowledge the origin of the idea, but we both knew. I did anyway.

Today has been a lazy day, playing with the boys, clearing up the Cookhouse in preparation for a low-key lunch-time crowd.

There's no reason why any of this should change over the next pentad; thus subsequent diary entries may well become repetitive and unnecessary. Signing off...

26 December 2010, Bel Air

The way I recall it, Morgan Quincy oozed into the Cookhouse, her breasts like cantaloupes and her hair like fire. I mixed her a Bloody Mary and she held the cherry between her lips like a ripe corpuscle she'd sucked from my surrendering heart.

She mounted a bar stool and crossed her legs. The swell of her thighs shone bright as horse flanks.

She informed me lasciviously that her father was a billionaire electromagnet magnate from Chicago.

I declared my list of assets. It was short: a shack on the beach, proven criminal tendencies and a vapour trail of spent wives. She didn't seem to mind that much. When I went to refresh her drink, she grabbed me by the balls and kissed me like an Electrolux.

Here in this LA mansion, a love-gift from daddy, we have a view of Catalina Island, eight bedrooms, a cinema, a pool designed by Liberace after Herculaneum, and seven invisible servants. There may well be a kitchen; it's rude to pry. Somewhere there's a yacht, a jet, a corporation and a machine that dispenses cash.

I have a little gallery in Rodeo Drive which I visit once or twice a week to *waft*. I deal mostly in the abstract impressionists. We dine with stars and men with trimmed white beards, give money away through our ostentatious foundation and make love with urgency and delight in unusual places.

But still the fantasy leaves me cold.

*

Yesterday we exchanged gifts by the pool.

It wasn't easy to get it finished by Christmas, but a 1,000-baht bonus promised to each of the men did the trick. By the tree we raised our glasses to our completed house.

'Let's give it a name,' May said.

'Bel Air,' I replied, as if I'd just had the idea.

We kissed as our boys splashed about in the pool.

Now, from here behind the Cookhouse bar, I can see the tree lights in our garden. I've put on *Christmas in the Heart* as a thank-you to Bob for sticking by me from the beginning.

May is favouring a few hung-over customers with her golden smile. Bramwell, now nine, and Tyson, eight, are teasing a litter of beach-cat kittens under a table. Oscar, on vacation from college, is expected tomorrow; Gwen perhaps next year.

The perfection is a challenge to my dreams, but it couldn't be any other way than this.

Vice-Versa

The Magneto was busy for a Tuesday night. As with the other go-go bars on Walking Street, business at this popular establishment was generally slower during the week, when the hordes of tourists were joined by fewer local residents — the ones who had to get up early for work at least. Sam's friends preferred the Magneto on a quieter night; conversation was easier and there was less competition for the various services the bar provided.

Sam and Chris entered through the black curtain together. It was a regular haunt for a number of their pals and they were not surprised to find a third Westerner of their acquaintance already nursing a drink at the bar.

Before they even had a chance to sit down with their friend, a bustling waiter was hurrying them for their order. Sam went for a Bacardi Breezer while Chris asked for the usual gin and tonic. They found bar-stools and looked around to get their bearings: the customary dozen or so dancers were writhing languidly on the small stage, the edge of which served as a bar counter. Most of the performers were engaged in close eye contact with their own reflections in the mirror that lined the Magneto's walls. The main area of the bar was thronged with busy service staff, dancers waiting

169

their turn to go on stage and various types of professional companion awaiting an opportunity to approach a customer for a drink or, perhaps, a more intimate arrangement. To one side was the lady DJ who controlled the watts. At the back were a couple of speciality areas where customers could sit even closer to the performers and, if they wished, indulge in a hands-on experience with them.

Judy was the third member of the group — a long-time Pattaya veteran and faithful customer of the Magneto who had known Sam for nearly five years. Judy was in her mid-sixties, a similar age to Sam and Chris and, like them, she was carrying more weight than was strictly healthy. Hers was a familiar story — she retired early, came to Thailand looking for a last chance for adventure, and married an attractive Thai boy who she now kept in a reasonable level of comfort in a flat in South Pattaya. These days Judy socialised almost exclusively with Westerners — *farangs,* as they were known — and spent her evenings drinking, talking, shooting pool, playing around with the working boys and occasionally selecting one for a bit of light relief in one of the abundant short-time hotels that catered for women like her.

Judy's young husband Nok didn't mind; the husbands rarely did as long as the women didn't rub their noses in it. The men would mostly stay at home, watching television, chatting on their mobiles, eating or sleeping. They would occasionally go out with their own friends — exclusively male, and nearly all of them married to *farang* women. In their way, they were faithful to their wives.

Sam's story was similar, though she had first come to Thailand at a younger age to work as a computer programmer. Some years later her Oslo-based employer had laid her off and, when she had recovered from the indignity, she realised that the severance money would be enough to live on if she wasn't too lavish. So Sam stayed on, settling in a bachelorette condominium in Jomtien. Before long, she met Gai in a bar and, soon after, married him in a touching ceremony at his parents' village in Isaan.

Chris was the youngest of the trio, though not by much, and had settled in Pattaya after the others. After a painful divorce in England, Chris felt she needed a new start. A prurient article about Pattaya in one of those faux-moralistic papers that the British like to read on a Sunday — it could have been the *News of the World* — had alerted her to the city's existence and intrigued her with the pleasures it was said to offer. It sounded like an attractive bolt-hole and, in her restless state, she decided that Pattaya was the place for her. She sold up at home and had now occupied a comfortable townhouse in the northern suburb of Naklua for about a year. Officially, she lived alone, but the neighbours would testify to a constant stream of young, tired-looking men who left her house in the late mornings. These visitors were on approval, she would explain to her friends. She was seriously looking for a permanent partner but was determined not to be hasty — the mistake that had led to the collapse of her first marriage. Chris was taking her time, sampling what was available and in no hurry to commit to anyone just yet.

'Quite a nice selection tonight,' said Sam, nodding towards the dancers on the stage. One in particular had noticed her eyeing him and was gyrating along the narrow platform towards her in the hope of a tip or a man-drink. 'Look at the package on that.'

'Not showing much tonight, though, most of them,' remarked Chris dismissively. 'Are the police having one of their crack-downs?'

171

'It's early yet,' observed Sam. 'They've got plenty of time to get the goods out.'

'This is still one of my favourite bars, though,' mused Judy seriously. 'It's not as raunchy as the Doghouse, and not as big as the Locomotive, but I think the quality of the boys here is more consistent. There are some great-looking lads here, you have to admit. Look at the buns on that one.'

Sam and Chris turned on their stools to appreciate the firm buttocks of a dancer who had just mounted the stage.

'That's down to the papa-san,' said Chris. 'I heard he head-hunted that one from the Gridiron A-Go-Go. In fact they say he brought half his boys with him. They were the best ones too; it was a great opportunity to abandon the chinless wonders.'

'And the little peckers,' added Judy.

'That's true enough,' Chris mused seriously as she drew on the straw in her G and T. 'I see you've found yourself a friend there, Sam.'

The boy was squatting on the stage in front of Sam with his legs apart. He had taken hold of her hand and was rubbing it across his crotch, which was roughly on a level with Sam's face.

'Feels good,' Sam said to the boy to cover her unease.

'Beautiful lady,' said the boy, looking for eye contact.

'Handsome man,' countered Sam, smiling at her friends.

'You want boom-boom?' the boy asked. 'We can go upstairs. Nice beds.'

'Maybe later,' replied Sam. Then, pointing to Chris, she added: 'Or try her. She's not married. No boom-boom for a week.'

Sam and Judy laughed, but Chris corrected them: 'Not since this morning, actually.'

'Oh, sexy lady boom-boom in the morning,' continued the boy, turning up the charm. 'You buy me man-drink?'

'I'll buy you a drink if you come down here,' said Judy, patting the vacant quarter of her bar-stool.

'Cannot; dancing.'

'After you're finished then.'

The boy winked and strutted off back into the huddle of performers.

*

A few minutes later the dancing shifts changed and, like a shot, Sam's admirer was at their side, accompanied by two others. The men draped their arms around the necks of the three friends, kissing their cheeks and massaging their arms. Their attention gradually shifted to their breasts and thighs. The second man threw his leg across Judy's lap and began rubbing his crotch rhythmically against her hip. Judy seemed quite taken by this boy; she was soon running her hands over his smooth chest and shoulders and into the back of his dancing pouch.

'What's your name?' the boy shouted over the din.

'Judy. What's yours?'

'Gung. You buy man-drink for me?'

'Oh all right,' said Judy.

Gung had Judy on the hook and reeled her in a little further. 'And my friends?' he said quickly, while she was on a roll.

Judy relented. 'Yes, OK, go on then.'

The boys clapped their hands with joy, called over a waiter and ordered beers. The second boy had slipped out of his thong and Sam was caressing his thin, smooth penis as he stood beside her stool.

The women did their best to maintain their conversation despite the distractions.

'Have you been over there lately?' asked Chris, indicating the two areas at the back of the bar, away from the main stage. One was a small wrestling ring in which a pair of boys, their skin shining with oil, were writhing together in something resembling a wrestling match, but with rather more stroking and a lot more attention given to the genitals than would be observed in a Saturday afternoon all-in television show. A narrow bar counter encircled the ring and customers were encouraged to reach over their drinks to the wrestlers and fondle a body part here, slap another one there. From the most attentive women the boys collected tips in small wooden pots.

The other was a low stage on which was mounted a large engine—probably from an old bus or a lorry. Two naked boys with spanners were dismantling the machine, and getting their sweaty skin smeared with engine oil in the process. One had a grease-gun with which he was playfully shooting gobs of dark lubricant at the other boy. As with the wrestlers, customers were expected to join in with the mechanics in any way they wished, buying man-drinks and paying tips for particularly good service.

'Not lately,' said Sam. 'I used to, but you see the same bloody things everywhere now. Once you've seen one bus engine being stripped down and rebuilt, basically you've seen them all.'

'I like the wrestling though,' said Chris. 'In fact, I bar-fined a wrestler at the Brands Hatch A-Go-Go only last night. He was good, actually; he knew all the holds.'

'I was just thinking that sort of thing has become a bit of a cliché now,' said Judy. 'Wrestling and engine maintenance—they seem to be the only ideas anyone can come up with. Imagine if the sexes were reversed, you can't see girls bothering to take an engine to bits night after night.'

'With their kit off!' said Sam.

The others laughed and sucked their straws.

Chris responded, 'And I can't imagine men coming here to gawp at them either. Would either of your husbands pay good money to watch something like that?'

'Nah,' said Judy. 'As long as I keep Nok supplied with new clothes and the latest gadgets, he's happy as Larry. He's just not interested in this kind of thing. Why would he be?'

'Gadgets is right. I've bought Gai two watches this year. The first one—not a copy mind you, a proper Rolex—God knows what happened to that. He told me he lost it, but you have to wonder with the safety catch and everything. Anyway, I bought him a new Tag Heuer for his birthday, a sporty one. That shut him up for a while,' said Sam. 'But it's funny just to think about them coming to a bar like this, isn't it?'

'You do see some men in here occasionally.'

'Husbands, of course, and the Korean tourists, but don't they look bored?'

'What if the whole bar was for men, with women dancing, wrestling...?'

'And being bar-fined!' finished Judy.

The women fondled their companions and shook their heads slowly as they contemplated this possibility.

'The whole thing's ridiculous if you think about it,' said Sam after a pause, 'because of the basic reason that women come here. Think about it, girls; why do we actually visit places like this? Conversation? We can get that anywhere. Are you with me? We could be in an ordinary Breezer bar.'

The others nodded.

'It's not conversation. It's to get a good eyeful. Yes? To be honest, girls, that's why we come here: to ogle their pecs and their bums and, let's confess, their packages. Well, you wouldn't get men coming to a place like this to watch naked girls.'

'Of course not,' said Judy. 'But that's because men's bodies are just naturally more attractive than women's. Can you imagine a whole row of girls up there on the stage, flopping their tits about like jellies and expecting men to be interested? "Those things are for feeding babies, not ogling," that's what most men would say.'

'Gai likes to nuzzle mine,' confessed Sam after a pause. 'He says it makes him feel like a baby.'

'Oh God, they all do that. They all want to be like babies,' remarked Chris. 'But nuzzling's one thing; watching's another. No man ever said breasts were beautiful.'

'Give me a firm set of pecs anytime,' said Judy earnestly.

Sam said: 'And men actually agree with that. Seriously. They can appreciate the beauty in a man's body, but not so much in a woman's.'

'Exactly. But the big problem, and the reason a go-go bar for men wouldn't work, is that women don't have dicks,' said Chris, who was now stroking the second boy's penis with encouraging results. 'It's as simple as that. I mean, what is there to hold on to on a girl? If men had places like this, there would be nothing to look at and nothing to play with. Might as well go to a sports bar and watch a decent game of netball.'

'Pussies are just not going to do it for anyone,' agreed Sam. 'They're just...well, nothing. I'm not being funny. All pussies are is a place where a dick is missing, and no one's going to sit and look at some girl waggling a bit where something else is supposed to be. Do you know what I mean? It would be like watching a Cape Canaveral space launch with no rocket. I'm not being funny; it would.'

The women laughed.

'OK, listen,' said Judy, 'let's continue along those lines for a moment. Watching sexy boys is just the first thing we come here for. What about over there in the groping areas? If there really were such a thing as a girly bar — theoretically speaking; in some alternate universe, say — what would they do there instead of wrestling and engine stripping?'

'Now there's a question,' said Sam.

'It's got to be something soft and wholesome,' suggested Chris, 'something girly — a bit dopey — that men would think is really feminine. What about a bath? You could have the men customers sitting around the edge of a circular bath — I know, drinking beer — and they could be watching a bunch of women wash themselves.'

'Maybe with a shower, right here in the bar,' added Sam. 'You could call it a Jacuzzi show.'

'That's brilliant,' said Judy. 'The men could soap the women up and get their hands all frothy. Think of the bubbles.'

'Yeah, they're really going to go for that.'

'I don't think,' said Judy.

The women laughed wistfully, their excitement deflated as they visualised the impossible scene.

'Or what about a bed?' suggested Sam, as she tried to re-kindle the pleasure.

'A bed? What would you do with a bed?' asked Chris, looking genuinely confused.

'You could have sex on it, or at least foreplay — you could have girls groping each other. You could even get them to use dildos,' explained Sam.

'Or bananas,' added Judy, a little desperately.

'What about ice cubes?'

'Ouch! I don't think so.'

'What, just girls on a bed? Girls pretending to be lesbians and making out on a bed with bananas?' asked Chris. 'What earthly interest could that be to a man? I don't know any man who would go for that. You know, I think they have more sense.'

'Well, we like watching boys sucking each other off, don't we?' said Judy. 'Boys making out look good to us.'

'But that's different,' said Chris. 'That's artistic. Anyway, it's a well-known fact that women are more visual than men. I read that once: women get turned on by watching, men don't. Females are excited by visual stimuli, males aren't. It's in our nature, simple as that. *Ergo*, men aren't interested in watching lesbians. For us to watch boys acting gay is normal. How else would you explain pornography? If men were as visual as we are, there would be porn films made for men. You'd see pictures of naked girls everywhere, just in the same way as you have boys now. Whoever heard of a man buying a sex video? Or filling his hard drive with photos of naked girls? It just doesn't happen. They say that 90% of the internet is taken up with porn. Or 95%; it was definitely a very large proportion. And naturally the vast majority of those websites are for women.'

'You would know,' teased Sam.

'I'm proud of my collection, which has taken me years to amass, if that's what you mean,' said Chris indignantly.

'Wanker,' said Sam and slapped her on her back good-naturedly.

'I'm not ashamed. Porn enhances my erotic experience. There's nothing wrong with that.'

'You don't think it exploits men?'

'How can you sit there, groping that boy's cock, and ask me a question like that? The men in pornos get paid, just like our friends here. Anyway, lots of the people who make porn these days are actually men. Did you know that? The people who run the business side, even some of the photographers, are men; ex-models usually.'

'Really? No, I didn't know that,' said Judy. She sucked the dregs out of her Breezer bottle and ordered three more drinks. 'Anyway, the main reason we're here, what about that? I suppose in this parallel universe of yours men would bar-fine girls, would they? They'd take them to hotel rooms and pay them for sex?'

'Sure, they'd have to or the universe wouldn't be truly parallel,' said Sam.

'But don't you see how silly that makes the whole idea?' continued Chris. 'Suggesting that a man would pay for sex just makes the whole thing totally impossible, alternate universe or not. It's just a matter of economics; think about it. Why would a man pay for sex when he can get it whenever he wants for free? You've got women like us – and younger ones who are more agile and, let's face it, can go longer than us – gagging for it; why would a man need to pay?'

'It's a good point,' said Judy ruefully. 'And anyway, in this country it's the women who have the money, so the men couldn't pay even if they wanted to.'

'Women may have the money, but men have got it made, don't you think?' said Sam. 'It's ironic. There's us chasing around after them, buying them trinkets and putting allowances into their bank accounts every month. And on top of that we have to beg them for a shag.'

'Or end up paying for it,' added Chris ruefully. 'This town is a bloody paradise for men.'

'The world is,' said Judy. 'It's a man's world.'

'Dead right. But I'm afraid we're stuck with things the way they are,' said Sam. She took a suck on her Breezer straw as she simultaneously fondled the naked buttocks of the two young men standing by her side and added, 'whether you like it or not.'

Monkey Business

Martin stopped the rented hatchback in the visitors' parking lot at Khao Yai national park. He and Frank got out of the car, stretched after their drive from Bangkok and began to prepare for the afternoon hike. As Martin packed water bottles, camera and map into his back-pack, Frank hurried over to a group of food stalls and returned with a large bunch of bananas. Tucking their trousers into their socks to discourage jungle leeches, the pair set off at a leisurely pace up the gently sloping road. A number of paths into the jungle began along this route, each with a sign pointing into the tangle of shrubs and trees.

'I always feel very primal when I set out on a walk like this,' confessed Frank.

'Primal? You always were the imaginative one.'

'Yes, don't mock. We're going back into the jungle, back to where we started from.'

'I thought we started on the plains of Africa.'

'Don't be pedantic. Anyway, the African plains may well have been covered with jungle in those days; I don't see how we could have survived long on a bit of grassy veldt. These pathways into the deep forest, they're taking us back. They're doorways into nature itself.'

'Perhaps into our nature.'

'That's better. Now you're getting the hang of it.'

Before starting on their hike proper, Frank wanted to feed the bananas he'd bought to a troupe of monkeys he'd seen from the car. They pressed on along the surfaced road for half a kilometre or so until, on rounding a bend, they spotted the monkeys ahead.

The troupe was made up of about 20 animals of various ages. The monkeys' backs were covered in olive brown fur while their undersides were white. A dark brown furry skull-cap made the top of their heads look flat. They held their short tails up as they walked. They were being led along the road by an adult, though their progression was by no means orderly. The other adults, some of them bigger than the leader, followed each other more or less in single file, while the younger animals skipped and jumped about, tumbling and wrestling with each other and dashing to and fro among the adults. Two or three of the smallest babies, black in colour, clung underneath their mothers and watched the antics of their elder cousins closely, their dark, inquisitive eyes as shiny as buttons.

Frank stopped to take the bananas out of his back-pack and tore one from the bunch. He was the shorter of the two friends, with sandy curls and a classically handsome face that, to some, indicated a poetic disposition. Quickly, the monkeys gathered near him, though they remained nervous. The adults bared their teeth and chattered at the two hikers. They were clearly accustomed to encounters with humans though they couldn't be described as tame, maintaining a safe distance and, while appearing nonchalant, keeping their eyes fixed on the pair. Frank threw the first banana carefully into the midst of the troupe and a number of monkeys dived for it. After a lot of noise and tooth displays, the leader established ownership of the fruit and sat down to eat it.

'Hey, come and have a look at the tackle on this one,' Martin called to Frank, indicating one of the largest animals which was sitting at the edge of the group. Martin was the older of the pair and more down to earth than his friend. With rather severe straight black hair, he often took the role of parent to Frank's irrepressible child.

'Oh yes, he is a big boy, isn't he?' Frank observed. 'I suppose he's the troupe leader. Are you?' Frank teased as he distributed the rest of the fruit to the other monkeys. 'Are you the leader of this troupe of primates, big boy?'

'Seriously, though, he has got colossal balls,' said Martin.

'Not as big as yours,' noted Frank, who then turned to address the large male monkey: 'You may have enormous balls, old fellow, but they're not as big as Martin's here, are they, eh?'

'I don't see how I could possibly know,' replied the monkey, clearly tired of the human's taunting.

'What? Did you hear that?' exclaimed Frank, laughing in response to the shock. 'That sounded like speaking. "I don't see how I could possibly know,"' he mimicked. 'I didn't know monkeys could copy human language, did you?'

'No, I had no idea.'

'Here, pretty Polly, pretty Polly,' Frank continued to tease the old male. 'Let's hear what else you can say.'

Another adult, the one that had been leading the troupe along the road and had claimed the first banana, ambled over to the big male and sat down in front of him. She was clearly a female. As the old male casually picked at the fur on her shoulder, she turned to Frank and said, 'Just listen to yourself, human: "Pretty Polly, pretty Polly." You sound like some daft parrot. Show some respect, please. And, since you asked, I am the leader of this troupe, not him.'

'My god, Martin, this one's really speaking. I mean it; she's actually talking; it's not mimicry, it's language.'

'It's really not that surprising,' responded the female haughtily. Her voice was high and soft but easily understood in the quiet of the jungle fringe. 'Nine-tenths of our genes are the same as yours, and I have to listen to your incessant babblings every day along this road. I've done it for years. It would be odd if I hadn't picked up a smattering of your language in that time, don't you think?'

'You learnt English from the tourists?'

'Of course, if that's what they are. We call them walkers; sometimes they're carrying books to identify the jungle species. "Pig-tailed macaque," they'll say, "Look, over there, those monkeys are pig-tailed macaques." Is that the best you humans can do, compare us with pigs just because we have short tails? Which are, I hardly need point out, nothing like pigs' tails anyway. I mean, I don't really care; it's only a name after all, but I'd like a bit of respect for the sake of the young ones.'

'Sorry, I didn't actually know you were pig-tailed macaques. I agree it's not a very dignified name,' said Martin tentatively. 'What do you call yourselves?'

'We're the noble monkeys,' said the leader. 'It's because of this brown patch on our heads. It makes us look noble.'

'I think you're right,' agreed Martin.

'We don't even know what macaques are, do we, mate?' observed the old male. Another male had shuffled over to sit with him and join in the conversation.

'No idea, mate,' replied the other male. 'Sounds Scottish.'

'You call yourselves human beings,' the female continued. 'Beings? What's that supposed to mean? You're so up yourselves you can't even bear to describe yourselves with an ordinary noun. "Beings" means no more than "things" or "entities"; it's nothing. You're apes, is what you are, apes with a noticeable shortage of fur. What good are those patches you have? You should be called the thread-bare apes.'

'Or pig-eyed apes,' the old male suggested with a throaty chuckle.

'Right, mate. Pig-eyed apes,' agreed the other male. 'The blonde ones, especially.'

'It sounds as if you're not that fond of us – of humans, I mean,' said Martin.

'Us old guys, the grandpas, we're for reconciliation, aren't we, mate?' said the old male.

'We're for what?' asked the other male.

'Reconciliation. Letting bygones be bygones, forget the past, peace and harmony, all that.'

'Peace. Yeah, mate. Too old for fighting, us grandpas.'

'You pig-eyed apes have done some bad things to us, you know, that's what we're trying to forget.'

'I'm sure we have,' began Frank. 'I'm sorry about whatever...'

'Ha! No point in being sorry. We're safe here in the national park, but over that hill there the humans still steal the young ones and take them away.'

'Take your young? Why do they do that?' asked Martin.

'For pets,' replied the old male, 'and for medical experimentation. Nasty, that.'

'Coconuts,' chipped in the other male.

'I was getting to coconuts,' the old male snapped testily. 'Also for getting coconuts down out of the trees. They train our young ones to distinguish between a ripe coconut and an unripe one. That's a laugh.'

'Ha ha,' said the other male.

'That's obvious, knowing a ripe coconut,' explained the old male. 'We can all do that. The young ones that get caught pretend they need to be trained. It's to put off the day when they have to start work.'

'Hard work, climbing trees, mate,' agreed the other male. 'Just to fetch coconuts for the human beings.'

The female leader continued, 'Here in the park humans mostly just want to throw bananas at us. Why is it always bananas?' She looked behind at the old male who shook his head sadly. She went on, 'We may be monkeys but we'd prefer some variety. It's not good for our young ones to eat so many bananas. All that potassium. I like bananas, don't get me wrong, but at every meal? I don't think so. We prefer a balanced diet. Can't you humans understand that? Sorry if I sound ungrateful.'

'Not at all,' said Frank. 'What should we bring next time we come?'

'I'm quite partial to kiwi fruit,' said the old male lugubriously.

'Some of the ladies like watermelon,' said the female. 'It's sweet and very refreshing, but we very rarely get it. Mangoes are good too. Durian's OK if you peel it first; otherwise it's hardly worth the bother.'

'My wife likes papaya,' said the other male. 'She says there's nothing like a nice papaya.'

'Which wife's that?'

'The skinny one. Always moaning.'

'She's got no chance, mate,' said the older male dismissively. 'They never bring papaya.'

'Where is *your* wife?' the female asked Martin suddenly. 'You humans generally go around in mating pairs.'

Martin laughed at the observation. 'I'm not married. Neither of us is,' he explained, indicating Frank and himself.

'Girl friends?' asked the female.

'No.'

'Gay, are you?' asked the old male.

Frank's eyebrows shot up in astonishment as he turned and smiled at his friend and blurted out, 'Yes, actually, we're gay.'

'Thought so,' said the old monkey matter-of-factly. 'Of course, I was gay for a time, when I was young. We've all been there, haven't we?' The other male scratched his head and nodded thoughtfully, as if recalling some enjoyable experience from his youth.

'When I first joined this troupe, from another one over that hill, I had absolutely no luck with the girls here, not a glimmer. I'd check they were on heat; it wasn't that. I'd try to mount them but they weren't having any of it. I thought, what is this? Have I got bad breath or something? But we've all got bad breath so it wasn't that. Anyway, I was horny as a rabbit on Viagra, as you'd expect with balls the size of mine, so being celibate wasn't going to be an option.'

The humans laughed at this reference to their earlier indiscreet teasing.

'So I spent the best part of a season with the boys — we have a few superfluous males in the troupe, as you can see. We were a sex-starved bunch, full of beans and, you know how it is, one thing led to another. I don't need to tell you two. I didn't turn completely queer, don't get me wrong, but at the very least you humans would describe our rough-and-tumble games as *homoerotic*. For us, being gay is definitely second best, not something you'd do if you had the choice. Know what I mean? You wouldn't go with a boy if one of the girls would have you but for some reason with me they wouldn't, not that first season, so what's a boy to do? I expect it's the same for you two, is it? Neither of you manage to get a girlfriend?'

'Ah!' said the female sympathetically. 'Sorry about that.'

'No it's not like that,' said Frank. 'I didn't want a girlfriend. I never have. I only like men.'

'Oh, it's a lifestyle choice then, is it?' asked the female knowingly.

'No, it's not a choice at all, it's in my nature.'

'Oh, it's in your nature, is it?' she repeated. 'What about your friend here?'

'I was married before,' Martin confessed, trying not to look sheepish.

'Married, eh? To a female? So what happened?' asked the old male. 'Did she die or get stolen?'

'No, she didn't die. We discovered we had different interests and decided it wasn't going to work out.'

'Different interests, eh?'

'Yes, I was more interested in boys than I was in her.'

'Oh, dear,' said the female, with an intake of breath. 'That's not going to work.'

'No, she wouldn't have liked that,' agreed the old male.

'No, she didn't.'

'Probably in your nature, like your friend here,' mused the female.

'Probably,' Martin agreed.

'So anyway,' continued the old male, 'after a season of monkey business with the boys, I decided to give a couple of the girls another try and was accepted straight away by quite a high-caste female.'

'She was,' confirmed the female. 'He was a bit of a catch that second season.'

'And she banged like the clappers. That was a few years ago now, more years than I care to mention if I'm honest. Now I'm one of the oldest in the troupe. We do security, we big males, to keep the troupe safe and sound. It's mostly snakes and eagles but we deal with all sorts, don't we, mate?' He looked around at the other male who nodded in confirmation. 'External security and a bit of internal discipline, when it's needed. We prefer to use a light touch with the little ones, though, don't we, mate? Nothing too violent. Sorry to go on about it but I have to say, if I'm honest, keeping order in the troupe would be a lot easier if you humans didn't insist on always bringing bananas. Our respected leader here gets it in the neck from the kids when she brings us along this road and all we get are bananas. Then the old grandpas like us have to wade in and sort out the ruckus. Still, can't complain. It's a good life, isn't it, mate?'

'Yeah, mate,' said the other male as he pouted, nodded his head and scratched his testicles thoughtfully.

A smaller female approached the leader with a young baby clinging to the fur of her belly. 'Shouldn't we be making a move?' she said softly. 'Some of the little ones are getting tired.'

'Yes, quite right,' agreed the troupe leader. 'We got caught up in conversation. Anyway, it's been good talking.'

With that curt farewell to the humans, the female got to her feet and began to lope slowly up the road, keeping safely to the verge. One by one, the adult members of the troupe fell into line behind her, followed by the young monkeys, still more interested in play than in the journey ahead.

Frank and Martin watched the troupe as it slowly disappeared around the bend in the road.

They found themselves alone again.

'I thought the bananas went down well,' observed Martin. 'That was a good idea of yours. Aren't monkeys fascinating?'

Frank looked at his partner sceptically: 'That's funny. I had the impression they weren't that keen on bananas.'

'They ate the whole bunch though.'

'It was just that I thought they were trying to tell me something, something in their eyes perhaps. They're very expressive, don't you think? Almost like humans.' Frank paused and then said plaintively, 'You are happy with me, aren't you, Martin? You don't regret leaving her?'

'Of course not. I love you and it feels right, so what could be more natural? Now, don't forget we're supposed to be on a hike,' said Martin as he led the way off the road, onto a narrow path and into the jungle.

Guile and Gullibility

I'll tell you the story of Dao. As well as the central character—whether she is the heroine of the tale in any proper sense remains to be seen—there are a number of others who exhibit frailties you may recognise. I'm there too, though you're unlikely to notice me until the end.

Dao didn't feel heroic that evening when, weary from work, she turned into the unmade lane that led to her house in south Pattaya. Work is less tiring when there is something to show for it, some achievement to be claimed. But Dao had erased from her mind the results of her day's labours and all that was left was fatigue. Since that morning she had vacuumed three houses, scrubbed 11 toilet bowls, polished 22 windows (many, with the aid of a step-ladder, on both sides) and ironed 12 shirts, six dresses, at least 14 T-shirts and, unnecessarily (as she always tells me), ten pairs of underpants. Dao understands that everyone is different, even customers. She realises too that wealth beyond her ambition or desire can induce in people a craving for luxury, though what she fails to grasp is that rich people have their pants ironed not to satisfy a specific desire for smooth underwear but simply because they can.

Dao parked her scooter on the muddy patch of land beside her house and dismounted. The nine or ten steps to the front door were trudged with heavy feet. She could already hear the crackling artillery of a computer game, confirming that her two sons were back from school. Food would be required, not noodle soup as she had cooked last night, and not fried rice which she remembered making the night before, but something novel, sustaining and quick.

As she prepared dinner you can be sure there was a nature documentary playing on the kitchen TV. An eagle would touch down on a platform of twigs, and Dao would be watching from the corner of her eye as a bundle of white fluff huddling there sprang to life and became two strident chicks dancing, squawking and lunging at their parent's beak. Dao had no more thought of this as she served the food and realised she hadn't made enough for herself. In a way she was too tired to feel hungry and now there was the revving of a familiar motorbike at the front, though she hardly expected Joe to return from the bar so early. In response to a tentative double knock she went to the door and was surprised to find Ping standing on the lower step. Some distance behind her, posing with his foot on his bike, was Joe.

*

With an anxious look over her shoulder Ping asked if she could come in.

Ping was the person Dao would least have welcomed to her doorstep. Joe had worked at her bar for nearly a year and in that time Dao had heard nothing good about the woman. On the contrary, reports she had received of Ping from shoppers in the market or beauticians at the salon were of her vanity and untrustworthiness. Many told Dao that the bar she managed had been bought for her by her *farang* husband, yet she boasted copiously of her skills as an entrepreneur, the success of the business and her plans to develop a chain of upmarket watering holes across the city.

Others told of loans that Ping had extracted from her friends and not repaid. These were generally for small sums—a few thousand baht at most—small enough for refusal to be embarrassing but nevertheless large enough to be missed.

Of the relationship between employer and employee— between Ping and Dao's husband Joe—despite many gentle warnings from her friends Dao retained an unenquiring innocence. It puzzled her from the start that a small bar in a quiet road in South Pattaya should require Joe's services as a security guard. No other such business had a guard as far as she knew, except perhaps overnight, and Ping's bar looked no more attractive to criminals than any other. Yet, if this meant that Dao suspected her husband of infidelity, it was only a fleeting thought and one that she didn't develop. She seemed to believe that too much attention to the idea might somehow make it true and the consequences of this were too momentous for her to consider. There was the shame of facing her father, there was the house and of course there were the boys. Something told Dao in that dogged way she has that it was better to carry on with Joe and his obvious faults than to upset the awful equilibrium of their lives.

Ping wasn't even that attractive. She was younger than Dao, but not much, and she was a lot thinner, but not all men like that sort of thing. She kicked off her sandals, stepped through the door and found that Dao's modest but unyielding presence prevented her from moving further into the living room.

'I hope you are well,' Ping began with a quick smile.

'I'm fine.'

'And the kids have finished their dinner?'

'Yes, yes,' she said without turning to check.

'It's about the bar.'

'Oh yes.'

'Business is very slow. It's the low season and I'm certain trade will pick up around the end of the year.'

As Ping's declaration faded to nothing Joe mounted the front steps and loomed in the doorway, leaning against the frame. 'Tell her,' he prompted.

'Joe says I should ask you because he knows you're doing well with the cleaning.'

'Tell her.'

'I need to borrow your money. It's his job, you see.'

Dao looked at her husband who nodded slightly to confirm the situation.

'It wouldn't be for long,' blurted Ping as she warmed to her mission. 'Only a few months, six at most, and I would pay interest, monthly.'

'How much do you need?'

'It's the rent you see, that comes to quite a lot, and I need more stock. I can't do business at all if I don't have beer. And electricity's extra, it's not included in the rent.'

'How much?'

'Forty thousand baht.'

Dao's eyes widened. After a pause she said: 'That's a lot of money. Why don't you ask your husband?'

'I'm not on such good terms with my husband. He has other interests besides me. He won't lend me the money.'

'She needs it, Dao, or else I'm out of a job, and you know what that means,' whined Joe, his eyes fixed harshly on his wife's down-turned face.

In truth Joe's employment, or lack of it, meant very little to Dao or the boys. Joe made no contribution to the housekeeping and spent whatever he earned on himself. From the money she earned as a cleaner Dao paid the rent, bought the food and clothes and paid for the boys to go to school. Not only that, she frequently lent Joe money to tide him over to payday, to fix his motorbike after another crash or, as was the case only two months before, to bail him out of police custody when he failed a urine test for crystal meth.

Dao's loans to Joe were never repaid. Instead, each was replaced by another. If he lost his job the housekeeping budget would not suffer directly, but Dao would be called on to support him entirely until he found another job. He looked pathetic, lurking there in the doorway, but he was her husband and the father of her children. Despite his history of fecklessness she had never refused him before.

'It's a lot of money,' she repeated.

'I could manage with 35,000,' suggested Ping, 'and I can put up the bar furniture as security, including the fridge. It's a professional one with a glass front, bought new. If there's a problem with paying back the loan, you can have all the stuff from the bar. You could sell it.'

'There's no risk, Dao. We just don't know what else to do,' said Joe.

Dao noted the 'we' but chose to ignore it: 'No, well, there's probably nothing else you can do. Alright, I'll lend you the money, but I want five percent annual interest paid monthly and I want the money back in six months, with the bar furniture including the fridge as security.'

'Agreed.'

'Thanks, Dao,' said Joe.

Ping got onto the back of Joe's bike and they sped away.

*

Dao doesn't like to receive bad news, especially in public, so she was made very uncomfortable by her friend Nan who she encountered at one of the vegetable stalls in the market. This was nearly two months after she had withdrawn 35,000 baht from her savings account and handed it to Ping.

'Your husband's certainly throwing it about, Dao. You must be doing well. I expect you'll be trading up to one of those houses on Soi 13 before too long.'

Dao didn't want to know what Nan meant but the woman stood there like a statue with a plastic bag of aubergines in one hand and her change from 100 baht in the other so Dao felt compelled to ask. Nan reported proudly: 'My husband and I were on the beach at Bang Saray last weekend and we saw Joe there having a right old time: fried fish, squid — a big lunch — and a bottle of Sangsom whisky. That's not cheap. He was with that good-looking woman, the one from his bar.'

'Ping?'

'That's the one, married to the *farang*. She was looking very slim; designer dress; nice hair. She must have been to the salon. Don't you ever worry about her playing around with your husband like that?'

'No.'

'I would, the way they were carrying on like a pair of horny parakeets. I hear she's not getting on well with that husband of hers, but I'm not one to gossip.'

*

The next morning Dao had no work booked. When the boys had left for school, she began to clean the house. After a while Joe appeared from the bedroom.

'It's been two months since I lent Ping that money, but I've received no interest. Would you get it for me tonight?'

'I can try but I doubt if she can afford to give you anything this month. There aren't that many customers around at this time of year. It's quieter than we expected, very quiet since the military coup. She had to pay the rent and there are other business expenses.'

'There's rent every month; she knows that. Tell her if I don't get my money I'm going to take the fridge.'

'Where will we keep the beer?'

Joe was lifting the lids of the pans on the hob, looking for leftovers. He said casually, 'Anyway, why do you need it so badly? You get plenty of money from your *farang* clients. Borrow from them if you're hard up.'

'I'm a cleaner, Joe, I scrub their toilets. My customers don't lend me money. Besides, I don't need to borrow; I just need to get my own money back from Ping.'

'There's never any food in this house.'

*

The next week on her morning off, Dao visited Gung the pawnbroker at his shop in Soi Khao Noi. She had known Gung for three years now and often went to him for financial and other advice. She persuaded him to come on her motorbike to Ping's bar.

Dao rarely went into bars, so she felt uneasy and enclosed as she entered, even though the place was large and open to the road. Two men were drinking beer at the shelf at the front though it was barely past ten o'clock. Sitting alone at a table by the wall was an elderly *farang* with thin hair and dry, wrinkled skin. He was eating slices of cheese and sausage on black bread with a knife and fork. Dao's cleaning customers were nearly all *farangs* so she had come to understand many of their peculiar ways, but the food they ate would always be a mystery.

Joe was sitting in front of the bar, Ping behind it. Though they faced each other, they were both absorbed by their mobile phones, flicking the screens nimbly with their thumbs.

Dao moved to the bar and, summoning her courage and keeping her voice discreetly low, said to Ping, 'I've come to collect the interest for the last two months, as agreed.'

'It's difficult at the moment, Dao, isn't it, Joe?'

Without looking up Joe waved his mobile at the bar's few customers. 'You can see how little business there is.'

'This is Gung who keeps the pawnbroker's shop in Soi Khao Noi. He's come to take the fridge.'

There was a loud clink as the wrinkled old man by the wall replaced his coffee cup on its saucer and looked down at his breakfast. The two beer-drinkers turned back to watch the street.

Gung was already sizing up the appliance, running his hands over the misted glass, testing the doors and peering around the back. 'Is it including the beer?' he asked.

'We won't need the beer,' said Dao quietly. You can take that out and leave it on the counter.'

'Wait a minute,' Ping cried as she hurried around the bar to intervene. 'What are you doing?'

'The fridge is security for the loan. You haven't paid interest as you promised so I'm calling it in. The fridge is enough for now; I'll come back for the furniture if I have to.'

'Sorry, you can't do that. I've just remembered.' Flustered, Ping took a token bottle of Chang from the counter and returned it to the fridge. She slammed the door and stood with her back to it. Gung held back, looking to Dao for direction.

The wrinkled old man stopped eating and gazed intently over his black-framed spectacles at the developing row. His mouth was full of pumpernickel which he was too distracted to chew.

'That fridge isn't mine,' Ping extemporised. 'When I set up the bar my sister lent me some money and I used it to buy the fridge. I haven't paid her back yet so the fridge actually belongs to my sister, not to the business. You can't take it.'

Dao thought about the furniture. She looked around the room at the stained tables and motley collection of rickety chairs and wondered if they were saleable, except to the charcoal burner. 'What about the tables and chairs?' she asked Gung discreetly.

After a glance Gung shook his head.

'Also the furniture,' said Ping, seeing where Dao's attention had turned. 'The tables are my sister's too.'

Joe slid off his stool and began to put the beer bottles back in the fridge. 'It's not that much, Dao. It's not worth making all this fuss about. Why don't you take this chap back to Soi Khao Noi and just calm down?'

The wrinkled man swallowed his black bread with difficulty, drained his coffee cup and lit a cigarette, crossing one skinny bare leg over the other. His watery eyes were now fixed on the ceiling fan.

*

The next day Dao was cleaning a house in Khao Talo when the phone rang. The house owner was out at the time. Thinking it must be her customer wanting to give her some instruction, she lifted the receiver. It was a *farang* speaking bad Thai, but fast.

'Do you want to speak to Madame?' she asked loudly.

'Is that Dao?'

'Yes, my name's Dao. Do you want the lady? She's out.'

'No, I want to speak to you.'

'Me? Oh. Who are you?'

'My name is Rolf. I'm married to Ping, the lady who keeps the bar where your husband works.'

'Ping? How did you get this number?'

'Your madame and her husband are friends of mine. They told me you'd be working at their house this morning.'

'Is it about Joe?'

'Not really. I'd like to talk to you.'

'Talk then.'

'Face to face, not on the phone.'

'I don't think I could do that.'

'It's nothing to be afraid of. I have a suggestion to make.'

'A suggestion? I don't know.'

'I want to help you. I'll explain it when we meet.'

'I don't really have the time.'

'Didn't you have a morning off yesterday?'

'Yes.'

'Well then, the same day next week. I'll meet you at 9am at Big C, in the coffee area.'

'Alright, maybe. How did you know about yesterday?'

'I'll be waiting for you in the coffee area, wearing a yellow shirt. And Dao?'

'Yes.'

'Don't tell anyone about this, OK?'

'If I decide to come.'

*

It was the first time Dao had been to the Big C coffee area alone. She felt embarrassed and quickly sat at one of the white-topped tables to become less conspicuous. She looked around, went to the cooler for a cup of water and returned to her table.

After a few minutes she was surprised to see someone she recognised. It was the wrinkled old man she'd noticed eating his breakfast in Ping's bar when she'd gone to get the fridge. He was skinny and slightly stooped. The dark shades that clipped on to his glasses were hinged up like huge eyebrows. For some time he peered across the room as if through water. Finally, finding Dao, he waved as if to a child. He was wearing a yellow shirt.

Rolf ordered two coffees and began in faltering Thai: 'I'm sorry I overheard your conversation in the bar last week. I was having my breakfast so close to you I couldn't help it.'

'It's OK. I'm sorry to have strong words with your wife.'

'Not so strong. My relationship with Ping is not as it was, though we still live together. I gave her a lift to the bar that morning and stayed for breakfast. There's a good coffee machine at the bar. Ping remembers the food I prefer and still likes me enough to get it in for me from the German deli across the street.'

Dao must have averted her eyes. She is often uncomfortable to hear about the marriages of others.

'A couple of years ago,' said Rolf as he swirled the coffee in his paper cup with a thin plastic stirrer. 'A couple of years ago, we celebrated our fifth wedding anniversary. We were still in love; I think I can say that.'

Dao blushed and held her hand to her brow to conceal her growing embarrassment, yet Rolf was unaware.

'Yes, I would say we were in love; there were many examples of our affection. For example, to mark our anniversary I made over to Ping a certain amount of money. Part of this was to finance a new business. I suggested an upmarket fashion boutique, offering dependable brand names from reputable suppliers. I thought she could make an impact on the retail scene. But she wanted a bar. I considered this the worst business to be in, but she was going to have to run the thing, and I couldn't expect her to sell quality clothes if her burning ambition was to run a bar, now could I?'

Dao looked down at her untouched coffee. When the silence was unbearable she said, 'No.'

'So a bar it was. But I wanted to provide Ping for the future too, the distant future.' Rolf smiled and lit a cigarette. 'Can I smoke in here? No matter.'

He held the burning cigarette under the table and continued: 'I mean when I die. Don't look so upset, my dear, we all die, even the Swiss. So part of the money I arranged to keep for her in an investment account in Switzerland. This is where the surest investments can be made. I come from Switzerland, yes?'

'Oh.'

'So you see Ping is not as poor as she makes out, and as repeated parrot-fashion by that useless husband of yours. I'm sorry, my dear, I don't mean to offend, but let's be honest, yes? Incidentally, you do know that my wife is sleeping with your husband? I think that much is common knowledge?'

Dao suddenly felt helpless. She sensed her face flushing cold. She tried to swallow but her throat gagged on the dryness. She nodded weakly and tried to appear interested.

'Yes, well,' Rolf went on, 'the money in Switzerland is invested in my name — she has no official status there of course. It reverts to Ping on my death, but until that event I have total control. I noted from your overheard conversation and that amusing little routine with the pawnbroker that Ping has borrowed some money from you.'

'Yes.'

'The likelihood is that your hard-earned cash has already been spent, with the help of your dear husband of course. You won't see it again. Was interest to be paid? Was that part of the agreement?'

'Monthly, yes.'

'You won't see that either. My wife has many qualities but trustworthiness is not among them. You've been taken, my dear. You're not the first but you may be the biggest. How much is involved?'

'35,000 baht.'

'Yes, excluding her sister who comes into the category of family, you're the biggest. She's getting ambitious.'

'It was all my savings.'

'Yes, well, I sympathise. You're out of pocket because you fell for Ping's spiel, or perhaps your husband played a part? Whatever, she won't repay you and she'll say she has no money. I know that's not true and I have control over her savings.'

'Yes.'

'Do you see where this is going?'

'No.'

I like to see fair play. I am offering to extract the equivalent of 35,000 baht in Swiss francs from Ping's account and return it to you, to even things up.'

'What would I do with Swiss money?'

'I'll change it for you into Thai baht.'

Dao smiles at last: 'I'll get my money back?'

'Yes, my dear, that is exactly what will happen.'

'If you think it's right. I don't know how to thank you.'

'You're an attractive woman, Dao. I liked the way you held yourself in the bar last week. You will think of something. Perhaps we could meet on your mornings off, to talk about it. I have a flat in town.'

Dao was puzzled for a moment and then took her realisation calmly. Her eyes narrowed: 'You want me to come to your flat?'

'I do.'

'OK, give me the keys. After the money comes though, we'll see.'

'Perfect, my dear.'

*

This is the story of Dao. It was told to me in a whisper by the subject of the narrative herself. We had just made love quietly one night in her marital bed, the boys asleep in the next room and a wildlife documentary on the bedroom TV playing on mute. Joe was at work and, as usual, was not expected home until the early hours.

As honesty is one of Dao's defining qualities you can believe her account. Any inaccuracies in this version are my responsibility though I claim my concentration was compromised by her insistence on nibbling me in a place I had previously casually identified as particularly and gloriously sensitive.

It seemed like a happy ending of sorts, with the money returned and enough lessons learned to save my lover from ever again finding herself at the mercy of so unscrupulous a woman as Ping. She was confident too of being safe from Rolf whom she could spin along with casual words and apparent undertakings.

But there was a loose end.

We heard the familiar motorbike revved at the front of the house.

'Have you got the keys to Rolf's flat?

'Yes.' When she heard the engine she slipped on a robe and walked calmly to the door, reaching it before Joe had mounted the steps.

I heard him struggling with the catch and Dao's calm voice: 'It's locked, Joe.'

'Let me in.'

'It's over, Joe. This time you've gone too far. You cheated on me and stole my savings; you took the money that was meant for your sons' future to spend on your own partying with that woman. No more, Joe.'

'Where am I going to sleep?'

'I don't care. Go back to your girlfriend.'

Joe moaned pathetically: 'She's thrown me out, Dao. She found out about her husband paying you back the money and she gave me the sack from the bar. That *farang* raided her savings. That money was Ping's.'

'No, it was mine.'

'The bar will have to close. I have no job now and nowhere to go.'

'I'm sorry, Joe.'

By this time I was dressed and came to Dao as she stood by the front door. Outside, Joe was pacing about in drunken anger, kicking over flowerpots and swearing loudly.

'Open the door,' I whispered to Dao.

'No.'

'We can't leave him there.'

Dao turned the lock and Joe rose up in the dark doorway, a powerful but pathetic presence.

'Gung! What the fuck's he doing here?' he screamed, pointing at me.

'Keep your voice down. The boys have school tomorrow. He's a friend.'

'What's your pawnbroker doing in my house in the middle of the night?'

'It's my house, Joe. He stays here sometimes. He's a good man. Joe. I've tried for years to make this work, but it won't. You can push me only so far. Now you must go.'

'And leave you here with him?' For a moment Joe struggled with his frustration, then stepped forward and swung at me. He missed and landed on his knees, sobbing.

'I'll call a cab,' I said. 'Give him the keys.'

Riparian

After less than an hour of labour, Pairot is born. A week later his maternal grandmother arrives in Chumphon, the gateway to South Thailand, to view her daughter's child. She takes a glance, pronounces him small and, loudly enough for the baby's father to look up from his hand of cards and bottle of beer, weak. The old woman will not address her son-in-law directly, nor even make eye contact. The man's failure to improve the living standards of her eldest daughter after six years of marriage has confirmed her earliest impression of him as lazy, feckless and stupid and an unsuitable addition to the family.

The first two children—both girls—have turned out satisfactorily, it's true. While both of them *wai* their grandmother respectfully on her arrival and departure, putting their palms together close to the nose as they've been taught, the elder one now also fetches her walking stick and sewing glasses when required and looks smart enough in her school uniform and regulation page-boy haircut. But the old lady has forebodings about the boy.

'We shall call him Noo,' she announces over rice as the sun goes down on the evening of her arrival. 'He's no bigger than a mouse and is unlikely to develop into much. It's a shame your husband was unable to give you a stronger son. The child clearly has weak blood. He hardly turns his head or grips my finger. How will he satisfy a vigorous wife? Is he suckling properly?'

'Yes, Ma, he feeds well enough. As well as the girls did.'

'That cheap food you buy has made your milk thin and watery. It lacks goodness. How can you eat pork like this? It's all gristle.'

'It's all they had at the market for the price, Ma. We do what we can.'

Despite the warnings Noo survives on a diet of broken rice, tough chicken and pork gristle. His sisters teach him to be dandled on their laps, wear miniature English football-club shirts, walk in flip-flops and speak the words of the farm. They show him the paths through the trees, the more gently-sloping branches he should climb to pick ripe purple mangosteen, the plants that yield drinking water and the places favoured by snakes. They stand back, the smaller sister behind the larger, when the boys from the village come to kick their ball about, throw balloons filled with water or silently witness the marvellous dissection of Noo's father's motorbike engine, its secret, masculine innards glistening with oil and so tightly packed, like the convolutions of an open durian.

Noo is growing up. It is a joyous time. Like the fattening of a pig or the blush of a ripening mango, it's a time to observe the way things change, how nature places one foot in front of the other without consultation and the jungle and the village—the whole world possibly—matures into what it is supposed to become.

And yet there's something that isn't quite right.

Noo, like the rest of creation, is developing, but not along the old worn paths. He does spend more time now with the boys from the village than at home with his sisters. That is natural, as acknowledged by his parents and reluctantly confirmed by the hurt silences of his grandmother when she visits from time to time. Yet, as his friends get closer, plotting chancy adventures, he holds back. Some voice he hardly hears is whispering to Noo of another direction, dangerous but more alluring, one that leads into the dark areas of the jungle, along a track that has no signs, no scraps of red ribbon tied to the saplings and, so far as Noo can see, no fellow-travellers.

*

A few more years on and Noo rises with determination, showers and dresses in clothes he has taken from the room of his sisters. His mother is an early witness to these experiments and doesn't react, at least not outwardly, hoping it could be nothing more than a stage in the lives of all boys of which she has not been warned. They sit together, the two of them at a time when the girls have homework to do downstairs, to watch a Chinese epic on TV. When the warrior prince is sliced through by a gang of black-robed and masked assassins, she reaches her dry hand across the planks of teak and touches his arm. He turns to find tears in her eyes, but however much he hopes these drips of brine acknowledge his pain he knows they are shed for the prince.

Later she speaks to him with re-gathered strength. His father is going to town and will be gone all afternoon. She says she has enquired about the injections. He is at a fork in the road and the hormones will ease his body one way, into the shape of a woman. It's easier now when he is still young, as long as he is sure.

'I'm 100% sure. But the cost.'

'I can use some of the housekeeping money. You're more important to me than lean pork or unbroken rice. You are my prince.'

That makes him pause with realisation. 'But Father.'

'It will be some time before it's obvious. Wear loose clothes. Keep out of his way.'

He imagines himself hiding in the trees and wonders for how long. She adds, 'Finally you will have to leave. You know what he's like.'

In a while she has an idea: 'When we're alone you can *ka* me for practice; but you must continue to say *krap* to your father.' One is please for a woman, the other for a man. He will be permitted to use a woman's words. He is sure of her now as a champion in the epic battles that will surely rage, the fights he dreads with his father and, what could be worse, his grandmother.

*

My age of confusion finished not with war but with a name. Becoming Jane made my purpose clear, ending years of not knowing and replacing them with a future of identity and confidence. It was no surprise to find that my father didn't share my optimism. I packed my bag before his sullen indignation could turn to drunken rage as it surely would, and I certainly wasn't going to suffer a visit by my grandmother.

My mother came to the door as the taxi carried me away but she said nothing to her new daughter. I realised then that it was fear that drove her, as it had driven me before that time, in that house, the dark house into which she would turn her grieving face as soon as I was out of sight.

I dozed on the bus, my head knocking against the curtained window waking me in snatches. Thus between the journey and the dream I plotted my life in generalities. There was no detail and I didn't care. I knew no-one in Phuket, had nowhere to live and, beyond the price of a couple of bowls of soup, possessed no money, no means of survival. Yet I was free of something and that, like the hot sun that burst the yellow curtains of the bus, infused me with happiness. That was the point at which my life reached its peak. I became fully potentiated on that bus. That power would carry me for more than a year before leaking away as my dream ended in realisation and revulsion.

*

On her first evening on the island of Phuket, Jane meets Thierry, a rich, nervous boy holidaying from Switzerland. Using signs and a few words of English and Thai they develop a bond which endures dinner at red plastic tables in a brightly-lit KFC and the walk back to Thierry's rented chalet on the beach.

'I came to Phuket looking for a coastline, a certain vulnerability,' he tells her softly on the veranda, sipping Tiger beer from the bottle. They're both fascinated by the sea, close now at high tide with waves no taller than a duvet. He might as well be speaking French, though Jane smiles as she has been doing all evening. 'In Switzerland we have no sea.' This time he makes an effort to explain it more clearly and she wonders how it could possibly be true.

'My life is privileged,' he confesses, 'free of danger.' Jane wonders if she should be worried by this.

When it comes to making love, she commits herself with the confidence of the novice. Sometimes it's better not to think, but simply to live. Thierry seems fully satisfied, which dispels the only fear that Jane has allowed. For herself, she lies awake in the little room, the veranda light they left on in their haste piercing the dried palm-leaf wall with a pinkish, organic glow, feeling that she's just been born. She imagines her mother holding up the little baby and laughing through tears: 'It's another girl!'

Thierry is the first person she has ever met outside her family, the village and the school, she thinks, the first person outside herself that she can remember ever having met. Being with him is like making contact with the rest of the world. She turns to his cool body—silky, pale and dry in the conditioned air—and watches her hand wander on his smooth chest until she's asleep.

*

Thierry has booked the chalet for only three weeks but whatever commitments he has in Geneva seem fluid and he extends his stay without difficulty. When his visa finally expires he takes Jane to make a passport. It has to be in the name of Pairot, so fearing his knowledge of Thai girls' and boys' names she goes to the window alone to complete the forms, smiling nervously over her shoulder. He flies her into Malaysia for the day, simply so that he can start a new visa on his return. Over the months, it's a journey they often repeat.

Thierry is happy to foot the bills, uncomplaining when Jane orders lobster through not knowing or suggests another shopping trip to buy the clothes she needs. But she wants to pay her way and besides she has the constant knowledge that, in the leather folder he keeps on the night-stand, is a ticket for Geneva, undated he says but capable of being activated without notice. In a moment her lover could be gone, called away to whatever mystery Switzerland is, to a life beyond this, to family, friends, streets or houses she has touched but neither knows nor understands, to a land with everything but a coastline.

To earn the money that she thinks may keep him here, she takes a job at a bar on the beach, a rickety bamboo contraption put up for the high season and stowed under the palm trees at the top of the beach when the tourists thin out. She learns to mix contrived cocktails with ridiculous names and acquires enough of the key words of English to chat numbly with the customers. She notices that the bar loses some business in the early afternoon as the hungry midday drinkers drift away in search of lunch. When she suggests to the owner a barbecue, he agrees guardedly but nevertheless provides the equipment; Jane and Thierry shop for meat in the market and Jane rises early to mix the marinade and thread chunks of chicken on to bamboo sticks.

Thierry pays for another month on the chalet. Jane begins to think about the future. She is as happy as she has ever hoped, but will they always live on the beach? It seems temporary. To step out on to sand and lose your footprints by nightfall is not at all like the jungle where paths persist for generations. She asks him many times in her head and plans to put voice to it soon: wouldn't he prefer a house in town, with a tiled floor and a garden with fruit trees? A condo at least? And what about the operations? She longs to complete her development once and for all as is surely the right of nature's immature.

One day she thinks of them old together, an old woman and an old man, but says nothing. She's not going to be the first one to mention love; that's for the man.

Then she's walking home along the beach from the bar. He hasn't come to meet her after her shift on the barbecue as he usually does and she sees that he's not lounging on the veranda with a beer. Her footsteps creak on the wooden stairs, but inside he's unconcerned. She opens the wicker door straight into their room and the two of them are lying there on the bed, looking out of the darkness like rats caught in a hole.

Thierry smiles. He hasn't been compromised; he's saying that he's testing her boundaries, the ones they haven't discussed, learning what she allows, finding out just how vulnerable it all was.

Jane stands in the light of the beach and stares. Everything she believed was true is suddenly made wrong. Her life has collapsed, melted to nothing. She cannot speak. Her head feels cold as if all the love she has incubated in its warmth has swilled out through a drain. She bursts into tears and rushes away from the chalet. Thierry shrugs without comment and gets up from his lover to close the door.

*

She retreats into the trees, sitting at the top of the beach under the coconut palms in a place from where she can see everyone that passes. He doesn't come.

After an hour she goes to the beach bar and sits on a high stool, as a customer, and orders a tequila. Nit can spare little time as the bar is now busy but she asks Jane quickly what's wrong.

'It's Thierry,' she says, indicating another drink.

'Well, I guessed that. He cheat on you or stop your money?'

'Cheat.'

'Men are such bastards,' says Nit as she turns to take an order. She would say the same if it was money.

Jane calms a little as the tequila has its effect. The sea is dark now and the lights have come on along the shore. She cannot see the chalet from here with any certainty, but she can pick out the row of them from their veranda lights. The sand between is eerily light, reflecting the moon better than land or sea.

Suddenly he is beside her, their heads at the same height, her still on the bar stool. Before, he would have caressed her but he does nothing, feeling a little guilt now, hoping that a remorseful face will see him through, but her anger will not sustain the silence.

'I'm sorry,' he says at last. 'I was wrong. I should have asked you first.'

'Asked me? What would you ask me?'

'If our relationship is exclusive of course, whether you mind if I have other lovers.'

'Other lovers?'

'Yes. I wouldn't mind if you had other men. I didn't think you'd mind if I slept with other...'

'Yes, Thierry? Other what? If you slept with other what?'

'Men.'

Jane pulls a 500-baht note from her purse and slams it into the pot with her bill. With a renewed outflow of tears she strides away from the bar, out of earshot, before collapsing on the sand. Thierry follows and sits beside her.

'I'm sorry,' he repeats. 'I told you I'm sorry. I should have...'

'You're a bad man. You're a very bad man, Thierry.' It was the worst she had learnt to say.

'I know.'

'Your lover. Who is that?'

'Oh, him. He's just some boy I picked up. He's nothing, really. Honestly, I'm telling you the truth. It was just...'

'No, not just anything. I saw him, Thierry. He was a man. I caught you going with a man. That's disgusting. I can't believe it, Thierry, you're gay!' She's shouting now, becoming hysterical.

Thierry's face goes slack and his mouth drops open. His eyes scan her face for clues of forgiveness but there's nothing there but anger, hurt and jealousy. Confusion dries his brain. For moments he can think of nothing to say except, 'Gay? Jane, of course I'm gay. What...? Excuse me, but why did you think...?'

'I don't want a gay man! Why would I want a gay man? How could I love...? I want a real man, a straight man, a man who loves me, loves me because of what I am. I want you to love women – not sleep with them, though I could forgive you for that – I want you to look at them go by and tell me I'm more beautiful.'

'Sorry, Jane. I do love you, but as a man. I've never been attracted to girls, never. I'm sorry. Look, this is all quite a shock. I'd better go. You know me now. You know what I am and you know where you can find me. If you want to come back or if you want to get your things, everything of yours, it's all yours of course.'

*

Jane sits for a while on a slight rise in the pale sand. She is alone now. Thierry has gone and the few romantic couples who walk the shoreline in the evening have found their restaurants for dinner.

She pulls her dress over her head and lays it on the sand. She repeats with her bra. She sits with her knees up for a moment, her hands clasped around her shins. Confirming that she is alone she slowly unwinds and looks down at her breasts, their weight and shape. They don't look like a woman's breasts, she realises now – they're too high and hard. A woman's breasts are like water and flow into her body like a stream. I have a man's chest, a man's muscles.

Hoping she is mistaken she wriggles out of her shorts and panties. Who was he trying to fool? What was he thinking? That the injections would shrink him away to nothing and the proof of a woman would simply grow like a hibiscus flower?

He is nothing but a man in women's clothes. He couldn't fool anyone, not his mother, no-one in the street, not his beautiful Swiss lover even. He is ridiculous. Everyone has been laughing at him. He can't go back, there's nothing for him in Chumphon, no living to be made here in Phuket and nothing possible left of the future he has planned so carefully with Thierry.

He stands up and looks at his body in the pale light like something larval, yet to form. He doesn't want to be found like this. He slowly puts his clothes back on, brushes the sand from them and walks in a daydream down the gentle slope. As the welcoming water reaches his hands, he combs his fingers through the surface. Soon he is swimming a slow but determined stroke, straight out from the shore.

*

I was born on the land and will die in the sea, yet I lived my life — all of it that had any meaning — on the shore, that narrow strip of shifting sand where the waves wash and the tide flows. On the map it's no more than the width of a line of ink, the black space between earth and water, neither wet nor dry, neither here nor there, not one thing nor the other.

WILLIAM PESKETT

Kidnapped

It was dark when she awoke and she assumed for a few seconds that she was in her bed. She wondered why the darkness was so complete. No hint of dawn broke around the sides and over the top of the curtains; no glow seeped in from the street-lamp behind the mango tree that leant from the front garden over the road; no calming green numbers told her the time.

She had a headache. She desperately tried to recall the previous evening. She hadn't been on one of her rare nights out with her friends, so it couldn't be a hangover.

As her head cleared, she realised indignantly that there hadn't been a previous evening. She hadn't even gone to bed; she'd been on her way to Lopburi. She was wearing jeans and a shirt. Reaching behind, she found her backpack in which she remembered putting her monk's white shirt and skirt, and her wash-bag.

She was going to take a bus to the temple near Lopburi, where she had planned to spend three nights on a Buddhist retreat, praying, eating vegan food, sleeping on a rush mat, sweeping the wat and praying again. It was morning. She remembered pulling closed the heavy sliding front gate. From there it was a short walk to the main road where she would pick up a motorbike taxi. This would take her to Tops supermarket on Pattaya Road Two, to a stand on the corner where minibuses left for the temple every hour. She'd walked in the soi, but couldn't remember a motorbike.

She was uncomfortable, not used to sleeping with her knees bent. She stretched out, but met resistance. She extended her arms with the same result. It was like being in a box.

She began to panic.

Exploring feverishly with her hands, she found carpeted floor, gritty with dirt and strewn with leaves or bits of paper and crackling plastic, like crisp packets; a shaped metal roof; wheel arches. As she lifted her head, she heard an engine rev and sensed movement. She was in a car boot. The engine revved again. She was being driven somewhere fast.

*

Tukta couldn't help waking Mitch with the noise of the shower, but she knew he'd be asleep again soon. She checked her backpack, swung it over one shoulder and bent to kiss him on his stubbly cheek.

'I'll call you tonight, if I can get reception,' she said. Or it could have been 'tomorrow night'. It didn't matter either way, as Mitch didn't plan to go out. He would be around to receive her call on the house phone at more or less any time.

He rose late, around ten-thirty, fed the koi in the pond, made some toast and cafetière coffee for breakfast and checked his email. While tending the fish, he noticed that some of the shrubs dotted in the back lawn were becoming unruly. He fetched the secateurs and spent half an hour filling one of the dustbins with clippings. He stood back to appraise the results of his labour.

Mitch was a big man who carried a little more weight than was healthy. A lot of it was accounted for by his belly which he allowed to hang a little over the low waistband of his surfing shorts, but there was a fair amount around his unshaven jowls, too. Feeling the sweat beginning to break through his checked shirt, he abandoned the chore, took off his cap and went to sit beneath the patio fan for a while with a book on his lap. He dipped into it occasionally, but mostly he gazed out over the garden, thinking about Tukta.

This wasn't the first time she'd been away without him. She sometimes went to see her family in Isaan—when she wanted to spend more than the one night that Mitch could tolerate sleeping on the wooden floor of what he still thought of as her parents' house. And she had been to the wat in Lopburi before, too—being a lady monk for a few days, as she put it. Tukta's urges to immerse herself in Buddhist prayer came in waves, like sudden small enlightenments. Mitch couldn't see any logic to their timing—they didn't seem to coincide with religious festivals or phases of the moon—but then he'd lived in Thailand for six years now and no longer expected to find a rational explanation for such things. He was becoming accustomed to an element of apparent randomness in his life, occasionally welcoming the sense of surprise.

Mitch was retired, and received a pension from his former employer in the States that was sufficient for both of them to enjoy a high standard of living. It simply wasn't worth Tukta getting a job. Her lack of education reduced her earning power to the unskilled level and, although a job might have given her days a focus, such a commitment would have been inconvenient for them as a couple on the occasions when they wanted to go to Koh Samui on an impulse or drive up to Chiang Mai, perhaps to wonder about living at its cooler altitude one day.

Theirs was a close relationship. Mitch and Tukta spent most of their time together. Mitch felt this most acutely when his wife went away. He had to admit, when she wasn't at home, he found himself at a loose end.

Remembering an instruction from his wife, Mitch walked round the back of the house to assess the ripeness of the huge papayas hanging precariously from Tukta's two trees. He wasn't to let them fall and bruise on the pebbles. They still looked green to him. This is how Tukta would have harvested them, for the green papaya salad that was the speciality of her home region, but he preferred them ripe, with lime, for breakfast, so he left the fruit to mature a little longer.

He passed the letter-box on the gate-post and peered inside. He didn't get much mail, perhaps ten letters a month, and they usually came in lots. He'd received a batch only the day before so he wasn't expecting any more for a week or so. The item inside was a surprise. It wasn't an envelope, but a folded piece of paper, not addressed and a little crumpled.

He unfolded the lined paper furtively, like a message passed in class. It was in Thai, except for one word written in Roman capitals: TOOKTA. The text, which he couldn't read, included what appeared to be a telephone number, probably a mobile from the look of the code.

At the end of the message was a Thai word that Mitch recognised — baht — and preceding that the figure 4000000. He counted the zeroes carefully. Four million baht.

He knew he hadn't won the lottery.

Mitch took the note back to the patio and sat looking at it for a while. The words in script were roughly scrawled. He had tried to learn the Thai alphabet and had made some progress with the 44 consonants and 15 vowels but reading characters that were clearly printed in a book was a lot easier than deciphering these ballpoint squiggles. Anyway, even if he could read the words, he'd need a dictionary to extract the meaning from them.

What could that meaning be? His first thought was that the message must be from Tukta, a love note perhaps, hastily written and stuffed into the box as she left that morning for him to find during the day. He wondered: does she love me four million baht? But why the phone number? He took out his own mobile and brought his wife's record up from his contacts list. The number wasn't hers, nothing like it. And anyway, Tukta spelt her name with a U; he'd seen her practise signing her new name over and over again just before they were married.

Mitch decided that to decipher the note he would need expert help. With his mobile already in his hand, he scrolled down and called a friend's number.

Dennis was another American, though from the West Coast. Although this was a long way from Mitch's native New Jersey, Dennis and Mitch had overlapping worldviews and similar dining preferences that meant they'd see each other once a week at least. Dennis had lived in Thailand for more than 20 years and spoke the language fluently enough to run a successful law consultancy business in town.

'Can you read Thai handwriting?' Mitch asked.

'If it's neat enough.'

'What are you doing for lunch?'

They met in their usual place, the coffee shop behind Pattaya Tai, on the edge of the market square, and ordered sandwiches and beer.

'How's Tukta?' Dennis asked.

'She went away this morning to that Buddhist retreat I told you about.'

'You mentioned some handwriting?'

Mitch pulled an envelope from his pocket and took out the scrap of paper. 'It's this note. I found it in the mailbox this morning after Tukta left.'

Dennis put on some round reading glasses and examined the paper in silence. After a while, he looked blankly at his companion and said, 'This is serious, right? You got this in your mailbox today?'

'Yes.'

'Then, on the face of it, things are not good.'

Mitch felt the innards sink in his body. His skin went cold. 'Why so?'

'This is a ransom note. It's from someone claiming to have Tukta. They want four million baht for her.'

'For her? What do you mean, for her?'

'To return her. They want money to let her go.'

'What? Who do?'

'It doesn't say.'

'What does it say, exactly?'

'It says, "We have your wife, TOOKTA. Call the number today. Bring four million baht. No call, or the police come, she's dead." More or less. That's the meaning anyway.'

'Christ! Do you think it's real? Who would play a joke like that? Shit, Dennis, what the hell am I going to do? You think I should go to the cops?'

'Let's think about this awhile. As for the cops, probably not. They could make a pig's ass of this and put Tukta in harm's way.'

Mitch tried to work his way through the situation but his brain wouldn't think straight. The visions that came to him seemed fluid, like water flowing over rocks. He couldn't channel his thoughts in a coherent way. He was thinking of Tukta praying in her nun's white clothes, of men with knives at her throat, of having to tell her mother she'd been found dead, all because he slipped up on some small technicality in a deal with kidnappers he couldn't even imagine. None of it helped. What was he to do?

'What should I do, Dennis?'

Dennis was a small, dark man with a few days' stubble that gave his firm jaw a bluish sheen. His face revealed sympathy and confusion but beneath it all he seemed calm. For Mitch, his friend's composure was all he could rely on to haul him out of the quicksand he was in and on to some solid bank of reason.

'OK, look,' said Dennis. 'Do you have four million baht?'

'What's that, about 150,000 bucks? In investments, yes, in the States.'

'How quickly could you get it here as cash?'

'About five days I guess; it could take a week.'

'Right now we need to make some calls. Would you like me to call this number?'

'Well, yes, if you think, but not here.'

'No. Good thinking. Let's drive over to my office.'

*

After more than half an hour, the car slowed, made a sharp turn and, in a short while, came to a stop. Tukta heard the car doors being opened and slammed, then the lock on the boot popped and the lid swung up. It was bright outside and she couldn't recognise the silhouettes of her two captors against the white haze. The taller of the men reached in and grabbed her by the arm, pulling her up and over the sill of the boot. As she stood stiffly by the car, she looked up briefly at the men, one older than the other but both dressed in dark clothes—jeans and T-shirts. They had cloths tied across their noses, like bandits. She had to look at them again before it struck her. She frowned as her gaze flitted from face to face.

'Chusak, it's you! What the fuck do you think you're playing at?' she screamed as she yanked the handkerchief down from her brother's face. 'And Arkom, have you lost your fucking mind?'

Beyond being able to utter these words, Tukta was speechless with rage. She stood quivering before the two young men, stamping her feet in frustration. When she could, she let out a series of grunts and whinnying noises to show her anger with her brother and nephew. The boys had suddenly lost their swagger. They cringed in the light of Tukta's enraged fury, preparing at any moment to be dealt a blow from her swinging fists.

'How could you? You jump me when I'm on my way to the temple, shove a bag over my head and stick me in there.' She was indicating the filthy boot of Chusak's ancient Nissan. 'You know how hot it was in there? I couldn't move. I couldn't fucking breathe. You could have killed me. I could have died in there. And anyway, why was I unconscious? Did you hit me? Chusak, I swear if you knocked me out...'

Chusak's voice was feeble and ashamed, as if his sister's anger was giving him second thoughts about the whole mission: 'We chloroformed you.'

'Chloroform? What's that, poison? You bastards! What the hell do you think you're you playing at?'

'We need the money, sister, for our business.'

'Money? What money?'

'From the *farang*. You've been married for five years at least and we didn't see any sign of him paying up, so we decided to take matters into our own hands.'

'It was my idea too,' Arkom chipped in. 'We didn't have a choice. There was no other way we could see. And anyway, where's the harm? No-one's going to get hurt and it's no problem for him.'

Tukta blinked two or three times and tried to get this story straight. 'What do you mean, "I've been married for five years"? What do you mean, "It's no problem for him"? "He would pay up"? By "the *farang*" do you mean Mitch? You're talking about Mitch, right? Why's he going to pay you?'

Then realisation shone from the murky clouds of the bizarre situation she found herself in. 'You've kidnapped me. You've kidnapped me, haven't you? You're going to get Mitch to pay a ransom. You are, aren't you? Unbelievable.'

'It won't hurt him; he'd loaded and he's never given us anything.'

'It *will* hurt him actually and he's not loaded. In America, he's not rich at all; he's just like us. He's worked all his life to save for retirement and now you want to steal it from him?'

'I've worked my whole life too, and look what I've got — nothing,' said Arkom.

Tukta snorted. 'I beg your pardon? There are two things wrong with that, idiot nephew. First, you're only 20, so your "whole life" doesn't really add up to much compared with Mitch's. And secondly, you've never worked a day since you were born. When did you ever have a job?'

'I helped your Ma with the farm,' Arkom said sheepishly.

'So how much did you think you were going to get Mitch to pay?'

'Four million baht,' said Chusak.

'Four million baht? Are you out of your mind?' screamed Tukta, grabbing at the sleeve of her nephew's shirt. 'I could understand this young runt coming up with a plan as mad as this, but Chusak, you're nearly 24. You should know better than that. What do you think will happen to us — Mitch and me — if we have to pay you four million baht? Where would we get money to eat? And "your business"? What business anyway? You don't even have any business.'

'That's just it,' explained Chusak more confidently. 'We need the money to start a business, Arkom and me. We're going to be partners.'

'And what business is this going to be?'

'A motorbike repair business. We need a shop and we don't have any tools, so we've got to get the money for that.'

'You don't need four million baht for a motorbike repair shop.'

'No,' said Chusak, 'we thought we'd need a million to be safe; then Ma said she'd like two million herself, probably two and a half. We rounded it up to four million in case the *farang* tried to bargain with us.'

'Ma? Ma's in on this?'

'Yes, actually it was her idea originally.'

Tukta's face became blotchy and red. The blood in her cheeks had reached boiling point. 'And what does Ma think she needs two million baht for?'

'She's going to buy some land in Khorat and build a row of shop houses.'

'Why the hell does she want to live in a shop house in Khorat?'

'No, not to live in, as an investment.'

'I see. So your plan is to take Mitch's savings away from him and transfer them to our mother? Then steal more money from him to throw away on some half-arsed bike shop and top this off with a further half million or so if you can get it. What do you two layabouts know about motorbikes anyway? Why would anyone bring their bike to you? You've always been useless at fixing things, both of you.'

'We'd hire skilled mechanics,' explained Arkom. 'We'd just be the owners of the business, like managers. We'd manage the money and so on.'

'You're a pair of complete losers. I'm thoroughly ashamed of you, and of Ma. Now take me to her and I'll tell her what I think of her.'

'OK, but we have to tie your hands.'

'What? Why the fuck do you have to tie my hands?'

'In case you try to escape.'

'You're not tying my hands.'

Tukta struggled as they grabbed her but they proved too strong. Her brother held her still as her nephew bound her wrists with plastic twine. They took her mobile phone from her pocket, turned it off and bundled her into the back seat of the car, next to Arkom, while Chusak took the wheel. It was a three-hour journey north to the family home.

*

In the heat of the car Tukta seethed with anger. For the first hour she said nothing. In her mind she tried to make sense of her absurd predicament. How could they think this plan was right? Had the monks taught them nothing? And how could they possibly think it would work?

Before confronting her mother, Tukta needed more information: 'How do you plan to make contact with Mitch?'

'We gave him my mobile number,' said Chusak.

'And you expect him to call you?'

'Yes.'

'If he doesn't?'

'We told him in the note that we'd kill you. And no police; we'd kill you if he contacted them too.'

'If he doesn't call, you're going to kill me? Where will that get you? You'll be in jail with no sister and no money.'

'Of course he'll call. He wants you back, doesn't he?'

'How will you get the money?'

'We're going to arrange a hand-over,' said Arkom with some pride.

'How will you arrange that?'

'On the phone.'

'Mitch doesn't speak Thai.'

'We'll speak English.'

'That's a joke. You losers couldn't shout "help" in English if your dicks were on fire.'

'I came top in English in my class,' Chusak reminded her.

'You were twelve when that happened, dear brother; you could just about say, "my favourite colour is blue", though you'd point to the pink square. And you left school the next year.'

'It was two years later,' Chusak corrected her.

'Oh, so it'll be advanced English then. How will you disguise your voices?'

'What?' asked Arkom.

'Mitch has known you since you were kids. He'll know who you are on the phone straight away.'

'But he's a *farang*,' said Arkom, taken aback. 'He won't know Thai voices.'

'What? Why not? You think *farangs* are so different from us? He'll know who you are immediately.'

'We could put a cloth over the phone,' said Chusak, 'or fill our mouths with stones.'

'Or we could talk in a squeaky voice.'

'Boys, if you do that, Mitch will say to you, right away, "Hi, Chusak. Why are you using that funny voice, and why are you eating rocks?'

The two young men thought this over for a number of kilometres. Finally, Chusak came up with an idea: 'You could speak to him.'

'You want me to tell my husband to hand over our savings to me or else I'll kill myself?'

'No, you could pretend to be under duress. Say that we told you to say it. We'd rehearse and write it down. You could read it.'

Tukta had had enough of this. Ignoring the pain in her wrists, she put her head against the car window and tried to sleep.

By the time they reached the turn-off to the village of her birth, Tukta was wide awake. She hadn't driven down this old familiar unmade road for nearly six months now. Mitch was always reluctant to make the trip from their comfortable home in Pattaya, though he relented once or twice a year.

Her mother's house was the oldest in the village, a large old-style wooden shack on concrete stilts. Opposite were two more modern buildings, brick below with wooden upper storeys, where Tukta's aunts had raised their families. Seven or eight other dwellings completed the small community. As they approached, the place seemed deserted. The boys helped Tukta out of the car and, with hands bound, led her up the steps of her mother's house and into the room that she'd slept in as a girl. The room was windowless; what light there was seeped in between the vertical wooden boards which were placed a centimetre or so apart for ventilation. On the floor there was some bedding, a bottle of water and a durian on a plate. The acrid smell of the aromatic fruit was already strong in the room.

'What's this?' Tukta asked indignantly.

'I made your room ready for you,' said Chusak. 'I thought you'd like some durian if you're hungry. It was always your favourite fruit.'

'I'm going to be a prisoner?'

'Of course. Otherwise you might run away.'

'How am I going to open the durian without a knife?'

Chusak hadn't considered this. 'You'll have to bang it on the floor. You can't have a knife.'

'Why not?'

'You might try to escape.'

'Well at least untie my hands.'

As they cut the twine on her wrists, she asked, 'Where's Ma?'

'She's gone into Khorat; she'll be back soon.'

'Gone to look for land to buy, no doubt,' Tukta snapped sarcastically.

'Probably,' agreed Chusak. 'Anyway, you won't have to wait here long.'

With that, the boys left the room, securing the hasp on the door with a padlock.

*

Dennis welcomed Mitch into his office overlooking Pattaya Road Two and closed the door.

'First, I suggest we find out if this note is genuine. Do you want to call Tukta?'

'Yes, of course, I'll do that.'

Voicemail; Tukta's phone was switched off.

'That doesn't prove anything,' said Dennis, 'but it's supporting evidence. Now, about the number on the note—I don't think we have any choice, do we?'

'No,' Mitch reflected anxiously. 'Would you mind making the call? They're not likely to speak English.'

'Shall I tell them who I am? I don't think we want to be caught lying, they might react unpredictably.'

'I agree. Tell them the truth. You're my friend who speaks Thai.'

'What are we going to agree to? Shall I bargain over the money?'

'Yes, there's the amount and also the timing. I can't get it for a week.'

'OK, here goes.' Dennis took out his smartphone and dialled the number on the ransom note.

The conversation lasted some time and Dennis was, in turns, businesslike, insistent and apologetic. When he finished talking, Dennis put down the phone and turned to his friend to summarise, 'They have Tukta and she's fine. You're not to worry; they haven't harmed her. They're holding her in Khorat. They've reduced the price to three million. They were unhappy about the week's delay; I think they might go for a lower amount if it could be quicker.'

Mitch looked relieved. 'Thanks, Dennis. I couldn't have done that. I'm obliged to you.'

'Don't, Mitch. It's for you and Tukta; you're my friends. You'd do the same for me, though I hope you'll never have to. One thing—the guy had an unusual voice, very high-pitched, and it sounded like he had tissues in his mouth. They could be professionals.'

'Shit! What happens next?'

'They've gone away to consult and will call back on this.' Dennis picked up the glossy phone and said, 'Wait, let's see if we can narrow down their location in Khorat. I have an app here that can ping their cell phone and triangulate its position. We should be able to see that on the map.'

Dennis pressed a few keys on the illuminated screen and continued, 'Here we are. Oh, the fucking little liar, he's not in Khorat at all, he's in Pak Chong. That's the place just north of Khao Yai, the national park. That's about an hour from Khorat, isn't it?'

'Pak Chong? Yes. I know it well. It's an hour west of Khorat. It's where Tukta's family lives.'

Dennis shot his friend an astonished stare. At that moment, the phone began to vibrate in his hand. He took the call.

'It's them,' he mouthed across the desk. Mitch moved closer to try and make out the voice on the end of the line.

Dennis pressed the mute and consulted with Mitch. 'How much could you get by tomorrow?'

'God, I don't know, let's say half a million?'

Dennis returned to the call which promptly concluded.

'They will release Tukta at 8am tomorrow in exchange for half a million baht.'

'Where?'

'The parking lot of Tesco Lotus, Khorat.'

'And you reckon they're calling from Pak Chong? Tukta's mother lives less than five clicks from there. That's too much of a coincidence, don't you think?. It must be someone that knows me, someone from the village. If I think of the number of weddings and funerals I've sat through in that village, drinking Thai whisky with their family, smiling at the folks. Do you think someone was watching me all those times thinking, "he's loaded; one day I'll kidnap his wife and see what I can get"? It couldn't be her father. He was always around in the early days but he's a drunk; walked out on Tukta's mother a couple of years back. He moved in with some female about half a click away.'

'The voice didn't sound like an old drunk; seemed younger.'

'How would you judge the guy by his voice?'

'Impetuous, fickle, opportunist, nervous, he was very suggestible. He's young certainly. I'd say twenties. I think they want this over as quickly as possible and don't care how much money they get as long as they get some. They don't want to lose face,' Dennis replied.

'The little bastards. They're not getting any of mine, that's for sure, not even half a million.'

*

In her childhood bedroom, Tukta dozed in the heat. She was awoken by a scratching noise by the door. She sat up to see a dark outline in the gaps between the wall planks. Her mother was squatting down outside the room, in the area where they watched television.

The old woman spoke through a chink in the wall, softly, like a confessional.

'The *farang* called,' she said.

'Mitch is my husband, Ma. He's not "the *farang*", he's your son-in-law who has always treated you with love and honour and who has been a good friend to the family and has helped you many times.'

'I agree he's a good man to you. You live in a lovely house and you don't want for anything. I was pleased when you married him because of the opportunity it offered. But an opportunity for you is an opportunity for your family. You have lived with Mitch for, what, six years? I took care of you for 28 years. That must mean something in terms of a debt.'

'You know I always help you when I can.'

'But the *farang* can afford so much more.'

'No, Ma, no he can't. Mitch's money is invested to provide us with a living. That's what pays for our food and water and electricity. If you take our money away from us how can we live?

'And anyway, this isn't the way to get him to help you. If you're in need, come to us and ask. Mitch is a good man with a good heart. He would always help you if you needed something. You don't steal from him; that's not right. You ask; that's how honest families do things.'

'What's the point of marrying a *farang* if he won't help your family?'

'I've explained how it works, Ma. What you're doing is wrong; it's unforgivable. You're stealing from your only daughter and threatening my life. I can never forgive you. Your greed is damaging our family. Now, unlock this door and let me go and we'll never talk of this again.'

'It's fixed for tomorrow. You can go back to the *farang* tomorrow. He will pay us a derisory amount that shows how little he loves you.'

'I don't call four million baht derisory!'

'The *farang* will pay only half a million. He said you're worth no more than that.'

'Mitch didn't say that.'

'Ask him yourself tomorrow.'

*

Mitch knew he wouldn't be able to sleep that night. To reach Khorat by eight o'clock the next morning meant starting out at three-thirty, even with the most favourable conditions. He wanted to get into position early and worried about early-morning traffic around his destination, so in the end he departed shortly after midnight. Not wanting to be recognised by Tukta's captors should they be familiar with his car, he borrowed Dennis's pick-up. He thought the kidnappers, whoever they were, would appreciate the money being delivered in his old leather attaché case, so he took it down from on top of the bedroom cupboard, loaded and locked it and put the key in the top pocket of his shirt.

He arrived in Khorat shortly after five. Dawn was doing its best to break but it was still dark. Mitch drove past the Tesco Lotus and counted a dozen or so cars parked out front. He stopped at an all-night 7-Eleven for a coffee and a hot dog and ate it in the car. To kill time, he drove a circuit of the town. The lights were on in some of the shops and there were a few pedestrians on the pavements. He passed a pair of monks with alms bowls, a woman kneeling before them to receive a blessing, her flip-flops neatly placed beside her.

Shortly before seven, he returned to the supermarket car park, chose a space in the first row, faced the pick-up inwards on the lot, killed the engine and sat back to wait. Dennis's car had tinted windows and Mitch felt confident that he would not be seen from outside, though he had a clear view of the whole area before him.

They had agreed to meet in row G. It was shortly before eight o'clock and the number of cars coming and going had increased. Row G was beginning to fill up. Whatever was about to happen, thought Mitch, this hand-over is going to be a public affair. After a few minutes, he could see an old rusty saloon cruising down row G. Mitch's first thought was that this must be the kidnappers casing the rendezvous. His second was that he recognised the car. 'Shit,' he whispered to himself, 'that's Chusak's old Nissan.'

He watched as it pulled into a parking bay and stopped. Nobody got out. Mitch grabbed his attaché case, got out of the pick-up and advanced towards the car, stepping over the curbs that lined the parking rows. He reached the Nissan and knocked on the driver's window. A young man opened the door and got out. His face was swathed in scarves, like a worker on a building site avoiding the sun. The back door opened and he was joined by another boy, also with his face covered.

Mitch recognised Chusak immediately. It took him a few moments to recall the younger boy's name, Arkom. He bent down and saw Tukta on the left side of the rear seat. 'Come on, honey, let's go home.'

Tukta got out of the car and walked round to join her husband.

'What about the money?' asked Chusak.

'Why do you deserve any money?' Mitch demanded in English. 'You kidnapped your own sister.'

'He knows who you are,' Tukta told the boys. 'How wouldn't he? You're even driving your own car, the one he's seen parked outside our house for the past three years.'

'But he agreed,' Chusak said as he grabbed the briefcase from Mitch and handed it to Arkom. His nephew shook the case and listened to the satisfying thud as the wads of paper shook around inside, but he got nowhere with the latches.

'It's locked,' he said.

'We're done here,' said Mitch to his wife. 'Our car's over there, the silver pick-up. Let's go.'

As he turned to go, Mitch took the key of the attaché case from his pocket, handed it to Chusak and said, 'You boys have done a very wicked thing. What's in that case is a whole lot more than you deserve.'

*

As Mitch steered the pick-up out of the car park, Tukta turned to him and said, 'That's it with my family. I can never trust my mother again, nor those two layabouts. We have to move, somewhere they can't find us.'

'We don't have to decide about this now.'

'Yes we do. We have to sell up and go. I can't bear the thought that they'd know where we live. What about Chiang Mai?'

'OK with me, but...'

'I'm sorry my awful family did this to you.'

'Aw, Tukta. None of it's your fault.'

'And I'm sorry you had to pay half a million baht.'

'On second thoughts, I guess you're right; we should get out of town as soon as possible.'

'Why?'

'That attaché case was full of newspaper.'

WILLIAM PESKETT

Mist on the Jungle

The closer we got to Ranong, the heavier the rain came down. It lashed the car in sheets, the thud of the big drops on the roof making our hired Toyota sound thin and cheap, like a creosote tin. Cars slid slowly past, their windscreen wipers on full speed, some with their lights on. Soaked boys on motorbikes drove by one-handed; the other an eye-shield seeking a passage through the watery veils.

The rain hadn't let up for two days. That night the water beat on the steel roof of our hotel chalet, keeping the boys awake. In the morning, expecting the fresh air of a newly-rinsed world, all we got was another wash cycle. The puddles had coalesced in the night, forming the beginnings of a moat around the bungalow. To reach the car, we had to leap in our flip-flops from island to muddy island, across the new swamp of the hotel garden like water-hens skipping between lily pads. Back on the road, the low grey sky threatened the horizon, nursing clouds like painful purple bruises.

Ranong is Thailand's wettest city. Five metres of water pass through it every year. On its journey from cloud to aquifer, or out to the sea, that day the rain hammered Ranong's streets, flooding its gutters and swilling fervently down its inadequate drains. The people on the slick pavements waddled about in translucent plastic coats, fogged up on the inside. A gust of wind would swell them up like fat grubs, their arms inside like organs heaving, their skins glistening under the constant downpour. The world as seen from Ranong was sodden, heavy, saturated, like a dripping liver. The town's economy seemed based on rain; one squeeze and its currency would spurt out like blood.

South of Ranong, when we stopped on Highway 4 to admire the Nam Tok Ngao waterfall from the sanctuary of the car, the popular spectacle seemed at once unremarkable, no more than a continuous part of its surroundings, just another cascade in a wide landscape of deluge.

Further on, we turned left, east off the highway and into the heart of the Isthmus of Kra. It sounded like an imagining of JRR Tolkien, a monstrous empire, perhaps, where the laws of the universe conceded to magic. The road narrowed. After a few forks, the tarmac gave way for a stretch to poured concrete, then to pot-holed shingle and mud. The tracks of previous cars snaked around the largest puddles, but I couldn't avoid them all. Filled with water, there was no way of telling how deep a pot-hole was going to be, so I slowed the slalom to little more than walking pace.

We were in jungle now, a deeper landscape, magic indeed, cultivated sporadically on either side of the track with sweet corn, papaya, dragon fruit and some coffee bushes. Further back, the lush mix of palms, bamboo and taller broad-leafed jungle trees exalted in the rain and danced with the wind. Lashed with water, every glossy leaf dribbled and ran. Above, the clouds had settled on the hills, the vapour wisps below the tree-line like cigar smoke in a clubroom that the diners had left.

At a crossroads, there was a small village which had a modern school and a dowdy temple. Geng asked me to stop the car.

'You want to get out?' I asked.

'Just for a moment. I won't be long.'

'You'll get soaked. That little umbrella's not going to be any good in this.'

'I'll be OK.'

'Can I go too?' asked James.

'OK, but hurry. What about you, Michael?'

'No thanks.'

Identical twins brought up together and everything has to be different.

They dashed under the umbrella into the temple compound. I saw her run up the steps of the bot with James on one hip, step out of her sandals and duck inside.

After 15 minutes or so, the rain had eased and they re-emerged from the wat. The light caught Geng's face as she got back into the car. She looked concerned. She put her son in the back, settled beside me and said, 'I had a bad dream last night. A doctor was cutting my sister's leg. She was naked. It could mean she's going to get sick.'

'And the temple?'

'Insurance,' she said.

I looked at my wife, slack-mouthed. There was nothing to say that I hadn't said before, always when we were in Thailand. I slapped the steering wheel in frustration, took a deep breath, paused to allow the moment to pass, and started the engine. I wasn't really angry; just disappointed.

She asked petulantly, 'You understand insurance?'

'Yes, I understand insurance.'

*

I could sing a song for you, my love, with notes that resound to your heart's thrum and words that echo to your own. I could write a book about you, an encyclopaedia of Geng; the chronicles of you. I have watched you sleeping, held your sleepy head in my lap on tiring boat-trips over choppy seas, and seen you as lively as anything with breath. I know your biology. I have tasted your blood and held your vomit in my cupped hands. I have seen two boys slip out of you. I have questioned you in the dark, talked to you all day, taught you and learned from you. We have made love knowledgeably; from the first day I met you we have made love. I have loved no-one more than you, Geng. There's no-one I know better than you; I know every molecule of you. And yet I don't know you.

*

My wife is that rare thing: a beautiful, educated and travelled Thai woman. She is not unique in these characteristics, I am sure, but she is rare. She comes from a poor family near Ranong in south Thailand at a point where the isthmus is at its thinnest, no more than 100 kilometres from the Andaman Sea in the west to the Gulf of Thailand to the east. Like most of her village contemporaries, Geng got little from formal schooling. Drifting into bar-work in Phuket was also nothing unusual for the girls she knew. Many had already seen off one hopelessly young husband by the time they left, depositing a baby in the arms of its grandmother as they boarded the bus.

Geng had held out in this regard, hoping to find a more suitable partner among the tourists who flocked to Phuket's beaches and bars. She surprised herself, and her family, by choosing a Thai man to marry. He was indeed a tourist — down from Bangkok for a fortnight's golf with three business friends — but he was unlike any of the local Thais whom her friends had married so unsuccessfully. He was not only comfortably wealthy he was also, from what I have heard from Geng, loving and thoughtful. Nerng had what the Thais call 'a good heart'. He saw potential in his young wife and, settled in their new home in Bangkok, sent her back to school, financed her studies and proudly supported her progress to university in the city, where she read physics — the only woman in her year to do so.

Geng's ambitions were not satisfied by her degree. She was offered a place to study for a PhD in electrical engineering at Manchester. Nerng's business contacts helped her win a scholarship from an educational foundation, and he promised to help with any additional living expenses she might have during the three or four years she would be in England.

For a year it was a happy arrangement. Geng flew home the first Christmas and Nerng visited his wife in Manchester the following Easter. But in the summer, when Geng again returned to Thailand, she noticed a change in her husband. He was ready to start a family, he said. He wanted children. Geng would have to abandon her doctorate and return to Bangkok. She couldn't be a proper wife at such a distance. He hadn't realised how long her studies would take. He missed her presence at company functions. He felt let down and confused. Geng knew what this was about: his family was pressing for grandchildren. It was pitiful, she thought, to see a man who commanded such authority in his business life reduced to trotting out the unthinking demands of his ageing parents.

Geng had to endure an angry scene with Nerng's mother in which the matriarch fed her roughly the same line that she'd received from her husband. However, Nerng hadn't gripped her by the wrists, slapped her face and thrown her to her knees as his mother had done. Unable to respond, she cowered on the floor in the position traditionally ordained for Thais in the presence of a superior.

Geng tried for a week to change her husband's mind, to convince him that there would be time enough to make a family after she had earned her PhD. Her qualification would open up wonderful opportunities for her, and for them. They could live abroad for a few years; she could earn good money.

The pressure in Nerng exploded. He couldn't go abroad; his business was in Bangkok. They didn't need any more money; he had income enough to provide for a family of any size.

It was hopeless. One morning when Nerng was at work, Geng packed everything she owned into two bags and left for the airport. She summoned the strength of purpose that resides in many Thai women in times of difficulty: she would carry on alone.

*

The pot-holed road continued for four or five kilometres. Over one stream a new concrete bridge had been constructed. Over the next there were still the two railway sleepers that I remembered. With the final run down into Geng's hamlet, the sun at last burst through the sky's sodden duvet of cloud. I pulled the mud-spattered hire car to a halt on the cement square — used in other seasons for drying coffee berries — across the track from her mother's house.

Geng's mother — I always called her Ma — approached us shyly. She wore a bright floral blouse over a bright floral sarong. Her natural reserve fought with her enthusiasm to meet her half-Western grandsons for the first time. Geng had trained them to *wai* their grandmother, holding their hands, palms together, up to their foreheads. Ma smiled gracefully, squeezed my forearm in the cross-cultural way she always did, and led us into her house.

Ma's home is typical of the area, indeed of most of Thailand, a two-storey wooden building with an open ground floor used for sitting out in the evenings, storage, free-range chickens and occasionally a caged pig. Wooden steps lead up to the main living quarters, four or five windowless rooms that are mostly bare of furniture. In one, there is a fridge, in another a large television, aged appliances which indicate roughly the functions of each area.

The steps were sprinkled with fresh blood in honour of our arrival and, I have been told in the past, to warn off any spirits that might consider doing us harm. The previous owner of the blood had been plucked and neatly chopped and was boiling in a grey broth over the open wood fire in the kitchen, an area beside the house protected by a lean-to plastic roof. A clawed chicken's foot, I recall, projected from the surface of the stew.

The bird was to be our lunch, served as we sat on wooden crates and stools around a low table while the village shaman, hired for the occasion, incanted scripture monotonously in some unused but sacred language. With Geng helping the twins, we stretched out our hands palm-down to spill any residue of bad luck that might be in us. Then we turned them over to receive the good luck that falls from the sky like enchanted rain.

After lunch, Geng came to me looking grave. Her aunt, she told me, had been taken ill and Geng had offered to drive the old lady to hospital.

'I knew this would happen,' she added dramatically.

'Actually, you said your sister would get sick,' I pointed out.

'She's my mother's sister. It's not 100 per cent accurate, how could it be?'

'How could it be one per cent accurate?'

*

My darling Geng, what is it about this realm, this soil, this idea of Thailand that strips you so completely of what you have strived all your adult life to achieve? I'm thinking now of your curriculum vitae: physics graduate, doctor of electrical engineering, production director – clear evidence there of your aptitude for rational thought. Is it the pesticide spray they dispense on the plane? Does some insidious fog enter your mind when you step through passport control? Does the metal detector wipe your hard drive? As you approach the Isthmus of Kra, do I hear your memory banks degrade, like Hal in the movie 2001: A Space Odyssey? *'Daisy, Daisy, give me your answer, do.' 'Don't do that, Dave.' What a shock it always is to find that ten years of education, self-motivated against what most people in your position would consider impossible odds, count for so little in the mystical kingdom.*

*

We met in the first term of Geng's second year. Although her scholarship was paying her tuition fees and rent, she had taken a waitressing job to make up the rest. I had been alone for four years following my wife's premature death. I liked Thai food. She served me at my table-for-one.

In those four years I had seldom felt desire for a woman and certainly there had been no relationships, no intimacy. Of course pretty girls had served me before, in banks, bookshops and burger bars. I had delighted in their beauty, but had never received that essential insight, the one that puts us together in some future tableau. This one is attractive, but what would she see in me? I sell insurance, for God's sake. Or that one? Can I imagine myself introducing a woman like her to my father or my daughter?

But it happened with Geng. I was polite to her and friendly without, I hope, giving her the impression that I was trying to pick her up, which I wasn't. She was friendly back. We permitted silences longer than is usual with waitresses. When I settled the bill, she hovered by my table so long I thought I'd botched the card transaction or insulted her with the amount of the tip. After an awkward pause, she told me she finished work at 11.30. I said I'd wait outside.

I found the nearest pub and counted off the two hours in a passion of uncertainty. What the hell was I doing? I'd hardly spoken to this woman except to discuss the spiciness of the food and the availability in Manchester of green papaya. She must have been 20 years younger than me. The test: could I imagine myself presenting her to my father or my daughter? Actually, no.

When I met her outside the closing restaurant, we hardly spoke.

'Where should we go?' I asked feebly.

'Most places will be shutting up soon,' she pointed out.

'I live quite close. I don't suppose you'd like to come and get some coffee? Really, you should say no. I mean, the risk.'

'It was my idea,' she said calmly, holding my gaze. Indicating the restaurant, she explained, 'I told my friend that I was meeting you. We have your credit card details. I think I'm safe.'

Within two hours we were in bed together. I had only the sketchiest notion of who she was, but somehow it worked.

In a year, we had travelled to Thailand so that she could complete her divorce. After a further six months we were married. The twins came along when she was a couple of years into a job as production manager at a packaging company. Four months later she was back at work, shortly to be made director with a place on the firm's executive committee.

Geng fitted well into the life of a Manchester businesswoman and wife. There's an oriental supermarket not far from our house where she could buy nearly everything she needed to recreate the food she loves... the food we love. The more esoteric fermented fish pastes and dips were perhaps an exception and I drew the line at trying to prepare our own at home.

Geng had been trained as a scientist to a high level and was now applying her skills in the unforgiving world of commerce. Her coinage was the electron; her tools were circuits, chips, robots and human relationships. Her environment was the factory floor, the control suite, the engineering lab and the meeting room. Academic as she was, it was a down-to-earth commission. She couldn't afford to have her head in the clouds.

My wife was raised a Buddhist, or at least into that amalgam of Buddhism, Hinduism, animism and superstition that Thais collectively call Buddhism. But she didn't seem to be an active adherent of the creed. I suppose I took her for a lapsed Buddhist in the same way that I was a lapsed Jew, that is, it was something our parents seemed to believe in. Geng had Thai friends in Manchester, almost exclusively young women married to Mancunians. We were occasionally invited to parties that had a Buddhist element — a new house would be blessed by a group of saffron-robed monks with northern accents, a baby would be similarly welcomed into our midst. But apart from that, Geng seemed to show no interest in practising the religion. She had British citizenship; she worked as a Westerner and seemed to think like one. In England her dreams went uninterpreted; the spirits of the earth and air, unattended, remained benign; she survived without making merit; and as for the lottery — an important focus for superstition for the average Thai — she could take it or leave it. The dimensions of her life — and of our lives together — seemed to obey the laws of physics.

*

Geng's aunt was brought out from one of Ma's bedrooms. She looked sleepy and pale. As Geng helped her to the front-door steps, Ma took a small bowl from the fridge, dipped her thumb in a dark liquid and applied a dab of it to her sister's forehead.

'What was that?' I asked Geng later as we processed towards the car.

'The rest of the chicken's blood.'

It was mid-afternoon by the time we reached the outpatients' entrance to the hospital. An efficient porter with a wheelchair met our car at the dropping-off area. Geng and the boys went inside with the invalid as I parked the car. I found them upstairs in a waiting area.

Before too long, Geng's aunt appeared through a pair of swing doors, her chair pushed by a young nurse in a freshly-pressed white uniform and white shoes. A more casually-dressed woman in a white lab-coat walked behind. This woman, who I took to be the attending doctor, approached Geng and they conversed briefly in Thai.

A bill was presented and I paid some money at a counter.

'It's an ear infection,' Geng translated the diagnosis for me. 'They've given her some antibiotics. It should be gone in a few days.'

'They didn't think much of your mum's medicine,' I remarked.

'What do you mean?'

'They washed the blood off her forehead.'

As we drove back to the village, the light was beginning to fade. The rain had stopped but the mist still clung to the wooded slopes above our route.

Back at Ma's house, Geng explained the doctor's conclusion to her mother. Her aunt was to finish the course of antibiotics and take it easy. She was placed at the table downstairs and, complaining that she was hungry, given some rice soup.

I went to get a bottle of Scotch from the car, found a plastic mug and came back to sit with the aunt. I noticed the bloody thumb-smudge had been re-applied. I considered remonstrating with Geng, but I could find nothing to say that would be new. Even in my own head, my unspoken arguments were beginning to sound intolerant and harsh. Really, what objection could I have to the way life was conducted out here in the jungle? None, but that wasn't it. It was Geng. It was my wife's accomplishment, the way she stood for what could be achieved with sufficient determination, which contrasted so awkwardly with the way as a minimum she accepted her family's hocus pocus and joined in with it at certain points. Already, I could hear her response: 'Let them; it doesn't do any harm.'

*

No, of course the stigma does no harm, but surely you can see that belief in it does. How can you and your family ever hope to benefit from the knowledge we have accumulated over centuries if you won't accept the immutable laws that govern the world? You, my darling, you of all people should see this, you who understand the physics of moments and the way of the pendulum, the duplicity of light and the repeatable properties of all things. You and your professional forebears have made us close to 100% certain of how materials behave. At home in England I know this is how you think. Yet here where the land threw you up the air is thick with humidity. Here, a steam of ignorance enters your lungs like a soothing balsam, and a mist descends on you as surely as it does on the jungle trees, blocking your view, occluding the light.

*

Three days later our holiday was at an end and we were on our way home. We returned our hire car at Bangkok airport and boarded a plane for Manchester via Schiphol. The boys and I had three seats together. During take-off, Geng held out for my hand across the aisle.

She said, 'Do you still want to retire to Thailand?'

I said, 'Of course.'

'We'll start looking for a house next year, yeah?'

'OK.'

'Somewhere that's not as wet as Ranong.'

'Good idea.'

'The rest of it,' she said, 'it's just insurance.'

'But you don't need insurance.'

'Don't let your boss hear you say that.'

The co-pilot welcomed us to Manchester. The ground staff, he said, had reported that conditions were clear and dry, with some cloud.

Letter from Nowhere

On the Wednesday evening, the third day, he found a note in a drawer of the desk. It was brief and to the point; it asked him to act as executor in the event of his brother's death. With the note was another, more recent, request that he do the same for Patrick's wife. In the same drawer there was an envelope containing his brother's will. He left it sealed.

In a filing drawer, in a wallet marked 'Songs', he found five typed sheets stapled in the corner. He scanned the document briefly and took it out to the patio. Back in the kitchen, he unbagged his litre bottle of duty-free Bushmills whiskey, found a glass and mixed a generous slug with ice and a little water. Back on the patio, he settled in a rattan chair and began to read.

*

'You always say you want us to die together. You tell me that you can't live without me, which I suspect is more a statement of financial or practical reality than a declaration of spiritual dependence. Either way, the odds are against it. No actuary would bet on it. I'm 58 and you're 32. Not so long ago, I was twice your age. You've caught me up a little in proportional terms, but arithmetically I'm still out there in the lead, holding you off with an inflexible oar as you struggle to be let into my ancient, leaky boat. I think perhaps you can picture us sitting together on the thwart, the waves chest-high as we sink into oblivion as into some sweet, inviting syrup.

'Let's be realistic. I'm old enough to be your — cliché alert! — bank manager. Just kidding. Seriously, though, I am old enough to be your uncle, your teacher, your lollipop man, your friend; yes, also your father. Your grandfather, even, if your forebears had got their skates on.

'Nothing has made me think so hard about my death as being married to a woman as young as you. If my wife and I were contemporaneous, more than likely we'd also be coterminous, or close to it. Under such conventional circumstances, the requirements of what insurers call the surviving spouse would not be so great. The house, yes, the car, the washing machine and so on, these would probably see the survivor out without the need for replacement. Also, money to live on and enough extra for a few treats — an ocean cruise as a final fling, perhaps, or a tour of Machu Picchu or the castles of the Rhine if arthritis can be held at bay.

'These would not be a huge burden on the estate. Under these natural circumstances — the way it's meant to be — affairs could be arranged to accommodate them, the capital would remain more or less intact and would be available to will to my grateful children. In this fantasy, I do not imagine that my chosen wife is the profligate type, waiting for my demise before blowing our savings on a few years of geriatric hedonism. I do not expect her to take an impoverished young lover who will roger her senseless and bleed her dry, though I have no objection to a dim but jolly stockbroker, say, or a retired colonel of independent means. I like the idea of a man with a limp or an eye patch; sock suspenders certainly. I do not deny her that.

'And I have no doubt that, contrariwise, if this imaginary wife were to predecease me, she would, in her sweet dying breath, extend to me the same level of trust concerning my conduct along the last furlong of the home straight. Should I find, in this event, that I have a handful of years left to roam the planet, I would do my roaming much as I had for the bulk of my life to that point—soberly, sensitively, intelligently, and with due respect for the value of my estate as it will be presented to my children on what's known as the second death. Why would I do otherwise?

'After a period of mourning, I might close up the house, perhaps for as long as a year, and set off on some modest adventure, largely unplanned. I would let the wind take me up like thistledown; I would be subject to the currents of the sea. I could spend some agreeable evenings smoking cigars on the veranda of a game lodge in East Africa, perhaps, as giraffes galumphed across the setting sun; or, tiring of the sheer splendour of the aurora borealis, drink mulled wine with dowagers in the saloon of an iron-hulled steamer coasting the Arctic fjords. I have often thought about Guatemala. This would be my opportunity to find out why.

'I don't have a particular fancy for women on this trip, as some might expect of a carefree widower let loose in a world of sin. I don't see myself lounging in fleshpots or carousing under moons. If ladies of a romantic disposition were to drift my way, providing they were up to muster I would bed them if bedding's what they wanted and so long as I proved up to the task with sufficient style and grace.

'The only thing I fear is gold-digging. I couldn't bear to be taken for a sucker. The truth is that there's not an enormous amount of gold to dig, but of course if the stories you hear are true, that fact is generally discovered only when what little gold there is has been comprehensively dug.

'To make things tidy, the length of my voyage would be determined to correspond as nearly as possible with my end. If I took too long a trip I could find myself meeting an undignified conclusion in a Cairo hotel room or while swaying giddily at the summit of the Sydney Harbour Bridge. I couldn't be doing with any of those sorts of death. I require a bit of *dulce et decorum*.

'On the other hand, if I made the journey too short, I could land myself with a residual eternity of boredom to tick away back home.

'No, it would have to be judged very finely. I'd come back, put all my papers in order, check the will, making the investments and savings accounts easy to find, and phone around the family, sounding cheery and positive. The point here would be to provide each of my relations with a common memory of me that could be conveniently referenced in later conversation. Then I'd water the garden, position myself on the rattan chair on the patio with a slim book of poems and a Scotch and soda on a side table and simply lie back to watch the sun go down.

'And down.

'The garden boy would find me in the morning before the flies had made a mess of me. It's the only way to go.'

*

Thomas removed his reading glasses and rubbed his eyes. He looked out over the swimming pool that abutted the patio and, beyond that, the tended precision of the garden: bottle palms, a lady palm, spindly dracaenas, the two ebullient cycads, all set in a neatly-trimmed lawn.

This was clearly some sort of letter, but it had no salutation and no signature. He had to believe that it was meant for Song, but why would Patrick fantasise to his wife about some other, imaginary spouse, some years her senior? It must have been some private joke they shared.

He wandered back through the living room to the kitchen. This house was so very Patrick, like his old home in England, but with tropical references. Patrick abroad; Patrick and Song; Patrick gone native; Patrick released, perhaps. He poured a larger measure of Bushmills, mixed it and returned to the garden to resume.

*

'But since I am married to you, none of this will happen. The truth is that I'm 26 years older than you, my love. That means that, everything else being equal, when I succumb to the inevitable, no matter how much you may wish for that event to trigger your own passing, you will have another 26 years to live, give or take. That's roughly a quarter-century, longer than an expected lifetime at some points in our history.

'What will you do?

'Your options are many. You could start again. When I've gone from your sight, it will not be long before I have gone from your mind. You have very few photographs of me; my books will soon become foxed and devoured by termites; my clothes by moths. You will be a clean sheet on which a new life, a second life, is waiting to be composed. Imagine how you were before we met. Recall the fresh hopes your heart contained.

'You could find another *farang*, my love, perhaps one as ancient as me, and embark on a repeat of our life together. Or you could set your cap at one closer to your own age and, after a suitable number of years have elapsed, and your love for him is as great as the one you now feel, again pray — more realistically this time — for the ideal you so often express of death together.

'I don't have your confidence that such an outcome is easily achieved, certainly not without unlucky violence of some kind. Couples die together in landslides, tsunamis, buffalo tramplings, plane crashes, freak events at theme parks or, more prosaically and much more likely given Thailand's dreadful road safety record, traffic pile-ups. The foolhardy practice of suttee is too awful to contemplate, even in my present light-hearted frame of mind.

'That this is what you are unconsciously wishing for, even now, sends a caterpillar of fear wriggling into my innards every time we leave the driveway in our car. Will she lean over and crank the steering wheel sharply to the right as we hurtle towards some speeding juggernaut? Will she tamper with the brake connections before we descend some peak on hairpin bends? How strong is your death wish, my *teerak*, this wish that our deaths should be as one?

'It's because you can't imagine those 26 years, perhaps; you don't have the psychic tools to project from the past or from the present to the future. There's no reason why those years, your next life, shouldn't be as happy as the time we've spent together. They may differ somewhat in detail, but the overall effect of being content with life and achieving some important examples of satisfaction, all that could so easily be repeated.

'I want you to understand, my love: I'm not that special. I'm not unique. I'm not. There are plenty of *farang* men with my capabilities, my patient and gentle demeanour, my capacity for loving, who could make you a good second husband. You cannot imagine this because I am the only example you have to go on. But take it from me: I've lived with many women, some of whom were fortunate enough to become my wives, and I can tell you that there are many kinds of happiness.

'Your own character is important in this. When I think back over my marriages, I see that the relationships I have enjoyed have been similar in nature. This is to be expected. Although the women were individuals, I was the same man. And, although I didn't have a supply of identical twins, triplets etc from which to pluck my brides, there were inevitably similarities between them. This stands to reason, since they had all been chosen by me to fit some picture of what was required in a wife. This ideal, determined perhaps by memories of some glamorous screen idol, a pert primary school teacher, or perhaps even my mother — I don't know — changed very little in the course of my life. So my wives were similar people and the marriages I had with them were comparable experiences.

'So it will be with you. Do not fear the future. Do not dread the difficulty of continuing as happily in the years to come as you live now. You will find a chap a bit like me and together you will have as much fun as we have had, all these years.'

*

Thomas put down the document, removed his glasses and glanced around, over the wall at the roofs of other houses and, beyond, to the tower and tall condominiums of Jomtien.

He walked to the garden wall, chest-high on his side, but higher than that as it looked over the road. On the other side, a Thai woman passed with a blond child. A nanny, perhaps? A step-child? This town accommodated every possible relationship.

261

He went back inside, filled a bowl with ice and carried it back to the patio with the whiskey bottle.

*

'I have put everything in order for you — the house, the investments, the widow's pension. With the right executor, it should be a simple matter to transfer these to your name. Together, they will provide for your comfort for the rest of your life.

'These arrangements, these plans for your life after I've gone, have made it much easier for me to think of my death with something approaching a level head. I don't see my leaving quite as everyday as remembering to put out the cat and milk bottles before retiring for the night, but it's closer to that than it was.

'Do we have some natural mechanism within us that prepares us for death, some drug that narcotises our fear more thoroughly the closer we get? It would make sense. Fear of death in the young is to be encouraged; it might keep them from teetering near cliff edges on their bikes, sticking their fingers in the electric sockets or drinking from the bottles under the sink. Likewise in young adults, a death at this age can disrupt the lives of many and so any means to avoid it would have considerable value.

'Not so with codgers. They have it coming. What would be the point of maintaining a fear of death in one to whom it will inevitably come so soon? It would be unnecessarily cruel. Any creator who designed such a feature into our makeup should be suspected of having a sick sense of humour. No, it's much more reasonable to allow the elderly to approach their ends with the sort of feeling you get as you edge the car into the garage after a long journey. It's not momentous, but as the conclusion of a tiring drive it stands for something.

'So it is with me. There's a job to be done for you which takes my mind from the fear of death. The necessary planning for your life without me has released the death hormone into my sluggish bloodstream and readied me for my fate.

'Death is nothing. When Christians say this they mean that the act of dying is a small inconvenience — nothing more — between a life here on Earth and its continuance somewhere else. I think some of them still believe in hell, though modish Christians these days seem to propose that, merely by having survived a lifetime in the considerable rough and tumble *de nos jours*, we've all done jolly well. In recognition of *our effort*, just as in Wonderland where everyone gets prizes, we will all take our places in paradise.

'Good man goes to heaven; bad man goes to Pattaya, if we are to believe the T-shirts, so we all win.

'You, my love, believe something similar. Well, you know what you believe.

'As a heathen, I am much more literal than you religious folk. For me, death really is nothing. It's an absence of anything. If it were a place, it would be nowhere. If anything, this knowledge should increase my fear of death for, while you and other believers have somewhere to go, I do not. Death will separate me from everything I know and everyone I love. My singular comfort, and the reason I have no fear, is that it will do this unconsciously. I will not know that I am not with my loved ones, because I will not exist.

'I have tried to explain why I cannot encourage your desire for us to die together, my love. However romantic it may sound, this event would have the effect of wasting your subsequent life and would, in any event, have no meaning. Far from *living* together in some afterdeath paradise, we

263

would be unconscious of each other and of ourselves. Don't wish for this; there's no *together* about it.

'Instead, please, my *teerak*, live now as if your life had no end. Look forward to the years we have left together and the different experiences that will be laid at your feet when I am gone. Live in hope, not in fear. Embrace life in all its facets and functions, and in all its inevitability.'

*

The fire at Noize occurred the previous Friday, close to midnight. News of it was on the BBC in the evening: 21 people known to have died; many more in a critical condition. Thomas noted it because it was in Pattaya. The name caught his attention and he wondered, fleetingly, whether his life was about to be touched by tragedy.

The next day, he received a call at home in Brighton from Patrick's neighbour and friend, a Dutchman called Matt. The police had been to the village, he said, looking for family members. They had knocked on Matt's door and told him that Patrick and Song were both in intensive care at Pattaya Bangkok Hospital.

By Sunday, Thomas was on a plane to Bangkok. On Monday afternoon, he took a taxi from the airport to his brother's village and located Matt's house. The neighbour gave him a set of keys, alarm codes and contact numbers for the hospital and for the police team investigating the incident. Matt offered the services of his wife, Toy, as interpreter if he wanted to question the police in the morning. He accepted this offer and Toy was called out from the kitchen and introduced.

Thomas let himself into his brother's house and made something to eat from the sad left-overs in the fridge.

In the master bedroom, the lights were on, perhaps for security. On the bed lay a towel and a hair dryer; Song had been getting ready to go out.

He set the alarm clock, crawled into the guest bed and slept.

*

On the second day, Toy called for him at 8.30am and they drove to a large police station, the Pattaya headquarters, presumably. She asked at reception for the officer in charge of the Noize fire on Road Three. They sat near the door and waited for someone to appear.

Soon they were greeted by a senior-looking policeman in a tight-fitting uniform. Standing in the reception area, Thomas asked Toy to tell the officer who he was and explain that he had flown over from England to care for this brother and sister-in-law. He would appreciate as much information as he could be given concerning the accident on Friday.

The policeman seemed to accept this request. He nodded and asked them to come into his office. He was a short man, with pock-marked cheeks and an angular jaw. Although his appearance was severe, he dealt with Thomas and Toy with courtesy. The sign on his desk said he was a colonel.

The policeman referred to papers on his desk, and to a computer screen. The fire at Noize discotheque, he said, had been started by a charcoal barbecue at a food counter. The building was of concrete construction, but the walls were clad in highly combustible materials—bamboo screens and wooden louvres—which quickly caught fire. The premises were licensed for 550 customers. Although the investigation was still at an early stage, there was evidence to suggest that more than 700 people were in the building at the time of the fire.

Exits from the disco were the main door and a fire door at the rear. The fire door opened outwards, but couldn't be used as it was obstructed by a pick-up whose driver was inside the building with his car keys. Twenty-six people were dead as a result of burns, smoke inhalation, and crushing. At the latest count which had been done the previous evening, 37 people were in various hospitals around the city, most in a serious condition.

The police were conducting a criminal investigation to determine responsibility for the overcrowding, the operation of the barbecue and the blocked escape route.

Thomas asked about Patrick and Song. The colonel looked through his papers and tapped at his computer keyboard for some minutes.

He referred to a report from one of his officers who had been present at the scene during the rescue operation. Mr Patrick had been seen helping people escape. He had moved aside tables and chairs to make a path to the door; then was known to have smashed out a window-frame using one of the high tables. With another man, a Thai according to the colonel, Patrick dragged furniture to the window, to provide a means of reaching the sill and jumping out. He and the Thai man helped many people, perhaps hundreds, to safety by this route.

Song's friends reported seeing her outside. They said she was darting about frantically, trying to get information about her husband from members of the emergency services. She was pleading with them. As the fire intensified, a woman heard her screaming that Patrick was still inside. Then she was gone. 'We discovered a little later that she had run back into the disco by the main door, to look for her husband,' the colonel said calmly. 'When the fire fighters could finally get inside, they found them both unconscious. They had medical insurance cards so were taken to Pattaya Bangkok Hospital.'

When the colonel appeared to have given all the information he had, Thomas thanked him and went outside with Toy. He was wearing jeans and a long-sleeved shirt which felt stifling in the heat.

'What do you want to do?' asked Toy.

'I'd like to go to the hospital, but they may not let us see them.'

'If it's the Pattaya Bangkok, they will let us.'

'OK, let's go. Thanks.'

*

At the hospital, they were greeted by a smiling woman in a white suit and white shoes. Thomas explained in English who he was and asked if he could visit Patrick and Song, from the Noize fire. The woman showed them to a row of white chairs and told them that someone would see them shortly.

Soon, a young doctor approached them and indicated with his hand that they should not get up. He sat in the next chair and turned to face Thomas. He was holding a white clipboard to which were attached some papers.

'You are Mr Thomas, isn't it?' he asked.

Thomas confirmed that he was.

The doctor exchanged some words of Thai with Toy. 'I just told him I was a friend of Patrick and Song.'

The doctor had a steady eye, but his hands betrayed his nerves. He gripped a ball-point tightly in his fist and repeatedly clicked the button in the top.

'Mr Patrick and Ms Song were admitted here on Friday night,' he said, glancing at his clipboard. 'They were both suffering from burns and breathing smoke. Mr Patrick was unconscious when he arrived; Ms Song was conscious but in a lot of discomfort. We placed them both in our ICU, our intensive care unit.'

'Are they still in intensive care? Is my brother now conscious? I wonder if it would be possible to see them, just for a moment. We won't stay long.'

The doctor let him finish. He didn't want to hurry the conversation, but let it proceed at its own pace.

'I'm sorry to tell you, Mr Thomas, but your sister-in-law Ms Song passed away last night. Her lungs were severely damaged by the fire. She died in her sleep. I'm so sorry.'

Toy gripped his arm with both her hands, then put one arm around him and squeezed. Thomas extended his arm to her and they sat for a moment hugging.

'Poor Song,' he said. 'She was such a lovely woman.'

The doctor's eye contact was steady, as he had been trained.

'And my brother?' Thomas asked, numbing himself for the response.

'Your brother is now conscious. His condition is stable. We expect him to make a full recovery.'

'Does he know about Song?'

'No, not yet.'

The Night is a Starry Dome

Being the travel journal of Nattaporn (Lek) Galanakis,
translated from the Thaiglish

I came to Crete because I was blue.

I married my husband Giannis Galanakis in 1997. I remember the first thing he said to me. It was 'Giannis, but call me GG'. I had asked him his name. That was always the first thing I asked. When I enquired where he came from, I didn't understand his reply, and anyway the music was too loud. I made him repeat it twice, then let it go.

I was working as a dancer in a bar in Pattaya. The bar was called the Dollhouse-A-Go-Go and was located in Walking Street. It probably still is, though I haven't been down that street for years. My job was to dance on a small stage — a bar really — for which I was paid a small amount. I could augment my earnings by appearing topless, by sitting with the customers and persuading them to buy me drinks, or by going with them to their hotels for whatever they wanted.

I never knew that not to involve sex.

That was OK; the bar attracted a reasonably well-behaved set of customers. I could sit with anyone I wanted to and be bar-fined by anyone I chose. If a man was too mean with the drinks, I'd quickly pretend that I was needed on stage. If he wanted me to go with him and I had a bad feeling—if he was drunk or smelt bad—I'd fast-forward to my period or, if that didn't work, tell him I had herpes. That always did the trick.

This flexibility put me in control of my career. The ones I didn't turn away became my boyfriends. The relationships I had with my boyfriends were very varied. Some lasted half the evening, others all night. Occasionally, a boyfriend would take me to Koh Samui for the weekend, or to Chiang Mai for the week. We'd go elephant-riding or white-water rafting and take photos of each other smiling against the scenery like young lovers. Some would later send me money from Amsterdam or Rome, others would write soppy emails in terrible Thaiglish, some of which I would show to my friends for a laugh.

When Giannis Galanakis walked into the bar, I was 23 years old. I had been working at the Dollhouse-A-Go-Go for three years and was close to giving up and going home. I had a dream, encouraged by my mother, that I would find my husband in Pattaya, but nobody I met in the bar came close. I worked seven days a week from evening to early morning so I had no other opportunity to meet men. The rest of the time I slept in the room I shared with a girlfriend from the bar. When I wasn't sleeping I was washing my clothes or eating from street stalls. I had no time at all for a social life. My only chance was to find a customer who could see me as more than a quick fuck or, at best, a temporary wife.

Giannis was sitting with his brother Emmanuel. While I danced in front of him, he looked at me tenderly. I went to sit with him. After a while he spoke to his brother and then he took me for dinner in a Thai restaurant on Road Two, after which we went dancing at Hollywood disco. He was a very gentle lover for a man of his build. The next day we climbed up to the Big Buddha to look down on Pattaya. The buildings appeared so ordinary from up there; it was hard to imagine what went on inside them. A week later Giannis hired a car and we drove to Surin where I introduced him to my family. I cried when he left. When he came back the following year, we were married.

*

Many men come to Thailand to live in paradise and abandon the duties of home. GG wasn't like that. After we were married, we lived together in Isaan largely out of our combined loyalty to my family. We settled in Khorat—as Nakhon Ratchasima is known to the locals—close enough to my family in Surin and far enough away to allow us to lead an independent life. Also, we thought the schools would be better in the big city.

All the time GG would dream about the beauty of the Mediterranean and the glories of Crete—its mountains, the encircling sea and its turbulent history. In the evenings, we would sit outside our house, with a few lights on around the garden, and he would speak to me softly from his heart about his boyhood in Almiridha, playing football with his three brothers, teasing his two sisters. The sky in Crete would be bright with stars, he told me.

It made me look up.

As a young boy he went to sea with his father to haul up the octopus pots and lobster traps, but only at the weekends

271

as his parents were determined that all their children would benefit from a proper education—an opportunity that had been denied most of their generation in the poor village. Crete was his distant paradise; Khorat was where he started his own family, so the foreign city became his home. Isaan was in his head, but Crete stayed in his heart.

GG felt a strong need to come from somewhere, not only a place but also a time, preferably long ago. If someone asked me: 'What are the experiences that have shaped you?' I would mention the births of my children, my marriage, possibly the evenings I spent under the house with my mother, debating family crises and the various rows that were taking place between my brothers and sisters about land, planting and the harvest. Giannis would say, 'Driving the Turks from my country.'

Or it could have been the Germans or the Venetians; there was always someone to be driven out.

My husband defined himself in terms of history, thousands of years of it, stretching back like an unrolled carpet. Over this time, the people of Crete have endured repeated invasions, occupations and battles for independence. This communal experience had been distilled into a precious liquor which was dripped at birth into GG's veins. He was who he was not because he was an accountant, a football fanatic or even a son or a father, but because he was a Cretan, an inheritor of a legacy of struggle and suffering.

*

When I took my children to the aquarium near Iraklion, we learned that an octopus can control its eight limbs independently. It can show emotion by changing colour and has eyes very similar to our own—an example of parallel evolution. Like other molluscs, it has blue blood. GG's father

272

Christos caught octopus off the rocky coast of Almiridha in the way his father had taught him, and countless fathers before that, by dropping earthenware pots on to the seabed, tied together with rope like gems on a necklace. A pot makes a good hiding place for an octopus and it will stay inside even when it is hauled up to the surface. Christos would land his catch and pound the animals against a rock to tenderise their flesh. He would hang them on a rope to dry, like starched laundry on a clothesline. The Minoans caught octopus in the same waters in exactly the same way thousands of years ago. There's something in the sea, GG would say, that endures and cannot be denied.

*

Giannis was surprised about how little I knew of my own country's past. I hadn't a clue about Thailand's kings, apart from the present one and perhaps Rama V, who is well known to all Thais and revered to the point of worship by many. 'What were you doing in school?' he'd ask. Really, I couldn't remember. I suppose we must have been taught Thailand's history, but none of it sank in, not deep enough for memory. At home, there was never any talk of the past. We lived for the present, not the past and not particularly the future.

My parents didn't save, they lived from day to day, sure that in the years that the rice harvest came up short we would be helped by my uncles and aunts who lived nearby. It was the same for all of them. They would assist each other at times of planting and harvest. They charged for their labour, but the money was quickly repaid when the favour was returned. The agents who bought our grain were fierce negotiators with eyes like knives, quick to criticise the slightest drop in quality, though my father worked hard to achieve the best crops of jasmine rice, the *hom mali* for which Isaan is so famous.

Even at times of bountiful harvest, when my father would come home with great wads of 1,000-baht notes, even this apparent wealth didn't lead to greater security or a better life. There were five children to feed and clothe and all the expenses of running the farm. The next payday would be 12 months off. It's only recently that my father has tried to squeeze a second crop from his fields, but the later yield is invariably smaller and less dependable than the main harvest. When I was a small girl, the box where my father kept his money was always empty before the next payday came around.

Part of living only in the present is that I didn't have GG's appreciation of old things. For me, a modern house, purpose-built, is preferable to a second-hand one. It's clean and undamaged and you don't have to think about breathing the air of others. GG saw things very differently. For him, a new house or a piece of modern furniture had no patina, no accumulation of experience. An old house, he argued, showed the wounds from the generations of families who had lived there. How could you look at the scarred skin of a whale without wondering about the fearful threats it had seen off in the ocean? It took him a decade of gentle but repetitive encouragement before I came to realise he was right.

*

After we settled in Khorat, Giannis satisfied his own need for a connection with the past and tried to interest me in the same by reading widely about Thailand's history, drawing parallels with his own. 'Invasion,' he'd say to me darkly. 'Our two peoples have bred with so many invaders, it's a wonder we know who we are.'

The great Minoan civilisation, the one that Crete can claim is truly its own, was the commercial powerhouse of the Mediterranean 4,000 years ago. It took a huge volcanic eruption on the island of Thira to bring the empire down. After it, Crete became dominated by Mycenaeans and others. By the time Buddhism was spreading across Southeast Asia 2,000 years ago, the Romans had over-run the Greek world and Crete was bundled into one of their provinces.

A thousand years ago, the Khmers were the major power in Southeast Asia, ruling from their capital at Angkor. They took control of the wide plains and established Lopburi as the centre of Siam. GG once took me for a weekend there to show me the ruins of the temples and palaces. 'Just imagine,' he said. 'When this pile of stones was a grand house hung with fine silks and perfumed with jasmine and champaca, Crete was being over-run by Arabs.' To be honest, I was more impressed by the troupes of monkeys that rampage through Lopburi these days.

After the Arabs, in the declining years of Byzantium, Crete was lost to the Venetians. In the east, Thais came from southern China to challenge the Khmer empire and establish their first kingdom centred at Sukhothai. Six hundred years ago, the focus shifted to Ayutthaya.

In the seventeenth century, as the Venetian empire declined, Crete became part of the Turkish Ottoman Empire, reaching what GG described as its lowest point in history. Likewise, the Burmese looted Ayutthaya. It wasn't until the nineteenth century that modern versions of our two nations began to take shape.

The Thais rebuilt their capital, eventually at Bangkok, and founded the Chakri dynasty, which is the one still in place today. After a century of struggle, Crete finally won its independence and became part of Greece.

In the Second World War, Crete was occupied by the Germans; Siam—now Thailand—by the Japanese. For GG, brought up with his father's stories of Nazi atrocities, this was part of living memory; for me, it was something I'd seen on TV.

Fifteen years ago, with his heart shaking like water, Giannis, second child of Christos and Eleni Galanakis, set out with his brother Emmanuel from the airport at Hania, Crete, to take a vacation in Pattaya, Thailand. Giannis met and married Nattaporn (known as Lek), fifth child of Paradorn and Sukanya Tanasugarn, in Surin, Isaan. Later, they had a son, Paradorn, and a daughter, Eleni.

Giannis liked to think of himself as a pure-blooded Minoan—dreadlocked boxer, swimmer with dolphins, joyous tumbler over bulls. But he knew that the odds were against it. 'We had even forgotten the name of our people until an Englishman coined the word "Minoan" only a hundred years ago. I know in my veins I have Greek, Roman and Venetian blood.'

'You have mixed blood,' I would tease.

'My blood may be mixed,' he would say, 'but it's a uniquely Cretan mixture.'

'Maybe Turkish and Arab, too,' I would press him, knowing how he would respond.

'No, that's impossible,' he would say as I mouthed the words along with him. 'Anyway, there's probably Burmese blood in you, along with the Thai, Chinese and Khmer.'

'That's all right. *Mai pen rai.* I don't mind. But what about Dorn and Eleni? They have inherited two halves of two wonderful histories. They're Eurasian.'

'They're children of the world. That's the future.'

Thais have cultivated rice for perhaps 5,500 years; they may have been the first people to do so. The first rice to be domesticated was the sticky variety, with long-grain strains such as the perfumed jasmine rice coming along much later.

Before I left home, at the age of 17, rice was my life, just as fishing dominated GG's early years. My childhood ended when my mother persuaded me that my future lay beyond the boundaries of the farm, as reckoned from palm tree to palm tree, and one day I found myself on the early morning bus from Surin to Bangkok, my heart fluttering with fear and the idea pounding in my head that I was to find a *farang* to marry.

There are many ways into poverty and, according to my mother, one way out. This philosophy was based on the experience of my sister Lalana, known as Oh. Oh was four years older than me and had left home aged 17, as I now was, to stay with a girlfriend from the village who was working in Phuket. She quickly found bar work on the island and, within a year or two, reported back to her mother that she had a boyfriend, a man who soon became her fiancé. Oh's beloved was Irish, which meant he was a *farang* and thus able to provide Oh with a home and possibly a little extra to send back to her family in Surin. A year or so later, Oh married her fiancé and they moved to Pattaya, where now I occasionally go to visit them.

It was a model betrothal that my mother was keen to repeat. She had three daughters. Butri, known as Noi, was a year older than Oh and so a more problematic case, but my mother did not shrink from the challenge. Two years before, Noi had been dispatched to Bangkok to seek her *farang* saviour, just as Oh had done. No success had yet been reported, but her room in the city was an asset my mother was determined to exploit. Noi's flat was where I was headed. It was to be the base camp for my assault on the pinnacle of happiness: marriage to a foreigner.

*

A Buddhist monk will shave his head and beard to show his detachment from the human world and his commitment to a holy life. A Greek Orthodox priest grows his hair and beard to show his devotion to serving God. They both reject vanity, one by having no need for a comb, the other by having no use for scissors or a razor.

When I lived in Pattaya, where the monks shaved their heads to demonstrate their rejection of the whims of the world, I noticed many of the *farangs* did the same because they thought it the height of fashion. Here in Almiridha, I have seen a priest with short hair and no beard. Perhaps he is eager to follow the vogue of the community he serves.

'It's as well we're not all the same,' GG would say. His hair was thick and black and covered practically all of his body. He was like a big bear. His chest was like a saucepan scourer and his beard was continuous with it—when he shaved, he had to decide how far down he would go and make a cut-off point there like the edge of a lawn. In the early days, I would sit in the bathroom in the morning to watch him shave, maybe with Dorn on my knee. As he made foam with a brush and carefully wielded the wet razor, I would wonder: How could I be so lucky as to have this big bear in my life? How can I make him stay with me forever? When he was finished I would kiss his cheek, smelling the soap. He would let Dorn feel his smooth chin. By the afternoon it was like needles again.

My vanity was perfume. Every birthday, when GG asked me if there was something I wanted, I would tell him perfume. He would ask me which one, and I would say that it was his choice, that it should be a surprise. The real reason was that it amused me to think of him in the Central mall in Khorat trying different scents, the assistant spraying some fancy French cologne on his big wrist and marvelling at the thick black hair on his arm. She would be longing to have arms as strong as his encircle her waist, but also she would know that he was buying perfume for another woman, his wife, me. I was at home basking in the warm glow of belonging, while shop-girls who didn't even know me envied me. This was one of the ways my love for Giannis worked.

*

There were six children in GG's household. All completed their high school education and all—all six—went on to study at the University of Crete. The more I learnt about GG's family, the more similarities I saw with my own. However, the most striking divergence from this parallel evolution was the importance that his family placed on education. None of my brothers or sisters stayed in school past the age of 16; all of GG's did. We are all poor; they are by comparison rich.

Giannis taught me the value of family. This sounds strange from someone who comes from Isaan where blood ties are everything. Like a 500-baht note crushed at the bottom of my handbag, it was in my possession, but I didn't know it until it was made obvious to me by my husband. Family present and family past; the melding of history and heritage with community and kinship. 'If you forget where you come from, you have no hope of seeing where you're going,' he told me more than once.

At school, GG devoted as much energy to football as he did to his studies. By the age of 16 he was considered an athletic prodigy and was given a trial at OFI, his beloved Omilos, the most successful team in Crete and one of only two island clubs to compete at the highest level in Greece. The year that Giannis walked into the Dollhouse-A-Go-Go, OFI had finished third in the national championship and had four players in the Greek national squad, but they were never again to achieve such success, a decline that GG ascribed — perhaps humorously, perhaps not — to their turning him down as a serious contender all those years before.

Giannis studied economics at university and qualified as an accountant with one of the big firms in Iraklion before joining the accounting practice of his brother Georgios in Hania. After two years, Georgios made him a partner. Galanakis & Galanakis.

*

The girls in the bar told me not to go with Arabs. They said they were disrespectful and could be rough. When first I saw Giannis and Emmanuel, I took them for Arabs because of their colouring. We prefer white skin to the coffees and chocolates of our own hinterland or which breeze into Walking Street from the deserts. But in GG's dark eyes I saw not disdain but a gentle longing, as if he'd been waiting for me. Because I had never heard of Crete, it was some time before I realised he was a European and therefore a proper *farang*, the kind my mother had encouraged me to pursue.

It may have been before the girls gave me that advice that I did allow myself once to be bar-fined by a young Saudi. I didn't much care for him, but he wanted to take five ladies together, so I thought there would be safety in numbers. He had a man with him whom he treated more as a servant than a friend. This man was sent to find a taxi big enough to take us all to his hotel. It was the Amari Orchid, where he had a suite of rooms.

The Arab was full of ideas. One was to lie in the bath while we five girls stood on the edge and pissed on him. When we didn't perform to his satisfaction, he got angry and made us drink a bottle of water each, wait and do it again. He wanted his servant to film it all, but we were afraid the movie would end up on the internet, so we wore our panties over our faces to avoid being recognised. It was quite amusing. Afterwards, he gave us all gold bracelets. I sold mine the next day for 8,000 baht. I felt cleaner for losing it.

I don't know why I'm writing this. My journal was supposed to be for Paradorn and Eleni, so that they would never have to be like me and know nothing of their family or their origins. How candid am I going to be?

I've decided to include everything that comes to mind. When the time comes to give the journal to my children, I will choose the sections that need to be removed. Maybe none will. In the end, the truth should not be feared.

*

Noi met me at the bus station and we took a motorbike taxi to her room in Bang Na, on the outskirts of Bangkok. She had a double bed, a wardrobe, some shelves and a fridge. There was a shower in the toilet. On the floor of a small balcony there was a gas ring and two saucepans. There were windows front and back and a big television on the shelving unit. There was a fan on the ceiling. The bed was unmade. Noi's clothes, a huge pink teddy bear and numerous other cuddly toys were strewn over the bed and around the room.

This was not how we lived at home in Surin and I was shocked to see what had become of my big sister. For her, it no doubt signified the freedom of having a place of her own away from home; for me on that first day it suggested a lack of self-control.

Noi was working in a Japanese electronics factory within walking distance of her apartment block. She said she could easily get me a job at the company. With my contribution to the rent, she said that together we would be better off. We'd be able to save some money from our pay and have enough to enjoy evenings out as well. It was clear to me that, before I came, Noi was living pretty close to the breadline. Factory work was poorly paid and, after deducting her living expenses and the money she sent home to our mother, there was nothing left.

Within three days I was wearing the company uniform — pale blue cotton pyjamas with a white cap and white rubber boots — and screwing circuit boards into the plastic casings of radio/CD players. I got on well with the other girls, most of who were from Isaan, and also with the supervisors. The work itself was repetitive and dull, but if I concentrated on the envelope that they would give me on payday the time passed quickly enough.

We did have some money left over for fun. If we were not too tired after work we occasionally went to a bar where they had live Thai music, or to a karaoke where we drank Mekong whisky. But we weren't earning big money, and we weren't meeting men. It became my mother's constant refrain: 'Are there many *farangs* there? Are you going to the right bars? Do you have a boyfriend? Who will take care of you when you are old? I want grandchildren before I die.' It got so bad I started to put off calling her. I'd pretend I had no credit on my phone, or no reception.

After a couple of years, I decided it was hopeless. Bang Na was a dreary Bangkok suburb. Nothing happened there. I was not going to make my fortune there. I was not going to find what I was looking for in Bang Na. Significantly, I had no more money after two years' work than I had when I'd arrived. My friends at the factory said I should go to Phuket or Pattaya. Since Oh had lived in both places, I called her to ask her advice. She said there was plenty of work either way, but if I came to Pattaya she could take care of me, so that's how it was decided.

Noi wanted to know what I was going to do in Pattaya. 'Work in a bar,' I replied. 'With tips I know I can make more money than here. Why don't you come with me?'

But Noi knew she wasn't cut out for bar work. She was a quiet girl who looked as if she was thinking about something; that's not what people want to see behind a bar. She said she'd carry on at the factory for a little while yet; then possibly move back to Isaan to help our mother with her work.

*

When my mother was not helping my father with the rice planting or harvest, she went to a silk weaving co-operative nearby that produced some of the best fabrics in Thailand, some even being graciously accepted by the royal palace. Fine silk fabric has been woven in Surin for over 2,000 years. Local designs often depict soldiers fighting from the backs of elephants, reflecting Isaan's turbulent history. While working at the loom, my mother earned 200 baht for a nine-hour day.

*

At the age of 40, Giannis was practising as an accountant in Hania with his brother Georgios. He was living in a flat nearby with his younger brother Emmanuel who had a job with a firm of solicitors in the town. Emmanuel had studied law at the university. Unusually for Cretans of their age, both Giannis and Emmanuel were unmarried. Three years GG's senior, Georgios had a wife and three children and lived in a large villa overlooking the sea at Kalathas, on the Akrotiri peninsula.

Giannis would often spend Sunday afternoons with his brother's family, playing with his kids, admiring his faithful wife Anastasia and coming to realise that life was passing him by. After seeing a travel programme on television, he devised a solution. He would take a holiday in Thailand. Giannis had never before been outside Europe. As an inexperienced traveller, he was apprehensive about going to Asia alone, and persuaded Emmanuel to accompany him. They chose a package tour to Pattaya.

*

When I arrived in Pattaya, I stayed with Oh and Dermott for a couple of days, but their house was small and I felt awkward, so I moved into a room in an apartment block. I could afford the rent because I quickly found work in the You 2 bar beer in Soi 8. It was easy work and, while the pay wasn't any better than at the electronics factory, Pattaya is a tourist town and I was working mostly with tourists, which was one of the reasons I moved.

The girls in the bar beer were encouraged to entertain the customers with parlour games on the bar counter, or by teasing and flirting. We were also expected to go with men to their hotels if that's what they wanted. This wasn't as difficult as I thought it would be — no worse than a one-night-stand with a boy from the village — and it had the added bonus of generating a tip which was nearly as much as a week's pay from the bar, just for short-time. On a good night, I might be bar-fined twice; it depended how much I felt like teasing and flirting.

Although I was making good money on good nights at You 2, the bar wasn't always busy. Sometimes there were fewer than ten customers and only one of them might be feeling horny. Since we had six girls behind the bar, the odds of getting a customer were sometimes slim. So one afternoon I went to see the mamasan at the Dollhouse-A-Go-Go in Walking Street and she hired me as a dancer. The Dollhouse could deliver a much steadier stream of customers for me to charm, and these provided me with a higher, and more reliable, income.

*

We had been married for ten years. Our house in Khorat was equipped, furnished and decorated in just the way we wanted. Over the years, we had decorated some of the rooms twice. The garden was planted with palms, jasmine for the perfume, a mango and two limes. Each year, I put in two or three papaya trees to provide for *som tum* and GG's breakfast. My family was not far away in Surin, and we would visit them maybe once a month. Dorn and Eleni were enrolled in a good school in which we had chosen the English stream.

GG was busy working, as he had for the previous decade, for the accountancy partnership he had with Georgios in Hania. When Giannis first came to Thailand, he was not fluent in English, but in the following years he studied hard. He realised that it was going to be the lingua franca, the language in which he could best communicate with me and a language that would be useful for his

285

business. As tourism in Crete grew, more and more foreign businesses were appearing in the north-west, and these companies were looking for accounting services conducted in English. Much of the service could be provided via the internet and phone, which meant from GG's office in the corner of our living room in Khorat. Many of the firm's clients never knew that the advice they received on Greek accountancy practice originated in Isaan, Thailand.

During the day, GG worked in Greek and English. He learned some words of Thai and tried to teach Greek to the children. He spoke to me in English, with some Greek and some Thai. The kids were taught in school largely in English, but also in Thai. They spoke to me in Thai, and to their father in English, but also used some Greek. In summary, the two main languages to be heard in our house were Thaiglish and Engreek. 'It's like the United Nations in here,' Giannis would say proudly, surveying his brood.

One day, he returned from town and was quiet. He refused a glass of wine. When the children were in bed he told me that he had consulted his doctor about some symptoms he had noticed that concerned him. The doctor had referred him to the hospital for a colonoscopy. It sounded routine until I learned that the examination was to be in two days.

The colonoscopy revealed a tumour which they removed. However, the cancer had spread further into GG's body and chemotherapy was prescribed to halt its advance. As the treatment went on, Giannis became weaker and his pain grew worse. He declined rapidly from my big loving bear of a husband to a mouse. In ten months, he was dead.

*

I grieved for two years. I'm grieving still for the love of a man who gave me everything—a home, two beautiful children, air conditioning, a love of roast lamb and red wine, two histories and the idea that, with an ambitious and enquiring mind and an appreciation of what has been achieved by others in the past, I can do anything.

It took me two years to realise that he would have wanted me to take our children to Crete. It's really not my home, but in a way it is the homeland of my children, at least in part. Before he got sick, Giannis enthralled them with tales from ancient Greece and from the fight for Cretan independence. I knew it was my duty to bring our children here and show them where half of each of them came from.

It was a long journey, particularly for Dorn and Eleni who had never flown before. We stopped in Cairo and Athens, spending hours in those airports. When we landed in Hania, Emmanuel was there to meet us. He had arranged an apartment in Almiridha for the four weeks of our stay, close to the house where his parents lived and he and Giannis had been born.

I brought the children to Crete so that they could meet their father's family and get to know the country he told them so much about. For this I needed a guide, and Emmanuel became our constant companion. The older brother Georgios had come to Thailand both for our wedding and for GG's funeral, so I knew him quite well. He and Anastasia had children who were similar in age to Dorn and Eleni, and we spent the weekend afternoons at their house so the kids could play. Although I had met Emmanuel only once before—years ago when he came to Pattaya with Giannis—I felt a special bond with him because he knew the circumstances of our meeting. He knew my past, or at least could guess at it. He had seen me dance naked in the bar. Sometimes with Emmanuel, I found myself imagining my dress was transparent, like polythene.

On days when Emmanuel had to go into the office, we would stay in Almiridha. The children never tired of playing on the beach. I would visit GG's parents at home or in the minimart that Georgios had bought them. The shop was on the seafront and close to the parents' house, where Eleni senior sold groceries to the tourists. GG's sisters, Stella and Irene, would help on the till at busy times. Their father Christos would sit outside on the pavement constantly clicking his *komboloi*, his worry beads. There were two chairs outside the shop, shaded by an old tree. As often as not, the patriarch would be joined by some other old man — it wasn't always the same one — and the wrinkled old friends would pass the time by exchanging bursts of conversation between long periods of looking out to sea in silence.

Giannis would have been pleased with the itinerary that Emmanuel devised. He took us to Iraklion to see the reconstructed ruins of Knossos, the capital of the Minoan world, where we could marvel at the spirited murals and decorated ceramics that these remarkable people created so long ago. That same afternoon, as a complete surprise, he took us to a football game at the OFI stadium, where GG's beloved Omilos (they were Emmanuel's team too) played Cretan arch-rivals Ergotelis. When his team won, there were tears on Emmanuel's cheeks, just as there would have been on GG's.

The thought came to me that Emmanuel was a big bear of a man.

After the game, he took us for souvlaki in a restaurant where a man played mournful music on a bouzouki and the tables were overhung with vines.

With Emmanuel, we always met memorable people. They would talk to us gently, Emmanuel and me, as if we were a couple and as if Dorn and Eleni were our children. In Hora Sfakion, on the south coast, we chanced upon an Isaan couple who ran a Thai restaurant in Paris. In a jewellery shop in the square in Yeoryioupolis, Emmanuel bought Eleni a pair of silver earrings from an extraordinary Englishwoman called Linda, who had an old friend living in Thailand.

In Rethimnon, we met a curator at the museum who had known Giannis and Emmanuel at university. He welcomed us warmly to Crete—the Mediterranean Land of Smiles, he called it with a twinkle. He took us for coffee and baklava at a pavement café near the museum.

'Why did you never marry?' the curator asked Emmanuel while stirring his cup. 'You must be 50 now. Don't leave it too late, my friend.' He was joking, but I thought his comments might have been thought rude if the two men hadn't known each other well.

Emmanuel looked at me with doleful eyes. He seemed to be full of longing. His look was like GG's the first time we met in the bar, as if he'd held his breath since that moment.

*

Two days before we were due to fly home to Thailand, Emmanuel arranged a dinner for the two of us in Hania. Anastasia came to collect the children who were to spend the evening and sleep over at her house. I wore my best dress and put on some silver jewellery borrowed from GG's mother. I waited for Emmanuel's car like a nervous teenager on a first date. I had the feeling that he was going to propose to me. I didn't know if it was a hope or a fear. Even if it was a hope, I was still scared.

We drove to the town and took a small boat across the harbour to a restaurant on the opposite quay. From our candle-lit table, we had a romantic view of the broad sweep of Venetian buildings that lined the waterfront. The town at night was lit up as if by fairy lights, the different shades of cream, yellow and ochre of the houses reflected off the still waters.

During the meal, Emmanuel talked about his life, the importance of his family and his legal career. He had led a happy life, he told me, though I wondered if what he really meant was 'contented'. He had never married, he said, simply because he had not yet met the right woman. She would have to meet the exacting standards set by his mother and by the wives of his brothers whom he had seen made so fulfilled by their marriages. He paused and looked at me softly. He didn't seem embarrassed. He was quite calm as he reached into his pocket and brought out the small box. He opened the lid and placed it in front of me. It contained a ring with a diamond that sparkled like water.

I burst into tears.

*

I have never in my life felt such a surge of emotion. My loving husband Giannis was everything to me. He was my protector and provider, my brother and my lover. He was my big bear and the father of my darling children. Nothing could ever diminish the love I felt for that man. The grief that gripped me at the time of his death still overpowered me on occasion, yet I had grown very fond of Emmanuel. His similarity with his brother sometimes confused me. As he guided us around his beautiful island, I had to stop myself looking at him in a certain way, the way I might have looked at Giannis, yet I knew in the end it was something I would not be able to resist, something that would become natural. Emmanuel cared for my children—his nephew and niece—tenderly, as if they were his own. At that moment, all these emotions came together and burst out in an embarrassment of tears.

The grief, the love; the memories of Giannis, the possibilities of a life with his big bear of a brother. It was more than my little Isaan heart could carry.

WILLIAM PESKETT

The Sea Isle of Itsara

After W B Yeats

Verse 1

When the time comes I will go there, to the far Koh Itsara.

There will be no house there, but the time to collect exactly the right materials to build one will stretch ahead like all the opportunities I never took. I will gather them all together as required: stones from the headland, lime from the earth, sand from the beach and hardwood dragged from the interior, sawn straight and square and good for the beams.

There surely must be tools there because I cannot bring my own. It's tempting to believe that the memory of tools will be enough—the trusted tenon saw that served my right hand, gnarled now, all my adult life, my rule, my oiled pliers and my claw hammer, half-rusted but still ringing true. My bricklayer's trowel, no longer sharp at the edge but worn at the tip to the curve that makes a perfect grout, I will hope to see washed bright and laid out on a rock. My power tools, the grinder, drill and saw, will work without their cables.

And there will be no haste there, for time is all I have, time to build my cabin, to prepare the ground, sink good foundations and fit the stones exactly, offering each one up to

293

its position in the wall, knocking off a corner here or a swelling there to improve the bedding in. I will not hesitate to put one stone aside for another if it doesn't fall into place without effort. Admiring the Mayan masons, I might risk slipping a cigarette paper between my stones as the ultimate test of my new patience.

While I am building, a temporary shelter of some kind will shade me from the sun and deflect the tropical monsoon rains, providing me with a dry place to sleep, if sleep will come. Branches stripped of their leaves and wedged across two or three trees with a thatch of coconut fronds should do the job; it's only for a while after all, though what is a while when time is immaterial?

I've decided that I shan't restrict myself to conventional working hours, but build when I have the notion, tidy my bivouac when its disorder offends me and rest when I'm tired or feeling lazy.

And I shall need some food there, for whatever stores I am allowed to take with me can hardly be expected to last forever. Clams and mussels will mass on the rocks, abundant for the taking; oysters if my luck's in; winkles if I care to pick.

There will be fish of course and the traditional methods of catching them are sure to be the best. A spear! I must have a spear and this weapon will surely be one of the first things I will make, perhaps even a small quiver-full to trial a number of different techniques. Bamboo may work, with a sharp piece of shell bound in at the tip, or some likely sapling with its buds removed, whittled to a point, may be just the thing to stab at the succulent, taunting shoals.

I like to see myself stalking the azure, white-sand shallows like a thoughtful heron, the dark schools of sprat parting before me and closing behind like a skirt.

I can't live on fish alone; I'll have learning enough to know that I need green vegetables to stay in good condition until the end. I wonder if I shall be granted the necessary folk knowledge to distinguish the nourishing gifts of the jungle from the emetic or deadly, or is this a skill I shall have to acquire after arrival? If it has to be learned it can hardly be by trial and error, the way the folk themselves must have worked. I'll be on my own and will have no room for error.

Some herbs and spices I hope to recognise — sweet basil and coriander certainly, ginger and cardamom are possible — but many staples I shall surely have to grow myself. Rice would be a natural for the climate, but with its need for irrigation I'm not confident of the viability of paddy on the isle. It may be better to think along the lines of potatoes — they're easy to grow and so versatile in the kitchen; besides, they're in my bones. Spinach and broccoli would be nice, and carrots and parsnips of course; then there are Jerusalem artichokes — well now, if I could propagate such things as Jerusalems my eternal happiness would be assured.

Fruit is the crowning glory of any harvest display. I would like to take papaya for breakfast, doused in lime juice naturally, and a choice of melon, mangosteen, longan or lychee for after dinner. That will be my plan at any rate. Bananas are a given; I'm depending on their being indigenous for I have no idea how to grow bananas from scratch.

A clearing in the jungle will be required — more hard work, I know, but that's a virtue; after such toil I shall be assured of good sleep at least. I shall hack away at the shrubbery, tug out the grass and be sure to dig deeply enough to remove all the roots to prevent them coming back.

After an eternity of natural mulching the soil will be dark, rich and peaty.

I shall save a suitable percentage of my foraged seeds for planting—corncobs, grass ears, fruit pips and beans—and sow them all in plough-straight rows.

For ready protein I could do no better than to keep livestock. The species will depend not only on what's available and what I can catch, but also on what I can effectively domesticate. Rabbits are a possibility and chickens are for certain, but the prize would be to develop a small herd of bush pig. I will not keep bees; their infernal buzzing would be an annoyance and besides I can't bear the taste of honey.

My animals will also do for company of a sort, though it is my paramount wish to be alone—the pigs in their corral, the chickens in their pen and I in my half-built cabin in the glade.

Verse 2

It won't be all hard work there. There will be time enough for contemplation, for walking in the margins of the sea, climbing the rocky outcrops to look out to the unpeopled horizon and exploring the luscious, wooded, mountainous interior of the isle.

I fancy settling near a stream, a thread of vivacity running from some mossy, gurgling place in the stillness of the jungle downwards to the sea. Of course I will need the water itself as a domestic commodity, but I'm thinking of an aesthetic and recreational resource here too. I shall divert the flow into all kinds of races, waterfalls and ponds using an ingenious system of pipework and aqueducts fashioned from hollowed-out tree-trunks and useful-shaped rocks hauled back from the beach. The visual effect will be entertaining;

the constant tinkling music of the water, a reminder of eternity, will be a comfort in periods of doubt.

It may be that, after a while, I will develop a diurnal routine. In the early morning I might work on my cabin, occasionally taking time away from the weight and mineral hardness of stones to tend the animals and weed the rampant vegetable beds.

Later in the day, I shall move undercover to avoid the sun and prepare food for the evening or, sitting at my workbench, put my mind to fashioning essential items from the bounty of the forest—a toothbrush from a frayed twig, a comb from a spined palm stem, spoons from tree-bark, knives from flint. It will be a time for testing my past, assessing what was needed and what, when said and done, was no more than a flippant luxury.

The early afternoon will be a time for rest. After a lunch of baked potato or sweetcorn and bacon fried in its own fat over a wood fire, I'll have no mind for building.

Evening will bring a chance to appreciate the beauty of my isle. The sunsets will be wide and magnificent, the dying sun skittering diamonds in to me off the sea like a jeweller on his velvet cloth and the night a rash of stars. Sometimes I'll sit alone on a high white dune behind the beach and wonder where all the other isles might be. The quiet will be a deafening buzzing in my ears as from a shell, the peace so loud it will be broken only by the lapping of tiny waves and the flurry of mynah wings.

Verse 3

When the time comes I will go there. With the destination so fully imagined, all that remain are the details of departure. I have the ticket; I have the visa; I will go, but the dates are open; I don't know when. It seems premature to pack my bags just yet, but there are times I admit when I feel such a yearning for my journey's end that it's hard to resist at least laying out my clothes.

For this is all I know now: there's something deep in us all that hankers for peace, for the simplicity that we are denied just by being human. I've seen it at the edges of our world, on a wild cliff-top perhaps, where people stop to consider where else there is to go; in a crowd where an angry populace surges together; or at a party where a woman's attention drifts. You see the same in cities where, occasionally, some small person who is unloved or victimised at work or drawn into cheating on his wife looks up and sees himself standing on a small block of grey cement, his pockets full of mobile phones, in a galaxy of stars.

And then there is regret, repentance for a life lived in impatience, approximation or compromise, a making do. Somewhere, sometime, there is surely a chance, if not to make amends, at least to put the lessons I have learnt into practice, to polish the technique, to have another go.

There was a less complicated time — childhood perhaps — a time in the memory when we were free of all this. This is what I hope to regain by going there, to sing with the leaves and be silent under the sky, to recall what my memory has recorded for me as good and true and worthwhile.

I long for it because in the end it is to simplicity that we are bound to return, because peace is an isle in a welcoming sea, because freedom is the first poem I ever learned by heart.

WILLIAM PESKETT was educated in Belfast and at Cambridge University, where he read natural sciences. He has worked in teaching, journalism, marketing, design management and corporate relations. He now lives and writes in Pattaya, Thailand.

Peskett has published two volumes of poems, *The Nightowl's Dissection* and *Survivors*, the first of which won an Eric Gregory Award. These were followed by novels, collections of short stories, verse, a radio comedy and two volumes of essays about ex-pat life in his adopted country.

You can find out more, contact the author and follow his blog on the official website www.williampeskett.com.

ROBERT JOHNSTONE was born in Belfast in 1951. He won the Walter Allen Prize and the second Beck's Bursary for poetry and published two books of poems, *Breakfast In A Bright Room* and *Eden To Edenderry,* the second of which was a Poetry Book Society Recommendation.

Johnstone was author of the prose books *Images Of Belfast* (with photographs by Bill Kirk), and *Belfast: Portraits Of A City.* He also edited a book of animal poems, *All Shy Wildness* and co-edited *Troubled Times.* He was co-editor of *The Honest Ulsterman*, a literary journal, and deputy editor of *Fortnight* magazine, an independent review for Northern Ireland. He also wrote studio scripts for television. He now lives in London and studies jazz guitar and jazz singing.

Made in the USA
Monee, IL
25 April 2022

95430637R00173